The Whaler's Forge

by

Christine Echeverria Bender

To Jan,

*Thanks for joining me
on another adventure.*

Warmly,
Chris

Illustrations, including the book cover,
were created by artist Cindy Duft.

Published by
Caxton Press
312 Main St.
Caldwell, ID 83605

I.S.B.N. 978-0-87004-474-8

Caxton Press is a division of
The Caxton Printers Ltd.

Printed in the United States of America.
178033

This book is dedicated with infinite love to my dear children Nicholas, Anna, Adam, and Gideon Bender. May the richness and beauty they've so generously given to my life be found in much abundance within each of their own.

Table of Contents

Acknowledgements

While investigating and writing this story, welcome surprises seemed to greet me at every turn. Thanks in part to a research grant bestowed by the National Endowment for the Arts and the Idaho Commission on the Arts, I was able to embark on two journeys of discovery to eastern Canada and retrace the footsteps of the early Basque whalers. Now, after traveling to five Canadian provinces and gaining insights from our northern neighbors as well as experts from Denmark, Spain, and the United States, there are a number of people who deserve recognition and sincere gratitude.

I must begin with my traveling companion and occasional rescuer (a certain airport security incident comes to mind), my life-long friend, Helen Berria. Helen shared this undertaking from its earliest conception to the completion of the book. I am fortunate indeed to have benefited from her warm-hearted, wise, tolerant, and optimistic company throughout such an eventful journey.

My research began with the study of works by people who've been captivated for decades by ancient Basque whaling. Initiated by the dedicated documentary research performed by Selma Huxley Barkham, incomparable historical knowledge was gained upon the unearthing of 16th century Basque terrestrial remains by Dr. James Tuck in 1977 and the discovery of a sunken Basque galleon in 1978 in Red Bay, Labrador. The director of the diving team that found the Red Bay whaling ship, Robert Grenier, now Chief of Underwater Archaeological Services for Parks Canada, agreed to meet with me at his headquarters in Ottawa. Once there, Robert allowed me to record him as he shared accounts of his experiences from the past thirty years, shedding light on many previous mysteries. His assistant, Ryan Harris, was kind enough to let me inspect underwater plans and replicas derived from their finds in Red Bay.

While in Ottawa, my research was enhanced by a visit with Peter Rider, Atlantic Provinces Historian and Curator at the Canadian Museum of Civilization. His generosity of time and expertise, then and afterwards, not only influenced this book's authenticity, but also led to the creation of a 16th century whaling exhibit at the Basque

Museum and Cultural Center in Boise, Idaho. For all you've done, Peter, please accept earnest thanks from me and from the thousands of people who now enjoy the whaling exhibit, which couldn't have come to life without you.

For months prior to, during, and after my trip to Red Bay, Labrador, Cindy Gibbons, Supervisor of the Red Bay Historical Site, took precious time out of her schedule to provide uniquely valuable data and to answer my endless questions about the archaeological history of Red Bay. Cindy is one of the true authorities on early Basque whaling in eastern Canada, and without her help my research undoubtedly would have taken longer and been less comprehensive. Also, Cindy reviewed my book in its draft form, graciously suggesting and questioning here and there on fine points.

Historic site interpreter Phil Bridle, an associate of Cindy Gibbons at Red Bay, was both patient and informative during my stay. He escorted me along the paths of Saddle Island, allowing me to study the remains of cooperages, tryworks stations, and the unmarked cemetery that cradles the graves of over one hundred and forty 16th-century Basque whalers. Phil even was thoughtful enough to give me time to walk amid the lonely graves in quiet reflection, to sense the presence of the men and boys now long gone.

Due greatly to the welcoming, open-hearted people I encountered at Red Bay, I firmly hope to return to their lovely town one day.

Upon leaving Labrador I journeyed to Grand Manan Island, New Brunswick to observe great whales in the wild, predominantly northern Right whales, or, as they were known for centuries, Viscaino whales. Laurie Murison, Director of the Grand Manan Whale & Seabird Research Station, proved to be a wonderful guide for those aboard her vessel *Elsie Menota*. To have the chance to sail among those magnificent whales, to watch and film them, and to learn the details of their biology and nature, was a rare privilege. Laurie was also available before and after this voyage when questions relating to Right whales arose. The written works of Roger Payne, who has been called the world's leading expert on whales, also provided vast and varied information on Right whale behavior.

After landing once again on the New Brunswick mainland, I consulted with Robert M. Leavitt, Director of the Mi'kmaq-Maliseet Institute at the University of New Brunswick in Fredericton.

With the aid of his book *Maliseet-Mi'kmaq-First Nations of the Maritimes*, through email and telephone communications, and during our meeting we delved into many topics related to Labrador's early aboriginal people. Robert's involvement together with the anthropological records of the late Frank G. Speck on the Naskapi people proved to be invaluably helpful.

A specialist in the field of historical linguistics, Dr. Peter Bakker of the Department of Linguistics at the Institute of Anthropology for Aarhus University in Denmark shared discussions and his many written articles related to similarities in Basque and Mi'kmaq languages as well as works of art, adding to my understanding of early interaction between these two cultures.

This novel's research drew to an end at a remote, wind-swept archaeological site in eastern Quebec. Dr. William Fitzhugh is the man responsible for my being there. Bill, the Curator of Archaeology and Director of Arctic Studies at the Smithsonian Institution, learned of my prior involvement in the whaling exhibit at the Basque Museum and Cultural Center, and invited me to become a digger on his team of archaeologists at a Basque whaling site. I didn't hesitate long before accepting the invitation. For three weeks I traveled and worked with the industrious crew of the *Pitsiulak*, all ten of us living in close, informal quarters aboard the eight-man research vessel. Several times a "nor'easter'" chased us to a safer anchorage to wait it out, but most mornings the diggers headed to Hare Harbour's boulder-strewn shore overhung by a granite cliff and the divers descended into the murky waters of the St. Lawrence. In the evenings we met back at the boat and told of the treasures we'd uncovered. Much to my delight and fascination, we found many artifacts that will help shed new light on the history of the early visitors to North America. The friendships of Bill and the other crewmembers, Will Richard, Abby McDermott, Ben Ford, Laurie and Alix Penland, Christie Leece, Vincent Delmas, and Perry Colbourne were the unexpected treasures I found in that lovely bay. To say the experiences gathered on the dig were merely memorable would do them a gross injustice.

When I think of Scott Gipson, my editor at Caxton Press, I can't help smiling gratefully. Scott's professional assistance is always blended with a kind and generous manner, and he never fails to make himself accessible when I need his counsel and support.

For her belief in my work and for her conscientious efforts on my behalf, I am indebted to my agent, Edite Kroll.

People very, very dear to me who so kindly took the time to read, edit, and provide feedback on this novel are my father Isaac Echeverria, my daughter Anna Bender, my sisters Debra Geraghty and Teresa Townsend, and my friends Andy Franco and Alice Tracy.

To Doug Bender, my husband and partner in life's delights, trials, miracles, and riddles, I wish to express my deep love and appreciation for being the one I can turn to first and last during the course of any endeavor.

Author's Notes

Capturing the essence of early Basque whalers presented several distinct challenges, not the least of which was keeping my 21st century views about whaling tucked aside while investigating the world of six and a half centuries ago. It was essential that I embrace the truths of that long ago time rather than cling to the status and prejudices of my own. How vastly different were the numbers and needs of the people and creatures that inhabited this earth back then. The dangers and hardships faced by those bold whalers can scarcely be imagined when compared to our present day securities and comforts.

The enterprise of Basque whaling diminished greatly after the 16th century. These whale hunters were followed by men from England, France, Germany, Denmark, Holland, New England, Russia, Norway, Japan, and other regions. By the first decades of the 20th century the invention of modern ships and bomb-tipped harpoons made whaling remarkably less hazardous and more efficient. Now the number of great whales has diminished to a point where they are in serious need of man's protection. It is my hope that the current condition of these magnificent creatures will be recognized so that support will be offered in time to insure their survival.

The date chosen for this story arose in part from Basque oral tradition that tells how their people hunted whales and fished for cod off North American shores for hundreds of years prior to the voyages of Christopher Columbus. The first known transaction related to Basque whaling is documented by a bill of sale for whale oil to a French abbey in 670 A.D. In 1497 John Cabot reached Newfoundland and named the bay of his anchorage after the fish found in abundance there: Bacalao Bay. The word bacalao, meaning codfish, is believed to be of Basque origin. Recently, Robert Delort (University of Paris VIII) uncovered Bristol shipping records that show Basque ships unloading cargos of beaver pelts between 1386 and 1433. The descriptions of these pelts imply that they may have been treated and stored in rolls, using methods similar to those used by natives of our eastern coastlines. And these cargos were delivered during a time when beavers were virtually extinct from most of Europe, although still present in Russia. If indeed the Basques were trading goods with native North Americans by 1386, it is reasonable to believe that whalers could well have preceded the traders.

Looking much farther back in time, archaeological evidence obtained over recent decades by Dennis Stanford of the Smithsonian Institution points to the possibility that the Solutrians, people who once inhabited what is now known as the Basque Country of southern France and northern Spain, and who may have been the ancestors of the Basques, landed by sea upon the eastern coast of North America as long ago as 15,000 years.

This book opens in a place known today as Red Bay, Labrador, where four 16th century Basque whaling galleons have now been discovered. The native people encountered by Kepa de Mendieta are recognized in modern times as Innu, formerly known as Naskapi. As mentioned in more detail in my acknowledgments, I owe a great debt of gratitude to the National Endowment for the Arts and the Idaho Commission on the Arts for the grant that helped send me to the places where these early people once lived.

On the subject of killer whales, some of the most dramatic accounts of orcas working side-by-side with whalers come from Twofold Bay in Eden, Australia. There, over centuries orcas developed a well-established relationship with human hunters of great whales. Although they were undoubtedly more plentiful in ages past, orcas still occasion the waters near Red Bay.

Christine Echeverria Bender

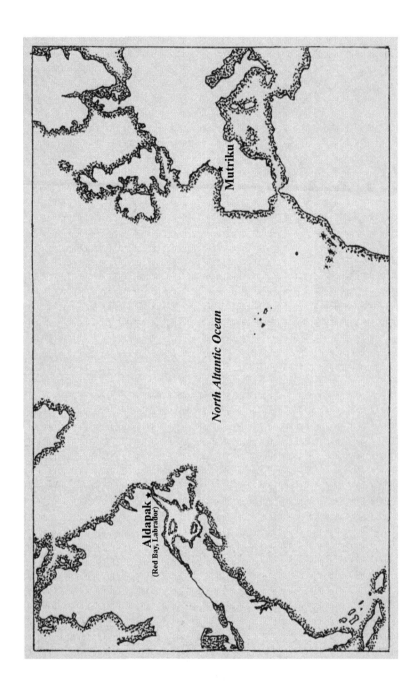

North Altantic Ocean

Mutriku

Aldapak
(Red Bay, Labrador)

Bay of Whales

1

June 26, 1364
A Nameless Bay off the Western Atlantic Coast

He stood motionless on the wooden deck, stripped of every compulsion but instinct. It was this alone that forced the harpooner to brace his stance before a surfacing black mass ruptured the water with explosive spray and heaved its bulk against the crippled ship. The hull groaned and quivered beneath Kepa de Mendieta but he neither reached for a weapon nor took a step. His arms hung unmoving at his sides, as lifeless as the canvas-shrouded body at his feet.

When the whale shoved the starboard bow again, swaying the decks and provoking shouted curses from the crew, Kepa's drawn face and reddened eyes sank to the stump of *La Magdalena's* main mast. Only the day before it had been a pillar of oak with a nine-foot girth that towered proudly above them. Now the jagged wood gaped back at him, broken, as he was broken. Unwanted images rose in his mind of the tempest that had attacked them at sunset with winds strong enough to snap their mast like a twig. Kepa felt again the helpless rage that had seized him as yardarms and riggings crashed down upon his crewmembers and trapped him against the rail. His ears still rang with the harsh echoes of human cries that had pierced the howls of the storm as a wave flung four flailing men overboard. He fought the terrible memory of the watery cavern that had appeared behind the small fleet and yawned thirty feet then fifty feet above them. It had hung there for an instant before it collapsed with a rolling, thunderous roar, swallowing their two companion ships and a hundred and three men.

It had taken longer for the storm to claim his younger brother. He'd died from his injuries not two hours ago. Kepa's fingers could still feel each stab and pull of the needle he'd forced through the rough shroud to draw it closed over the pale, damaged form that had been Gotzon de Mendieta.

In response to the whale's nudgings, the ship rolled gently and rocked the shoulder of the swathed body against Kepa's foot. At this touch Kepa stiffened, his boots rooted to the deck, his bearded face suddenly fierce and protective. The whale surfaced again, then gracefully curved its massive back and dove with its fluked tail lifted high, descending unchallenged save for Kepa's vengeful stare. Other men hurried to their positions throughout the ship but even a shouted command from the boatswain could not dislodge Kepa from his chosen station.

Coming up close, a younger man with a bandaged neck spoke with quiet respect. "We have been called to the lines, Kepa. We must bring her in."

Kepa's chin motioned toward Gotzon's body. "I will stay with him."

He will not be disturbed, cousin," said Urdin. "Come, you are needed. Come now."

Kepa moved heavily as he was tugged toward the rail. Glancing back, he took his place along with the others and reached for the hemp lines. He began to pull hand-over-hand.

With the physical demands of hauling in the sails his mind slowly began to return to the world of the living, to look with clearer focus at what lay around him. They were maneuvering the ship past two small islands that nearly touched in the center and toward a larger rocky island also barren of trees. Kepa could feel the ship moving sluggishly because of her wounds, and how she responded more slowly to fewer hands doing greater shares of the work.

As *La Magdalena* circled the western end of the larger island and turned northward, the inner arc of a protected bay revealed a treed ravine, suggesting a river. Every intake of breath was heavy with the smell of fish, and the skies clamored with the cries of seabirds roused by the ship's arrival.

If the strongest among them could guard against attacks from anyone claiming this hilly land the men of *La Magdalena* might be granted the water, food, and time needed to recover their health and restore their galleon. They might survive this unknown land as they had survived the storm. They could fill their hold once more and return home.

Yet Kepa harbored no hope of ever reclaiming his soul. The last of it, that shred he'd clung to for nearly a year, had escaped with the release of Gotzon's final rattling breath. And since Kepa could no more will his own breathing to cease than he could now disregard the boatswain's calls of the water depth with each lowering of the sounding weight, his arms and back and legs kept working.

La Magdalena eased to a quiet anchorage just north of the island while huffs of a lessening breeze snapped the nearly furled sails and billowed the linen shirts of the men. After checking the belayed lines Kepa's cousin straightened, wiped his forehead with a torn sleeve, and stared out at the waters around them. In a voice grave with irony, Urdin said, "So we find the whales here, at the end of a storm that has killed most of us and blown the rest half an ocean off course. Look at them. There must be a thousand."

"We can let our eyes have their fill," said Kepa, his bitterness unconcealed. "We've paid dearly enough for the sight." Kepa watched as the great whales spouted and breached in every direction, some within harpoon range, all mocking the tragedies of men and the frailties of their wooden ships.

"The whales could not be this great in number if men were hunting them," said Urdin. "This land might be uninhabited. Perhaps God will be merciful and we will be left undisturbed to rework the ship."

Kepa made no comment concerning God or his mercy. "Without Gotzon," he faltered, "with the loss of the others and the state of the wounded, the ship's crew is in need of repair as badly as she."

The cousins were given no more time for reflection before commands assigning new duties were called out. Showing a cautious alertness in this strange land, their captain ordered the ship's only two cannons, swivel guns mounted on the fore and stern castles, to be loaded. Bows and arrows were distributed to four men chosen to stand guard.

Returning to his post beside Gotzon's body, Kepa saw a small pile of tools near the stairs leading to the half deck that needed sharpening. His grinding stone was close at hand so he picked up an ax and tried to examine its edge, but his eyes seemed unwilling to focus. Letting his gaze drift to the canvas bundle, he swallowed twice then said in a barely audible voice, "Well, brother, at least I can work beside you a little while longer." He studied the shrouded face until his vision blurred further and his chin descended. His chest rose and fell as if his lungs were battling to break free. With sudden impatience he wiped harshly at his welling tears, scowled at the tools, and bent to his task.

Not many minutes had passed before the cook was busily tending a fire that would produce their first hot meal in days and a boat was being lowered for a landing party to explore the island. The men aboard *La Magdalena* were already removing the stump of the main mast, refitting yardarms and railings, mending sails, and reworking the rigging, but everyone found time to cast a glance toward the mainland in search of any movement. Even Kepa occasionally slowed his grinding to scan the ridgelines and valleys. He scrutinized the red-brown rocks clustered along the shore as well as the patches of groundcover that rose up the slopes and then gave way to the forests mantling the inland hills. Other than drifting clouds, reeling sea birds, and intermittently swaying trees and shrubs, all was still.

As his gaze fell he realized that Urdin had again come to stand beside him. No words were spoken but their eyes, when they met and held, filled the silence.

Kepa was the first born of the three de Mendieta men, two years older than Gotzon and four years older than Urdin. Yet the age difference between Kepa and Urdin was felt little. The boys had been raised almost interchangeably by twin sisters, and a low stone wall marked a shared boundary between their families' lands. All three of them had thick, straight hair of the darkest brown and skin that bronzed quickly when exposed to the elements. Their features were strongly chiseled, their eyes keen and alert above coarse beards and beneath formidable, tapering brows. On Kepa's neck, two inches beneath his right ear, a rust-colored birthmark, shaped like the wing of a bird, rose tip first above his open collar. Dirt darkened the beige linen of his shirt as well as his red tunic, faded blue breeches, and torn woolen hose. He appeared only slightly less shabby than most of the men around him whose clothes bore the earthen tans of a lower class.

Kepa's comparative leanness set him slightly apart from the ship's other two harpooners but less so than did his educated speech and quiet manner. He was a rarity among even the officers because he could read and write both Latin and Castilian. His native Basque was still passed down through its ancient oral traditions rather than the written word. The other languages he had acquired through years of schooling, and the possession of such knowledge by a harpooner was exceptional indeed.

Yet if the size and power of Kepa's body were just noticeably less than those of common harpooners, who were the largest and strongest of a hearty breed, he had quickly distinguished himself as one who could hurl his weapon with unmatched precision. Not a man in their three-ship fleet had questioned his value at the bow of a whaling boat.

Urdin bore the blue-gray eyes of his father, a remnant of a long ago Viking invasion, or so Gotzon often proclaimed when they were boys. For two years aboard a previous ship and for the past 14 months under Gotzon's diligent guidance on *La Magdalena* Urdin had been training to become a pilot. After Gotzon's injury during the storm, Urdin had capably relieved both the shipmaster and the captain when they'd badly needed rest. As young as Urdin was, Kepa felt that he had proven himself worthy of this office. Observing his cousin now, he could sense that Urdin had matured a decade in the last few days.

Taking a step closer and crouching down beside Kepa, Urdin said, "The boat is returning. We must discuss Gotzon's funeral."

Kepa tapped the knife he'd been sharpening against the palm of his hand. "I should have been carving his grave marker."

Urdin motioned toward the carpenter, working under the forecastle not far from the sick and injured men. "Benito has almost finished it. But there is something I would ask of you. Will you, can you play your txistu today?"

The flute-like instrument had been Kepa's companion ever since his fingers had grown long enough to reach all of the holes. Over the years he'd played at scores of weddings as well as funerals but this time he shook his head. "Not today. I am sorry, Urdin. The music has left me."

Urdin nodded slowly and let the topic shift to whom they would ask to sing and whom to dance, both essential elements of any Basque rite. Before they had finished, however, Captain de Perea approached them with compassion and his own grief furrowing his forehead. He had replaced his weather-beaten coat with a cleaner one, and he now removed the velvet hat that covered a receding hairline of gray.

Speaking softly, he said, "Several men have asked to dance during Gotzon's ceremony: Todor, Zeru, Bakar, Koldo, Ander, Kemen, and Jokin." Receiving nods of gratitude from Kepa, he strengthened his voice. "Well then, the grave is ready. The first boat is waiting for you two to board."

Three other seamen joined them as they took positions over Gotzon's body, bent low, and lifted it up. As Kepa, Urdin, and the others slowly carried their burden to the railing, every man and boy on the decks extended a wordless tribute by stilling his hands and rising to his feet. Carefully, they lowered the bundled form into a chalupa, one of the boats that they would use in their whale hunts. After Captain de Perea joined them, their chalupa pushed off and waited near the ship as a second boat was manned.

They had rowed only a few strokes away from the ship's side when the boatswain at *La Magdalena's* railing suddenly shouted, "Captain! Two natives on the northern hill!"

As heads pivoted and eyes darted to follow the man's pointing arm, Kepa spotted the motionless figures on the hilltop, one no larger than a young child. Excited voices rose from the ship. Men pushed tighter against the rail, nudging and shifting for a better view.

"Master Ansotegui," the captain called sharply and the shipmaster leaned out over the rail. "All other hands are to remain aboard. Set a double watch and see that armaments are readily at hand."

"Yes, Captain."

The boats advanced toward the island as Kepa cradled Gotzon's bound feet and watched the two figures on the mainland hill. The motionless pair was observing the men and their ship as intently as they themselves were being studied. From this distance Kepa could distinguish that their black hair hung long and loose down to their waists and that their full-length clothing seemed to be made of some kind of animal skins. He could detect no weapons. After a few moments the larger of the two natives lifted his arms straight and high before him, as if in salutation. Captain de Perea was glancing ahead and did not see the gesture. Before any responding signal could be delivered, the adult drew the child over the crest of the hill and disappeared.

The men in the boats murmured uneasily to one another. Kepa wordlessly asked his newly deceased brother, *Do you see them, Gotzon? What manner of people dwell in this land where we've brought you?*

After landing the boats the burial party processed solemnly to the gravesite near the eastern tip of the island. Here Kepa stood over the grave, listening and watching but unable to contribute as he knew he should. The funeral was conducted with reverence and ancient tradition, yet the passion of the ceremonial dancing was lessened by the absence of Kepa's txistu, and Captain de Perea's prayers were enjoined by men whose glances repeatedly strayed to the far shore, watching for whomever might next appear on the hills around the bay.

After the final prayer they lowered Gotzon's body into the shallow grave with his feet positioned eastward, toward home and the rising sun. The shovels that filled his resting place with dirt lifted and fell with more energy than might have seemed fitting under less uncertain conditions. Yet, when at last three large stones had been set lengthwise atop the grave, and a wooden marker bearing Gotzon's name had been pounded into the rocky soil, not even the captain seemed willing to leave the patch of ground. They stood in the breeze, dirty, battered, grave-faced men, and not a dry eye could have been found among them.

Letting his blurred gaze touch upon each of their features, Kepa sensed that they were remembering not only his brother but also the men who had died at sea, men who would never receive the funerals they deserved.

As if to confirm this speculation, Captain de Perea raised his voice loud enough for the crew on the ship to hear. "Men of *La Magdalena*, offer your prayers with me!" The whalers aboard ship paused in their work to bow their heads, and their captain prayed with great feeling. "For every good man who was taken by the storm, and for his family that will suffer because of his absence, please, dear God, have mercy."

"Amen," rose from those near at hand and aboard the ship.

"And, Heavenly Lord," the captain added, "please keep us under your watch in this strange land. Let those of us who stand here this day live to see our homes again."

Home. All that remained of home for Kepa were too many graves scarring his family's homestead, what now lay buried in this foreign ground, and the cousin standing at his side. He lifted a heavy arm and settled it across Urdin's shoulders.

As the others picked up their tools and headed toward the boats, Captain de Perea stayed with them. "Urdin," said the captain, "if you are ready, when we return to the ship I will announce your promotion to the office of pilot."

Urdin's face showed no emotion, but his voice held certainty. "I am ready, Captain."

"And you, Kepa, it would do me and the rest of the men much good if you would agree to accept the position you deserve aboard our ship. You know my feelings well, and yet I will not insist."

"I am sorry, Captain. I must decline."

"You were neither born nor raised to be a harpooner. You perform that task well enough but your education and your most valuable talents are being wasted. Will you not reconsider?"

"As I have said before, sir, never again."

The captain waited, trying to discern any weakness in Kepa's determination. But Kepa just shook his head, slowly and with finality.

Breathing a heavy sigh, the captain said, "Then, choose six men who can handle muskets and swords, and scout the mainland shore. If a village lies on the other side of those hills, I want to know about it before we establish our camp. But take every caution." This last he said sharply, as if suddenly fearful that Kepa might abandon his usual prudence.

"Of course, sir."

Captain de Perea held him with an assessing stare, then nodded resignedly before leading the cousins to their waiting boat. While Urdin rowed for the last time as a lower ranked seaman, Kepa watched the deserted grave marker shrink with every pull of his oar.

Beasts of a Strange Land

2

Wooden bowls were still being gathered from a meal of codfish soup when Captain de Perea ordered the men to the main deck and announced Urdin's promotion. The crew responded with mutterings of satisfaction and relief, and almost immediately turned conjecturing glances in Kepa's direction. Giving no hint that he read their expectations, he quickly approached Urdin to offer his formal congratulations. In the strength of Urdin's handshake Kepa found understanding, or at least acceptance, of his refusal to resume his former role. For the first time in their lives, Kepa was surrendering the leadership position between them.

When the captain made no further promotional announcements as Kepa stepped away from Urdin's side, Julian Urresti, *La Magdalena's* physician, stared pointedly at him and pursed his lips in disapproval. After merely nodding in acknowledgment, Kepa avoided the doctor's eye and kept moving toward the stern of the ship.

He wasted no time selecting six men strong enough to accompany him ashore, mostly those who regularly rowed his boat, and loading the arms and supplies they would need. Keeping his hands busy and his expression blank, Kepa concealed the battle he waged with his haunting grief, both new and old. He found himself soundlessly thanking his captain for sending him on this mission, any mission, any assignment whatsoever that would keep him occupied.

Before finalizing his landing preparations Kepa searched out the ship's normally gregarious cook, but today found Paulo Batista gruffly ordering two cabin boys to cast fishing nets over the port railing. Gotzon had been a favorite of Paulo's, as had Kepa's father a generation earlier, and Kepa knew that the old cook's mourning must run deep and sharp.

9

Kepa approached him from behind and asked, "Paulo, how many barrels do you wish us to fill?"

At the sound of Kepa's voice, Paulo struggled to keep his first words even. "You have other things on your mind this day than filling water kegs, sir. I can not help thinking the captain a bit harsh to be sending you off scouting at such a time."

"I am grateful that he is sending me."

After sweeping Kepa with a perusing glance, Paulo said, "I see that you are, sure enough. In that case, sir, one or two barrels would be most welcome."

"Two then, but you must not address me as 'sir', Paulo. You know this better than anyone."

"Old habits, sir, and fond memories. Some things a man finds hard to surrender."

"Yes, yes, at times very hard." Feeling the heaviness pulling at him again, Kepa forced his head a degree higher and said, "We will leave shortly."

"The barrels will be scoured and waiting, sir."

"Very good."

"Tonight, sir, you can toast to your good brother with fresh water in your wine."

To this Kepa could only nod and turn away.

When all was ready he boarded the chalupa and positioned the long steering oar to serve as both tiller and rudder, keeping the weapons close by. From his youth he had been trained in the use of muskets but found them more troublesome and less accurate than his twenty-inch crossbow. He preferred it despite a loading process that soon tired a weaker man. It required him to slip the toe of his boot into a stirrup slung at the end of the bow, brace his foot against the ground, and pull upward on the string until the dart could slide into its groove. He'd learned through much practice to load a crossbow faster than any other man aboard *La Magdalena*. And once the arrow was set, Kepa's aim was deadly. As he sat in the boat awaiting his men, his crossbow's strap lay across his chest, its reassuring bulk against his back. The other firearms he would dole out once their boat landed.

Closely watching the tree lines, Kepa steered toward the farthest curve of beach near the mouth of the river.

The many spouting Right whales took little interest in the

chalupa's passing, and the men had crossed most of the bay without an encounter when the water twenty yards ahead suddenly churned with the thrashings of a bull whale. Kepa shouted, "Hard astern!" As arms and backs strained, every eye locked on a pod of orcas that had appeared from the depths to encircle the Right whale.

Possessing baleen to filter its food rather than teeth to tear it, the Right whale's powerful body was its only defense. With deadly grace the whale lifted its fluked tail high above the water and brought it crashing downward, slapping the ocean like a Herculean spade and spraying two foaming plumes into the air. But the orcas quickly reformed, leaving the Right whale to twist and maneuver in a desperate attempt to keep them from closing in.

Rowing swiftly until they'd reached a safe distance, Kepa and his men stared in awe as the tall pointed dorsal fins and white-patched black backs revealed the herding movements of the predators. Systematically, patiently, they squeezed the encircling trap tighter and tighter. The orcas, only a quarter of the size of their prey, now began to dart in and bite chunks from the Right whale's hide, each time escaping the slamming reach of its dangerous flukes. Again and again the orcas struck, singly and in pairs.

It was a well-executed hunt, Kepa saw, its precision sharpened through ages when survival depended on the collaboration of the pack and the determination of each member, much as it did with men. Suddenly, one of the largest orcas shot forward and clamped its jaws onto the flesh near the whale's left eye. It clung there as the wounded Right whale rolled in a full rotation, lifting the orca completely out of the water once, twice. On the Right whale's third revolution the orca finally tore free, landing fifteen feet away with a massive chunk of skin and blubber still in its mouth. The rest of the pod wasted no time. High, echoing cries of pain and fear rose from below Kepa's boat, broke the surface of the water, and filled the air. Blood that had started as a crimson smear now spread in a widening pool as the Right whale's movements grew slower and more feeble. The orcas did not ease their attack until all of the Right whale's struggles had ceased, and then they congregated near its head to feast on the giant tongue.

Although they were hardened to the art of killing, and they knew their roles to be more akin to those of the orcas than that of the victim, neither Kepa nor his men spoke until they were nearer the shore and had slowed their rowing somewhat.

"Well," burly Todor Eiguren said at last, "that's a sight I'd not ask to see again. Besides, if there's a whale to be caught, it should be us that does the catching. Surely there's enough small fish in the sea to feed those black and white devils without them chasing the baleen whales."

Another man spoke up. "Devils or no, those are fish to keep at a respectable distance."

Kepa did not join in the edgy chuckling of the other men. His gaze had not left the orcas. As the pod greedily fed, only one drew away from the kill. It was the large one that had inflicted the deadliest wound on the Right whale and it now began swimming slowly but directly toward their chalupa.

"One's coming, men," Kepa called in warning. "Pull toward shore." The chalupa leaped forward and skimmed rapidly across the water but the orca was faster. Kepa could see the black and white dorsal fin racing toward the span of water that lay between the chalupa and the beach.

Surrendering the steering oar, Kepa grabbed and loaded his crossbow. The orca approached the front of the chalupa, maneuvering to match any shift the men tried to make in its direction, forcing the boat to reduce its speed. The devil fish, as the men would call it from that day forward, swam within ten feet and paused, holding them in position. Kepa, his muscles tight but steady, held his aim at a spot three inches in front of the blowhole. The orca was large and sleek, and its skin bore few of the scars that came with age. Distinguishing it from the other large orcas, the white marking at the back of its dorsal fin climbed almost to its tip.

Kepa listened acutely as he stared, awaiting the creature's piercing calls and whistles that had signaled the rest of the pod during their hunt. No sound came as the orca maintained its short distance, but Kepa's gut began to constrict as he perceived that the creature was studying him, considering. His shoulder twitched yet he held his fire. His shot might merely wound the killer and bring its rage down on his men, and even if he wounded it fatally, its death throws might attract the rest of the pack.

The orca began to circle the chalupa and, at Kepa's cautioning order, the rowers gently dipped their oars. The shore was so close, not fifty feet away. Keeping even with his moving target, Kepa slowly rotated in place with his crossbow aimed at the back of the sleek black head. After making a complete circumnavigation of the steadily advancing chalupa, the orca stopped behind them and dove forward from the stern. Every man tensed, knowing the whale could breach upward from beneath the boat and fling them into the sea. But no sudden blow hit their feet, and when the orca lifted its head directly in front of them Kepa called out, "To starboard, men." While the rowers shifted direction slightly, aiming for a different stretch of shore, the orca remained where it was, watching. Then it unhurriedly dove again, surfaced thirty feet away, and swam back to the pod.

Kepa lowered the crossbow, uncocked the string, and replaced the arrow in his quiver. It was then that he glanced back at the ship and saw Urdin and several others standing alertly beside the stern-mounted falconet canon still pointed at the pod. They too had been prepared to defend the chalupa. Offering a wave of thanks, Kepa sat down and again took the steering oar. The pod paid them no more heed, and while the chalupa increased its speed slightly its crew dared to breathe a collective sigh as it rowed.

Argi, the youngest among them, revealed that his apprehensions had gradually drifted ashore when he asked, "Do you suppose we'll find many natives, Kepa?"

"We have only three hours of sun left," Kepa replied, "but their village might be close. It is also possible that a group is already heading toward us, now that we have been spotted. Then again, hundreds of them could be watching us right now from those trees."

The men shifted uneasily. Courage was a thing that no whaler lacked, not for long. He knew that the odds of an early death ran high for those who pursued an animal so large it could crush a chalupa's crew with one slap of its flukes. Before ever boarding his first ship he'd heard stories of whalers freezing or staving to death after being separated from their ships as the sun set or the fog lowered. They faced these dangers year after year to feed their wives and children. And this particular crew had recently witnessed the violent destruction of two fellow galleons. More than a hundred men, many of them friends and some of them family, had drowned before their eyes. And yet, they'd never before had to fight their own kind. Kepa knew that his men had greater confidence in facing a familiar foe, be it whale or storm, than a foreign one. He too shied from the idea of killing another human being.

"Whatever we find," he said, "keep level heads. No shot is to be fired carelessly."

Nods and mutterings of assent circled the group as they rowed.

The chalupa slowed as it slid through the shallows, gliding the last few feet with silent grace until her keel scraped the sand and Kepa leaped into the water. He waded ashore with the bowline in his hand. A small hermit crab skittered through the foam-washed shells of sea urchins and mussels to evade his feet. He paused long enough to check for movement on the knolls above and to scan the ground near the mouth of the river. His men kept close behind him, watchful and silent as they hauled the chalupa high above the tide line and secured it to a boulder. Seeing no immediate danger, Kepa approached the river's edge, knelt beside the rushing water and scooped a handful to his lips to test its flavor. It was so cold and pure that it lay sweet and tingling on his tongue before he swallowed, and drew a low moan from his lips. Before drinking more he signaled to his men and every one took a few gratifying gulps.

"It tastes better than the finest wine right now," said Kepa, his chin dripping, "but drink sparingly. After we have explored we will have our fill."

The crew obediently left the riverside and belted their swords. After checking their own muskets, they held the loaded weapons up for Kepa's inspection. All was ready. Resettling his quiver and crossbow so their straps rested securely at his chest Kepa said, "Whatever we meet, stay close together."

Argi, his eyes uncertain, asked, "Kepa?"

"What is it, Argi?"

But the young man only hesitated, shook his head, and then lowered it.

Giving a nod, Kepa led them up the gentlest slope in a single file. Unfamiliar wildflowers shared the soil with various grasses, their bright colors swaying amidst the greens as Kepa and his men took the path that followed the river toward the tree line. They climbed steadily and soon Kepa spotted a set of footprints on the trail ahead of him, first only the one set but then many. At a glance he guessed them to be several days old but he was far from certain.

He had had little experience with such things. Choosing to press on, he did not pause to discuss the prints with his followers. Though the men of his scouting party surely saw them as well, they too said nothing as their boots trod upon the prints of their predecessors.

Their weariness and anguish brought about by the last grueling days encumbered their pace, and they took longer than Kepa had anticipated to draw within bow range of the forest. Here they halted, breathing hard. This close to the trees Kepa could smell the mingled perfumes of the balsam firs and black spruces, their strangely needled forms and scents so different from the oak forests of his homeland. Just uphill from where they stood the fluttering of aspen leaves, also foreign to them, produced a soft rustling sound. Nothing else stirred.

"Keep to the trail and go quietly," said Kepa, once again taking the lead. With his eyes and ears straining he crept cautiously into the woods but nothing showed itself. The footprints disappeared as the trail thinned and this made Kepa even more wary. But before long the men began to talk in low tones, relaxing a little as they absorbed the raw beauty of the land. Kepa remained watchful, and hushed the men when their voices rose too high. Coming upon a sizeable stream that fed the river, he took the trail that ran along its ascending eastern bank.

No more than a quarter mile up this stream Kepa came to an abrupt halt at the sudden sound of a loud slap. His men froze behind him, scanning with wide eyes in every direction. There was a long, paralyzed pause before the sound came again; a wet, echoing clap. Two men jerked violently but held their positions.

Kepa inched ahead and around a curve until he spotted, close beside the path, the stump of a tree that had recently been hewn by a primitive ax. Less than ten feet ahead stood another stump, and a little beyond this, another. Kepa signaled his men forward until they saw the stumps too, and he drew an arrow and loaded his bow as they lifted their muskets. At the sound of another slap, muscles flinched tighter. Very slowly, Kepa motioned them on.

The next clap burst so loud and near that all six men spun to their left. Kepa could see little through the trees except the stream that had veered away from the path. Walking softly toward the flowing water, noting that the stream had grown too broad to ford easily, he slowed and crouched within the cover of the last trees. His men crept up on either side of him. As he let his gaze travel upstream he spotted a sleek brown animal swimming in the gentle current, then several more of its kind. A couple of seconds passed before one of these creatures turned directly toward them, raised a dripping paddle-like tail and slapped it soundly against the water.

Todor let out a bark of surprise and began to sputter with laughter. His chortling quickly spread to the others until it grew so boisterous Kepa was forced to quiet them all. "Remember what we are scouting for," he warned even as he shook his head at his own foolish trepidations.

Wiping at his eyes and trying to catch his breath, Todor said, "Sorry, Kepa, but what a scare those little beasts gave me. I'll pay for it twice if my wife ever hears about this."

As Todor's voice subsided Kepa watched one of the water animals swimming to a structure made of logs, sticks, and mud, which had evidently caused the widening of the stream. Trailed by his men he made his way closer to inspect the dam. He could see that it was ingeniously constructed from the trees he had wrongly assumed had been chopped down by men. Somehow these furry carpenters must have done the felling, but just how was not clear until one of them climbed up the opposite bank and began gnawing on a tree already partially hewn.

"Heaven above us, look at those teeth," exclaimed Todor. "Those creatures may be small, but with teeth like that I'm glad they're on the far side of this stream. The rest of the crew will never believe us."

"Well, the captain certainly will not thank us for returning with wild stories and empty hands," said Kepa. "On our way back we will corner at least one of these and take it to the ship." He moved reluctantly away from this fascinating discovery and retraced his steps through the trees to the path.

They trekked on for forty minutes to reach the top of the fourth and highest hill, and here the men spread out within the cover of the trees crowning its ridge, panting as they took in the view before them. The vista revealed a valley with a wide, green meadow bisected by the river and dotted with several small ponds, but there was no sign of human occupancy. Disappointed as well as relieved, Kepa glanced to the west and assessed the height of the sinking sun

16

as his heartbeat slowed. "We must head back, men. We barely have time to fill the barrels before—"

A musket exploded at the eastern end of the line, followed by a shout of panic and pain. Men near Kepa crouched and swung their muskets up as he loaded his crossbow and rushed in the direction of the cry. Argi was scrambling to rise, pressing his right arm tightly to his chest while pointing frantically with his other arm toward the forest up the trail. "Hurry, Kepa! Hurry! It's wounded!" He heard branches crashing ahead and forced his tired legs on in an effort to catch up with the other men already running toward the noise.

Kepa managed to reach them and take the lead but with his strength almost depleted, he knew he could not hold his pace for long. Just as he was about to slow, he spotted a large, rolling splash of brown just off the trail. With weapons poised he and his men drew nearer until they had surrounded a struggling, antlered deer the likes of which they'd never seen. Wild-eyed with terror, the deer tried to gain its feet but toppled to the ground. Argi's musket ball had torn open the front of its chest. Kepa raised his bow and, aiming at the heart just behind the shoulder blade, he loosed his arrow. The animal jerked, kicked once, and lay still.

When Kepa saw Argi standing at the edge of the group cradling his injured arm, he asked, "How bad is it?"

"Not so bad," he said, but Kepa could see the pain in his eyes. "I fell when I fired, and twisted my wrist."

He walked over to Argi and examined his wrist, which appeared to be broken rather than merely twisted, then tore a piece of linen from the bottom of his shirt and bandaged the young man's lower arm. "That will do until Dr. Urresti can bind it securely. Bakar and Todor, stand guard while we get this animal gutted. That musket shot could have been heard by anyone within miles."

No more words were needed to get the men bustling. Kepa did not reprimand Argi for firing his musket. It had been an imprudent act considering the potential danger, but the lad had been through more in the last few days than some men endured in a lifetime. Exhaustion and hardship had taken their toll on them all. And if they made it back to the ship unchallenged there would be fresh meat for the entire crew this night.

While directing the cleaning of the strange deer, Kepa observed the grayish tinges on its dark brown body and head, the purity of the white collaring its neck. But this creature was more impressive in size than in color, and it bore antlers that divided over the forehead into a short stem overhanging its face and a longer branch arcing back then forward as it rose, reaching at least four feet above its head. Both ends of each antler fanned out to twice the size of a man's hand, facing inward. The muzzle was more squared than tapered, and its hooves seemed overly large for its body.

As soon as the deer's body cavity was emptied, the knees of the beast were tied together and a sturdy branch was slipped between them. Grunting under the weight, two men hefted the front of the pole while two others lifted the back. Now they must make haste, before the light or their endurance abandoned them. With Kepa directing them back the way they'd come and Argi and Todor guarding the rear of the line, they headed vigilantly downhill.

The sun's brilliant golds had dimmed to rust by the time the heavily laden chalupa returned to *La Magdalena*. Its occupants had failed to find any natives during their exploration, but they had brought back the clean, icy water Kepa had promised Paulo, along with a strange water creature and enough meat to provide the men with a meal to relish. None would decline the chance to taste red meat after months at sea.

Soon after the men and bounties of the land had been brought aboard, Kepa heard Captain de Perea invite Urdin to rejoin him and the other officers at his table. The new pilot accepted, as he must, but Urdin cast an uneasy glance back at his older cousin, who had not eaten since their anchorage. Kepa motioned him on reassuringly, then watched Pilot de Mendieta leave, mount to the half deck, and enter the captain's cabin.

Just before the hearty stew was ladled into their bowls the men received a cup of wine diluted, for a change, with untainted water, causing many aboard to smack their lips with approval. There was plenty of stew for all and the men had hardly tasted their first bites before loudly praising first the hunters and then their cook. Paulo accepted these tributes silently. With his huge ladle still in his grip he spotted Kepa watching him from the far railing. Setting the ladle back in the caldron, Paulo reached for his own full cup. Facing Kepa, he lifted it with formal dignity. He held it there without uttering a word, his chin high and his expression bearing immeasurable respect. The talk on the main deck died away. Bowls so greedily cradled a moment before were abandoned as men got to their feet and cups quietly rose until they hung elevated in the hands of every man and boy on the deck. At last, Paulo said, "To Gotzon, and to his older brother."

Kepa dropped his head to conceal the sensation that struck him like a wave, too raw and powerful to understand or name. He took four gasping breaths while he fought for control. With a great effort he forced his eyes higher and laid his anguish and his gratitude bare before them. Fumbling slightly, he managed to take hold of his own cup and lift it to the height of his shoulders, meeting their salute. After a moment he brought the cup to his lips, forced his tightened throat to swallow the last of its contents, then turned away and climbed the steps to the forecastle. There he remained in solitude against the prow, staring into the darkness that hid his brother's grave.

The evening had grown chilly so he pulled his beret lower and folded his arms across his chest. Why was it, he wondered, that he must still feel cold, and hunger, and thirst, and fear when he so dearly wished to feel nothing at all? But the answer came too quickly; a man is not often granted his desires.

Unbidden, the memory of two young boys running recklessly down a sloping field washed over him. He heard Gotzon's voice shouting, "Someday we will sail to far lands, Kepa! We'll find wonders and riches that will amaze even Father. Wait and see, Kepa. Wait and see!"

On this night all Kepa could see, or imagined he could, was the dark outline of a wooden grave marker, small and forlorn in the moonlight. Gradually, he pulled his gaze higher and traced the stars across the vastness of the night sky, drawing his sight high over the ship and then downward until his tired eyes came to rest upon the stars hanging just above the ridge where he'd stood not long before.

"How many wonders and riches does this land hold, Gotzon? Can you see them?"

It seemed that the evening breeze caught the words and swept them into the sky, lifting them higher until they passed beyond the listening moon to be gathered in by the waiting stars. As Kepa stared upward he felt Gotzon's presence. The awareness grew until it was undeniable, and he understood.   His brother would never leave him completely.

He closed his eyes and breathed in the smells of the sea and forest, breathed them in for Gotzon as well as for himself.

Whale Hunt

3

In the days that followed the ship's arrival Captain de Perea kept even his harpooners and coopers laboring to make repairs and replenish provisions. He forbid any whale hunting until *La Magdalena* was capable of escaping an attack from an undefeatable force. With the whales so close and so numerous, their calls and splashes resounding across the bay day and night, the whalers were surrounded by an unprecedented incentive to complete their tasks with feverish efficiency. Their individual shares of the whale oil brought safely back to their homeport would support their families throughout the coming winter.

While aboard, Kepa assisted with the finer work on the metal tools, fastenings, and fittings of the ship, but these activities were suspended when he was sent ashore on several scouting and gathering expeditions. The captain gave strict orders to travel inland no more than a couple of miles. Although traces of the natives' earlier presence were occasionally found, during none of the trips did Kepa spot human inhabitants. None had been seen by anyone on the ship or the island either, although many eyes frequently scanned the tree lines. New guards were posted at each turning of the sandglass.

Kepa spoke less and less as the days passed yet the pain from the loss of his brother grew more tolerable. This he attributed to the land itself, which seemed to possess an almost mystical quality. Most of his tasks were performed with quiet concentration and little interaction, which suited him well. The excited anticipation building within the men around him, especially that exhibited by the other two harpooners, he shared not at all.

The hunted game brought back from the forest by Kepa and his men and the codfish caught from the sides of the ship were so bountiful that Paulo soon had plenty of food to salt and pack into newly scoured barrels. One early afternoon Captain de Perea, after inspecting the hold and its more than adequate stores, ordered the barrel makers and one of his carpenters to row to the island and begin constructing a cooperage.

These men set out at once and, near the top of a small hill in the center of the island, they began to lay out their workplace. Their captain had already chosen the future site of the rendering station, so the coopers planted the corner stakes thirty feet above and twenty feet to the west, upwind of where the rendering would be conducted at the water's edge. Such judicious placement would allow the coopers to roll their barrels downhill to the point where they would be filled, while sparing them from most of the harsh black smoke generated by the tryworks.

When the roof and walls of the structure were almost finished, most of the coopers began hauling barrel staves and willows for hoops ashore. By noon of the next day several heavy oak barrels, barricas, had taken shape, each of them capable of holding fifty-six gallons of oil.

Captain de Perea had kept a close watch on their progress, as well as the advancements made by the ship's workers. Within hours of the coopers rolling their first completed barricas to the side of the cooperage, he commanded his mason and renderers to proceed to the island. Members of the rendering crew were men and boys trained to strip the thick blubber from whales and to extract its precious oil, and those of *La Magdalena* performed their dangerous and grueling jobs unflinchingly.

Once ashore the renderers marked off their station, dug a shallow trench, and helped the mason gather rocks and mix clay. They built a rectangular, open-backed chamber and spaced out a line of four circular top-openings to cradle huge copper kettles, each measuring two and a half feet in depth and four feet in diameter. Beneath each kettle, fires would be stoked to an extreme heat to bring the juices of the minced whale blubber to a boil. Stacks of wood, cut and gathered by Kepa and his chalupa crew, soon rose high and wide on the wooden platform constructed behind the stone tryworks ovens.

As the workstations took recognizable shape and *La Magdalena* grew proud and seaworthy again, some of the men were permitted to remain on the island at night after their shifts ended. Kepa was among these few. His lodging was far from luxurious, little more than a shallow cave dug from the hillside, but he relished the relative solitude his small hollow provided, the freedom to stretch his legs upon the earth, and the opportunities to visit Gotzon's grave. The island possessed several freshwater ponds, natural stone basins that caught and held the rainwater, and these Kepa and the others took full advantage of as places to bathe and wash their clothing. Since the large pools were also utilized by countless sea birds, however, neither he nor any other man dared to drink from them.

The wounded and sick aboard *La Magdalena* responded quickly to the fresh water, food, and rest they were given, and within two weeks most of them were becoming as restless to be filling the oil barricas as anyone else. Edginess caused by the need to test their regained vigor escalated steadily until Captain de Perea at last announced that the first hunts would begin the following day. All was to be made ready.

That night Kepa took his txistu to his island cave and held it to his lips for the first time since Gotzon's death. The first notes, coaxing, reassuring, rose from his mouth and fingers with more ease than he had expected. From inside his dark recess he couldn't see the appreciation mingled with relief on his cousin's face or the pleased expressions of the other men who stilled their activities to listen, but he felt his own spirit lifting with the graceful voice of the much-loved instrument. He needed its comforting music tonight to hold his forebodings of the day to come at bay.

La Magdalena had carried a fourth harpooner when they'd set out from Mutriku for the northern seas in April, but he was one of those who had been taken by the storm. The ship's young apprentice harpooner had not yet earned enough money to purchase his own whaling boat, as was the custom, nor had he gained the experience needed to command the more seasoned whalers who would comprise his boat crew. For now, only three chalupas could be used and all of the whalers must adjust their well rehearsed methods to this less efficient number. With one fewer boat the danger of fatal mishaps increased. Nudging such misgivings from his mind, Kepa let the txistu's melodies possess him.

The eastern horizon was only lit by a gray, foggy glow but Kepa was already crouched on the rocky shore beside his chalupa, coiling a drogue line with great care and lowering it into the boat. His hemp line could run several hundred feet behind a harpooned whale, at a speed that might well twist off a man's hand if it became tangled in a loop. The coiling of this length required a delicate touch to reduce the chance of such accidents, so he alone performed the task for his chalupa. When Kepa came to the last few feet in the line, he reached for the drogue, an inch-thick oak board cut three feet square and fitted with a wooden shaft at its center. He threaded the end of the line through a round eye drilled through the stem, and knotted it firmly.

He'd inspected the whaling tools and lines the night before, but now he scrutinized them again in the chilly morning mist. He kept his weapons sharp enough to slice skin much thinner than that of a whale, prompting everyone who dared to touch them to do so with respect. As usual when studying the readiness of the tools, he took up his harpoon first.

Although Kepa could wield the harpoon with extraordinary accuracy, it was a heavy, clumsy implement in unseasoned hands. Its six-inch double-barbed tip capped a yard-long iron shank, the cone of which fit snugly over the tapered head of an oak handle. The harpoon's handle alone stood almost as tall as Kepa. In the growing light he checked the single iron pin that held these two formidable pieces together, hoping it would remain fixed for the short period in which it was intended to last. Sitting down upon a large rock and carefully balancing the harpoon on his knees, he tightened its warp. This section of oiled rope was bound snugly around the base of the shank, then ran most of the length of the handle and was secured again, ending in a larger loop to which the drogue line could be tied.

Whenever a whale was harpooned, preferably in the muscle just behind the shoulder, the handle of the harpoon would commonly snap away from its metal shank just as the whale plunged forward, and the drogue was thrown free of the boat to act as a drag to slow the whale's progress. Then the rowers would seize their oars and call upon the overdeveloped muscles of their arms, backs, and legs in a furious attempt at pursuit.

Next of Kepa's tools to be examined was the lance. Testing the sharpness of its edge with his thumb and then eyeing its securing pins, he nodded with satisfaction. With its foot-long pointed head crowning an iron shank that extended a full fifty-four inches, it was even heavier than the harpoon. Its wooden handle was longer as well, resulting in a device that measured nearly ten feet from tip to butt.

The last of the hunting weapons to be inspected was the louchet, built much like the lance but with a wider and rounder head. Both the lance and louchet would be held back until the whale tired enough for the whalers to come up beside it. Then a harpooner needed the great lengths and weights of the lance and louchet to deliver lethal stabs that could reach the heart or lungs.

Setting the louchet aside, Kepa tugged free the rag he'd tucked into his belt, poured a few drops of olive oil onto it from the vial at his feet, and began conscientiously rubbing the metal parts of each tool.

When he finished resettling the whaling tools in the chalupa, he raised his head and saw that the light fog was lifting. All was ready. As his gaze drifted lower to settle on the bow of his boat he paused and reached out to run his fingers over the emblem he'd carved on the stempost months earlier. It was a lauburu: a spinning wheel with four curved and thickly headed spokes, the ancient symbol of his people. The small insignia stood for home during the best of times, of pride, and courage, and happiness. He was still staring at it when he heard Urdin call out, "Kepa, a moment." He straightened and turned.

Watching his cousin draw closer, Kepa could see that he had something serious to discuss.

Urdin started tentatively, as if to test Kepa's mood. "It is nearly time. The men have been as anxious as bridegrooms for this day."

Kepa said only, "They have," then waited.

"The whales seem to sense the danger of our activities. Look how many have moved farther out of the bay."

"I see. Perhaps they do feel something different about this morning."

"And you, cousin," Urdin asked, eyeing him more closely, "how do you feel about taking up the harpoon again?"

"It is how I make my living."

"Now, yes, but only since—" A sharp stare of warning from Kepa silenced him for a moment, and then he pushed on. "Cousin, I have kept quiet too long, hoping you would come to see things differently, but I will do so no longer. This — ," he paused, spreading his arms to encompass Kepa's chalupa and the two boats anchored farther down the shore, "this killing does not fit your nature. I have seen other whalers who respect the whale, even admire the creature, as any good hunter admires his prey. But with you it's different. You *sympathize* with the whale even as you harpoon it."

Kepa shook his head but Urdin would not accept his denial. "I know you almost as well as I know myself. You didn't choose this life out of need for money or adventure. I suspect that you hunt to ease some thirst for vengeance, against fate, or God, or I don't know what. That, or you simply hunt to torture yourself."

"Urdin, stop. That is enough."

But he didn't stop. "I see how you struggle with your demons after each hunt." When Kepa kept his lips defiantly locked, Urdin's expression and voice saddened. "Arima would despair if she were alive to see what you have forsaken."

"How can you speak of —?"

"I am afraid for you, and for myself! I do not want you taken from me too! Things were bad enough after Arima's death, but now, with Gotzon gone —." When Kepa tried to move away Urdin took hold of his arm. "Hear me, cousin. When you took up the harpoon, Gotzon and I told you it was madness but you would listen to no one."

Kepa, his eyes cold, eased his arm free. "There is no dishonor in what I do."

"For other men, no, but you waste greater talents and risk death needlessly. And you die a little with each whale you kill." A tense, painful silence stepped between them and waited. "I must ask you, Kepa, can I trust that you will return from the hunt today?"

Slowly, Kepa turned his face to him. "First, our captain feared for my soul, and now you ask if I intend to cast it away." He met Urdin's gaze fully and, seeing the anguish there, softened. "You need not worry, dear cousin. I give you my word that I will never court my own death."

Urdin listened to these words hopefully but Kepa could see that he needed greater assurance than this, so he continued, "The night after we buried Gotzon, I began to feel that there is something I am meant to do in the days ahead. I cannot tell whether this will be an act of good or evil but I mean to await its coming, whatever it may be. I promise you, if I do not return from today's hunt, my absence will be brought about by the whales or the devil fish or the hand of God, not by my own design."

Relieved now, Urdin allowed himself a smile as he said, "Then, my only wish is that I were going out with you."

"A price that comes with your new authority," Kepa said with a note of pride. "You'll be missed in my boat."

Their conversation was interrupted by the approach of Kepa's men. Argi arrived first, nodding respectfully to Kepa and Urdin before slapping his chest and taking in a huge breath. He let a smile break across his young face as he exhaled. "Good fortune is rising with the breeze, is it not?"

"I can smell the whales," Kepa said, "if that's what you mean. Farewell, Pilot."

As Urdin left them five other whalers neared the boat, one of them no more than thirteen years of age. Seeming to notice the lad for the first time, Argi, only six years his senior, burst out in mock dismay, "What is Zorion doing here? Have we grown so short-handed that we stoop to taking on children?"

Zorion glanced at his father for support but Todor merely lifted a bushy eyebrow and awaited his son's response.

Softly, but with his head up, Zorion said, "Kepa said I could join the crew."

"And did he say we'd throw you overboard if you gave us the slightest trouble?" Argi demanded.

"That, he didn't have to tell me," Zorion said seriously.

Argi gave out a hoot of laughter and slapped the boy on the back. "No, I doubt he did."

"Zorion will prove himself deserving to be among us," Kepa said, and saw the boy stretch his shoulders back a bit. "Stand ready now, you men. The captain is coming." His crew and those of the other two chalupas drew together to form an arc around Captain de Perea. Men at the cooperage, tryworks station, and aboard the ship paused in their early morning duties and faced the whalers.

"We have a fine day before us, men," their captain said as he scanned their faces. "Never has a whaling crew looked upon such bounty as that swimming in this great bay. But as you well know every whale within our sight carries a deadly threat. We must now ask God to bless our undertakings with his protection." He lifted his chin and prayed in a rough, reverent voice, "Oh Lord, You have brought us to this coast crowded with whales. Many of our kinsmen and countrymen were taken by the storm before they could reach this place, and they are sorely missed. Yet, keeping in mind the dangers of this life, our remaining whalers will soon leave the safety of land to again hunt the mightiest of fish to ever swim the sea. Please keep death from claiming any who stand before you now. Amen.

"I wish you good hunting, men."

Nods and murmuring followed the captain's prayer as most of the men moved toward their chalupas. The three harpooners met briefly to discuss the hunting strategy one last time, and several of their men listened as their leaders divided the bay into sections. As always, if a boat was in peril or needed help bringing in a wounded whale and another crew was nearby, aid would be given. Otherwise, due to the extraordinary number of whales in such tight proximity, each chalupa would work independently rather than in the usual pairs. Kepa agreed to hunt in the westerly portion of the bay.

As Kepa's crew boarded, each man, and especially young Zorion, maneuvered carefully to avoid shifting the lines and tools out of position. Todor took hold of the steering oar and motioned Zorion to the nearest of seven thin wooden boards braced across the length of the small craft that served as seats. Kepa shoved away from shore and leaped into the bow. The other two whaling boats pushed off at the same time and an unmistakable air of competition accompanied them into the water. A shout of challenge arose from Mikel, the harpooner of the most eastward chalupa, "Our wine shares to the crew that brings in the largest whale!" "Done!" roared Bakar, the second harpooner. The contagious enthusiasm had not failed to seize Kepa's crew along with the others, and he called out, "Agreed!" His men, their teeth gritted between grinning lips, tightened their grips and sliced their oars down into the water.

The nearest whale was a young one lying just off the western end of the island, but Kepa quickly spotted the largest creature in his section of the bay and pointed Todor in that direction.

The whales' songs and strange gunshot-like noises reverberated all around Kepa's chalupa as it flew across the surface of the choppy water. He could sense the tightly strung anticipation of his men with every pull of the oars. They were forced to slow, however, in order to row through a group of whales swimming between them and their target. Never before had they hunted in such tight quarters with their prey, and the men eyed the whales' movements warily as the boat entered this congested expanse of their realm.

The whales dove or moved off as the chalupa neared them, but the nose of each crewmember was abruptly assaulted by the stench of the water, and the rowers had to maneuver nimbly to avoid the floating wastes left behind by the enormous creatures. They'd just managed to pull clear of the stinking, bobbing obstacles when a whale suddenly surfaced very close to the boat. It exhaled through its double-nostril blowhole, a distinction of its breed, and shot a V-shaped spray twenty feet into the air, dowsing Kepa and his men with seawater.

Keeping his eyes on their target, Kepa saw the whale begin to move slowly toward the entrance of the bay. "Do not lose him, men," he ordered and the boat again surged forward.

The chalupa approached swiftly from behind, keeping just to the whale's left side with the hope of driving it toward shore when it ran. Reaching back, Kepa took hold of his harpoon and tied the drogue line onto its warp. He rose to his feet in the bow of the racing boat with the weapon clasped in both hands. "Ready the drogue," he hissed over his shoulder, but Argi was already lifting the wooden weight to the gunwale. Kepa stole a glance behind him and saw that Zorion's eyes were round with fear but the boy's jaws were clenched tightly shut. He gave him a quick, reassuring tip of his head then faced forward.

Watching the whale's movements, Kepa tried to read its intentions. He stared at the massive, unawakened power before him and questioned the sanity of every whaler ever born. They were forty feet from the whale's flukes, then twenty, then only ten. He braced his feet apart and balanced the harpoon in his left hand while keeping his right far back to maximize the power of his thrust. *Steady*, he told himself. *Steady*. The arms and legs of every rower tightened as they drew within striking distance, readying themselves for the reaction of a hundred ton wounded animal. In one continuous motion Kepa stood taller, his shoulders lifting, and released a guttural cry as he threw his weight downward to drive his harpoon deep into the shoulder of the whale.

With a swiftness that belied its size, the sixty-five foot animal arched its back and heaved its tail high out of the water. The chalupa turned sharply and darted out of reach before the twelve-foot span of flukes slammed down with enough power to splinter the boat. They were still pulling away when the whale lunged forward.

"He is running for open water!" Kepa yelled. "Hard after him, men!"

Still at the steering oar, Todor cursed viciously but he and the oarsman spun the boat around and headed after the whale. As the harpoon line fed out, the drogue was tossed from Argi's hands into the water. Kepa's harpoon proved how well it had been set by remaining imbedded even when the drogue bounced wildly on the surface then caught the water and forced a fountain of spray into the air as it trailed behind the whale.

Now Kepa leaped down and took up an oar, straining with the others to keep the whale in sight. Their bodies worked in unison, molding Zorion's movements with a tempo that had become intuitive to the experienced men. A grueling pace was maintained until Kepa, facing astern as he rowed, peered over his shoulder and saw the whale's flukes flash with reflected sunlight just before it dove. Now he and the other men could only pause, scanning the water while they sweated in the cool breeze, hoping the harpoon wouldn't work itself free, praying their quarry wouldn't charge upward from beneath them and shatter the boat. But then their whale spouted less than forty yards ahead, and amid shouts of encouragement the race resumed.

Kepa's crew passed many other whales as the chase stretched out but they kept doggedly after their original prey for nearly a half-hour. At last they began to gain on the drogue and within minutes the whale came to a gradual halt not far ahead. As the boat continued to close the gap between them, Kepa exchanged his oar for the lance. Lifting its considerable weight and steadying his balance, he again stood and held himself in position. For an instant Urdin's words of that morning resounded in his ears, *this killing does not fit your nature*. With a mental shake he tried to erase the claim from his mind. Urdin was wrong. This was what he was meant to do.

While the chalupa quickly closed in Kepa scrutinized every inch of the whale's monstrous back. It loomed larger and larger before him as he attempted to anticipate its next move. "Straight in, men! God keep us!" Todor and the rowers sped directly toward the

30

harpoon wound, pulling parallel at the last moment. Kepa aimed the lance precisely for the heart. From a spear-length away Kepa heaved and bore down with his full strength, burying his weapon six feet into the body of the whale.

An enraged, pain-stricken call broke from the depths. The whale thrashed wildly as Kepa's men struggled to swing away. The massive tail rose to strike at its tormentors but the flukes crashed down upon the water a foot beyond the stern of the boat. The churning waves rocked the boat madly, throwing Zorion halfway out before Todor grabbed the top of his son's tunic and hauled him back over the gunwale to the floor. Kepa grasped the louchet and fought to stay upright.

This is when Kepa's skill was needed most, for he knew every muscle and bone of the creature they battled. Lifting his louchet almost in unison with the whale's rising tail, Kepa let his weapon fly an instant before the flukes descended, biting deeply into the tendon that joined the fluke to the tail. His cut disabled the whale as effectively as one cripples a man by severing his hamstring. The tail swung sharply away, the injured fluke slightly askew, but Kepa sensed that this opponent would try to strike again. He yanked savagely on the louchet line and pulled the blade free.

The whale turned back toward them and bore down vengefully upon the boat. But before the distance between them could be eliminated completely, the chalupa suddenly whipped to the side and out of reach of the nearest fin, and then abruptly stilled to give Kepa his chance. Aiming for the whale's flesh just behind its blowhole, he hurled the louchet and watched it plunge deep into the black flesh. Again, a roar boomed from beneath them and the whale veered off and swam a short distance away. It held itself sideways to the boat, keeping them in sight, and Kepa perceived its indecision. He observed the creature closely as blood pulsed from its wounds, reddening the sea in a widening pool that eventually overtook the chalupa. *Soon*, Kepa thought. *It will die very soon.*

A few moments later the whale turned once more to face them and he ordered, "Lean to the oars!" But before they'd gained much distance the wounded beast reversed its direction and slowly headed off. The chalupa maintained a respectful distance for a quarter mile, until the whale lessoned its labored efforts, came to a full

stop, convulsed in its final flurries of death, and ceased all movements. Even then the whalers approached with watchful vigilance.

Closer up, Kepa could see that the whale's body was already
beginning to roll, so he turned to Zorion and announced, "Todor,
your son can claim a fine catch for his first hunt."

An exultant cheer erupted from the sweaty, weary crew, and the
men began to slap Zorion's back and offer coarse congratulations so
outrageous that one would have thought he'd killed the whale single
-handedly. The boy, his breeches still dripping from his partial
dunking, beamed as his cheeks flushed crimson.

They quieted a bit as the chalupa rocked gently beside the dead
whale, and Argi whistled in admiration at the incredible size of the
prey they'd conquered. "We've a good chance of collecting on that
bet, eh, Kepa? There can be few monsters of this size, even in this
bay."

Kepa nodded, "Perhaps, but at least two leagues lay between
our tryworks and this whale. A good deal of rowing must be done
before we can take its measure."

With that, they hauled in the drogue and began securing the
whale's tail to the chalupa. When the lines were in place Kepa took
possession of the steering oar, pointed the boat back toward their
island, and his men strained to set the whale's carcass in motion.

"Now, Todor," he said, "sing us to shore." Zorion's proud father
needed no more encouragement before lifting his voice for their
long pull back. His song was one that his great-great grandfather
had sung before him, and that the entire crew knew as well as their
daily prayers. They all joined in to sing of the valor of a whaler and
of his longing for the woman awaiting his return. The rhythm of the
tune set the pace of the oar strokes, creating a faultless uniformity
that encouraged the chalupa's dipping blades to add their own whis-
perings to the texture of the music.

After relinquishing their whale three hours later to the renderers,
men whose faces were already blackened by the tryworks smoke,
Kepa's crew was allowed to rest briefly before going out again. By
that evening Zorion could hardly stand and was able to lift his badly
blistered hands no higher than his elbows. The boy was almost too
exhausted to eat, an unheard of rarity. Kepa noted, however, that
Zorion was not so tired that he turned down the extra shares of wine

collected from the other two chalupa crews. He fell asleep within moments of taking his last swallow. The day had been successful for all three crews; one boat had been badly damaged but it had soon been replaced from spare components held in readiness aboard the ship, and no whaler had sustained a fatal injury.

After his other men had followed Zorion into a state of death-like slumber, Kepa stayed by their small fire and silently absorbed the night. Occasional words and laughter reached him from the renderers down the shore, the latest shift now filling barrels by torchlight. Blessedly, his crew's camp was upwind of the smoky fires so the breeze that brushed his face brought with it the sweet hint of spruce. Surrounded by snoring, Kepa sat in the sand amid his small group and stared at the glowing embers. Unbidden, the death roars of the first whale they'd killed came back to him with unforgettable clarity. He pictured the whale's final struggles, the water red with its blood. He rubbed his eyes in an attempt to rid himself of the images.

"Ah, Gotzon," he murmured to the spirit of his dead brother, "our cousin is an insightful man."

Deadly Prey

4

"Those demons from hell!" Todor shook a tight fist at the pod of orcas attacking the thrashing, wounded Right whale still bearing Kepa's harpoon. "That's the fourth catch, the fourth, they've stolen from us! And look there, it's that same white-finned devil leading them."

Standing in the chalupa with his lance held loosely in his hands, Kepa nodded as he too recognized the very orca that had circled their boat on their first day of arrival. "He watches us, that one, and waits for his chance."

"They drive us off after we've made the first strike," Todor still seethed, " mocking us all the while. If there weren't so damned many of them I'd be tempted to row in there and steal back what's ours."

"If they follow their usual tendencies, they will eat the tongue and surrender the rest to us," Kepa pointed out. "I doubt we will lose much of the oil from that whale."

"But they'll not give the carcass up 'til after nightfall and by then the meat will be of no use to us."

"Well, there is little to be done about them now." Kepa resettled the lance along the side of the boat, moved his spare harpoon within reach, and said resignedly, "Unless we are willing to risk our own tongues, we had better search out another whale. With this fog lowering we may not have much time."

After the first day of hunting, the great whales had dispersed somewhat, but not far enough to greatly reduce the success of the whalers. The hunting had gone so well, in fact, that Captain de Perea had announced that morning they'd be sailing within the next few days. In addition to hundreds of barrels of oil, a grand store of meat, baleen and even some of the whalebones were now being prepared for transport back to Mutriku.

And during these weeks only one whaler had been killed. His neck had broken when he was flung from his whale-tossed chalupa. His grave now lay beside Gotzon's.

As much as Kepa longed to see his home again, there was much he would miss about this bay they'd named Aldapak, in honor of the surrounding hills. The grandeur of the forest, the magnificence of the creatures that roamed its vastness or swam in its waters, these he would remember always. Lately, even the smallest of living things here had managed to capture his fascination.

For some time he had noticed Paulo leaving his cooking duties to wander the island and mainland to study the progress of a peculiar berry that grew close to the ground in profusion. A week ago Paulo had called Kepa to him and displayed a handful of the light orange berries, saying proudly, "These are from the first patch to ripen." The small fruits were roughly the size of garbanzos and looked like tiny sunset-hued clouds. Kepa had eyed them with a bit of suspicion but, acquiescing to the cook's insistence, he'd tossed the whole batch into his mouth. As he chewed, his taste buds absorbed a musky, savory sweetness that reminded him of ripe apricots. In response to such an unexpected pleasure he had smiled, and this had moved Paulo so greatly that the eyes of the old cook had blurred with tears. Until that moment Kepa had not realized how long it had been since anyone had seen him smile.

Paulo and his cabin boys had soon picked enough cloudberries, as they were rightly dubbed, to fill several barrels, and took turns standing guard over much of this golden treasure as it dried in the sun upon makeshift tables. Such delicacies would be welcome indeed during their return voyage.

Their return voyage. Once Kepa reached home again, what then? He'd begun to realize, no, to face Urdin's assertion about how little the taking of whales suited him regardless of how he'd tried to conform himself to the role. When he returned to his village he'd turn his hand to another endeavor, though he had no idea what that might be. With his share of the whaling profits, at least he'd have money enough to see himself through until he found an alternative means of making a living. Although he was old to begin training in a trade most boys started by the age of twelve, he could learn to build ships as his father had done. Perhaps he'd even grow accustomed to farming his family's land.

He was startled by a shout from the lookout positioned on the eastern hill of the island. "Whale! Whale spouting! A third-knot southeastward!"

His crew set to their oars with renewed vigor only a moment before Todor called out, "Bakar's crew is pushing off!" The men in the other chalupa flashed challenging grins and both boats quickly reached full speed, racing through the mist-blanketed water. Crews worked willingly together under tough weather conditions such as this, but a keen and long-held competitiveness existed between boats as to which would make the opening strike.

"We'll get you in first, Kepa!" Todor promised as he set a demanding pace for the rowers.

The fog was growing so thick that Kepa squinted and leaned forward in an effort to keep the whale in view, its black form floating ahead like the strip of a shrouded island. The other chalupa was not far behind but with Todor's break-neck cadence his men were closing in on their target well ahead of them. Kepa reached for the harpoon and rose up, scanning the whale's size, anticipating its behavior.

Before they'd drawn within striking distance the whale suddenly turned toward them and slapped the water menacingly with its flukes. "Slow the boat," Kepa ordered, sensing the aggression of the giant creature. Breathing hard, his rowers lifted their oars. "Pull back, men," Kepa said, but before they could obey, Bakar's chalupa crew hauled past them with a victorious shout. The whale again arched its back and slammed its tail into the sea, causing even Bakar's chalupa to glide to a pause. With no further warning the whale suddenly charged Bakar's boat. The rowers jerked their handles back and sawed madly at the water but Kepa saw that it was too late, his companions would not escape.

"Straight in!" he ordered and his crew drove their own boat right toward the impending collision.

They were still ten boat-lengths away when the whale lowered its head in a shallow dive and rose up under Bakar's keel. Unable to swerve out of reach, Bakar let loose his harpoon before his boat was struck from below and thrown high into the air, its keel splitting in half and men, tools, and oars flying in every direction. As the huge, dripping tail rose from the sea above two desperately swimming men, Kepa heaved his harpoon at the nearest fluke. The weapon struck powerfully enough to wrench the tail to the side but it still came crashing down with colossal force on top of one man.

Kepa grabbed his lance and aimed just as two other men from Bakar's boat reached his own chalupa. One of the swimmers seized the boat's side an instant after Kepa hurled his lance. The man's weight rocked the boat nearly to the water line and Kepa stumbled back, trying to right his balance, but slipped on a line looped at his feet and fell to his knees. With his eyes cast downward he saw that the harpoon line had been allowed to slacken in the bottom of the boat. He jerked his gaze up. Zorion had dropped the drogue to hold onto one of the swimmers clinging to the boat. Kepa scrambled to rise and loosen his feet as he yelled, "The drogue!" But the words had hardly left his lips before his feet were grabbed from beneath him and his left leg was stabbed with pain so intense it felt as if his limb were being wrenched from his body. The line viciously yanked him up and forward and his head smacked sharply against the chalupa's stem post as he was torn from the boat. Stunned and limp, he hit the water.

Icy wetness sped over Kepa at an unimaginable speed, his right leg splaying wide while his left stretched out ahead of him. Holding onto what remained of his breath, he opened his eyes and bright flashes of fiery light nearly blinded him. When he tried to kick himself loose his effort only worsened the agony shooting through his leg. The tension in the line made it stiff as iron. He struggled to bend over and reach toward his ankle but the water and pain pummeled him back. He could feel that his air was almost gone, yet he couldn't free himself. Near panic, his lungs burning, the rest of his body freezing, he remembered his knife. His hands tore at his belt and he managed to pull it from its sheath.

Just then Kepa felt the whale reducing its speed and ascending to the surface, and he stroked frantically upward in time to gulp a watery breath, then another before the whale dove once more, pulling him down with it. He fought to reach the line binding his leg but he could neither pull his ankle to his hands nor bend far enough to reach it. The sea grew darker and colder as they slowly descended. His arms gradually weakened and his lungs began to burn again. The hammering in his head thundered louder. His ears ached as if they would soon burst. His legs were nearly numb.

Kepa's struggles lessened as the chill settled into his bones. Oh, he wanted to rest, just for a moment. Air from his mouth trickled out in a tiny stream of bubbles that rolled up his cheek and into his hair. The water seemed to wait with soft, open arms for his surrender.

A small spark within him suddenly flared and his pounding brain cried out, *No, by God, no! Once more!* As he fought to bend down again he felt the line slacken slightly. With a desperate burst of strength he clamped his knife in his teeth and clawed down his hyper-extended leg, stretching, reaching, straining until he knew his muscles would surely snap, and then he grabbed it. With his lungs aflame he jerked his knife from his mouth and sliced with fumbling fingers at the line. Before he'd severed half the cords the line pulled taught again, but he clung to it and kept sawing even as he was tugged forward. The line suddenly snapped and he stopped moving.

He let his body float in the grey depths. He could do nothing else. His left leg had no feeling and, after making that last valiant effort, his arms could no longer respond to his wishes. He felt the knife slip from his fingers. His eyelids closed and could not be opened again.

I am too deep. The thought came to him as though through a haze. The battle was over. He'd lost. He'd lost.

With neither malice nor regret he opened wide the reaches of his soul and relinquished all claims to his earthly life.

He was rising very slowly now, but he was only just aware of this. One last hiss of bubbles escaped his lips. A gurgling spasm seized his body and he tasted seawater and bile.

Slipping into a realm of forgetful peace, he began to dream. Ever so gently he was being lifted from the lonely depths, ascending higher and higher until he broke free of the water's grasp to float beyond the cold, beyond the pain.

But as Kepa's sleep deepened and all wonder and desire faded, even his dreams died away.

Hut of Pain

5

It came as a soft whisper, the smallest murmur of awareness, creeping up Kepa's body to convey that his bare legs and chest were snugly molded to the warm back and buttocks of a naked woman. This perception had scarcely reached him when shocks of pain shot through him so ruthlessly that he let out a strangled groan. Breathing raggedly, he felt the softness beside him shift away.

He dared not move or open his eyes since the physical torture of doing so would surely kill him. Worse even than the agony forced upon him by his left leg was the deafening pounding within his head. He groaned again, weaker now. With his eyes locked shut he tried to retreat into his cave of unconsciousness, but instead of regaining his hold on slumber his stomach began to clench and sway. He was unable to swallow down a building, rising bout of nausea. Turning his head aside, he vomited again and again until there was nothing more to eliminate. He rolled back, sweat-soaked and shaking.

Voices hushed and strange hovered around him. Hands gentle and cautious brushed over his skin and shifted the covers beneath him. Only once, for an instant, did his eyes slit open but he was struck by so punishing a flash of light that he cried out and then lay as still as the dead, wishing never to move again. Before long, blessedly, a dark oblivion embraced him and let him sleep.

Several more times he stirred to wakefulness, always to feel the woman's body pressed up close or wrapped around him under heavy covers. And each awakening triggered the futile retching of his empty gut while his head and leg fell under painful assault once more. Afterward, completely spent, he slid back into darkness.

Now he awoke to outraged grumblings inside his stomach. He kept his eyes closed and let the pain in various parts of his body reveal its intensity before attempting to change positions. It was tolerable, just, but he was in no hurry to lift his eyelids. He could feel that the woman was not beside him.

Had he merely imagined her? Perhaps, but someone had treated him. His left leg was heavily bound, perhaps splinted, and it throbbed from ankle to hip as if it had ballooned to twice its normal size. Tentatively, he shifted an inch. *Good God, save us! Enough, enough, oh Lord above, please, enough.* With his chest heaving and his teeth gritted, he waited for the pain to relent. Very slowly, he cracked open one eye, and then the other. Trying to ignore the protests of his aching head, he lifted it a few inches and began to make a squinting scrutiny of his environment. It took a few moments for his eyes to focus.

The filtered light revealed that he was housed within a small conical structure, its long support poles coming nearly together at the top and covered with the light colored bark of trees. His gaze lowered to take in the primitive household items on the fur-covered floor and hanging from the curved wall. In a slow circling sweep Kepa noted various baskets, a pair of strange wooden frames rounded at one end and pointed at the other with leather strips crisscrossing their centers, and several animal pelts. Something was cooking in a stone pot over a low fire in the center of the room. Its smell tempted another growl from his stomach.

Lowering his head, he rested for a couple of breaths then lifted it again to continue his study of the chamber. He saw tools made from antlers, what appeared to be a shallow drum, three dried skulls of some kind of animal, and, with a start, one small and absolutely motionless young woman.

Kepa had not even suspected her presence. She held herself so still that he could detect no evidence of breathing, but her eyes, two oval brown crystals almost too large for her features, stared intently back at him.

Without thinking Kepa tried to sit up but a responding stab jolted through his leg with such violence that it drew a clipped curse from his dry lips before he fell back. The woman came quickly to his side, touching his shoulder and saying with gentle insistence, "Atlasmit, atlasmit."

He gradually forced himself to relax and turned his face toward the woman again. Her obvious concern for him eased a little when he didn't attempt to rise.

Far from naked now, if indeed this was the same woman who had shared his bed of furs, she wore a knee-length leather shift belted at the waist and a pair of leather shoes. She was petite, perhaps seven inches shorter than Kepa, but her body was fully, femininely formed. Her thick, black hair fell to her thighs and was bound by a thin band at the crown of her head. It framed a small, worried face with broad cheekbones and generous lips that seemed to Kepa, even in his disabled state, to have been created to perfectly balance her exquisite eyes. The color of her skin was what his might have been had he not spent so many hours baring it to harsh conditions, and its surface was smooth and lustrous. Upon this close inspection, Kepa was surprised that her appearance was not more notably different from the physical characteristics of his own people. This land was close to three thousand miles from theirs.

They studied one another, each trying to read clues that might reveal an inner nature. Kepa concluded from her direct, trusting gaze that she was far more comfortable with his presence than he was with hers. A moment later he was struck by the question of why she had held his body against her own for—how long? And if she was so free with her... her... herself just what had taken place between them? But then, he quickly recalled, he'd been delirious at the time. Surely in his condition he couldn't have... Unexpectedly, ridiculously, he felt his cheeks warming, and much to his embarrassment he saw that she noticed. She seemed puzzled by his discomfort but mercifully lowered her eyes and moved away to stir the contents of the pot over the fire.

While she was occupied, Kepa lifted the fur that covered him just high enough to peer beneath it. He was wearing nothing except a curious necklace he'd never seen before. He had only an instant to consider its presence before the round hide that served as a door was pulled aside to allow the entrance of an old man wearing a leather shirt and a pair of tight-legged breeches, fringed down the outer seams, that reached below his ankles. The man was followed by an older woman dressed similar to her daughter, or so Kepa guessed his caretaker to be. The couple, each of whom Kepa judged to be about fifty years of age, had streaks of gray in their long dark hair but they moved with fluidity as they circled the hut. They seemed to wear their age with subtle dignity. These older ones exchanged glances and a few words with the young woman as they sat down to face Kepa, showing a patient expectancy.

Uncertain, Kepa weakly raised himself up enough to lean upon a bent elbow, tapped on his chest and asked, "Are there others here, others like me?"

This query was met with looks of incomprehension. He tried again by making clumsy gestures of boats, men, whales, and hunters, and this triggered an impressive string of verbal responses from the old man, the meaning of which Kepa could not fathom. Then, with great care, the native used his hands to indicate that no others from the boats were close by. At least this was what Kepa interpreted the message to mean.

Well then, if no other whalers were near, how far was he from his whaling camp? He'd have to send word to the captain. In his present condition, however, trying to communicate so complex a request seemed overwhelming. Even the brief exchange that had taken place had tired him greatly.

He sank back down and tried to keep his eyes from closing, but failed. He'd almost drifted into sleep when he felt a soft touch upon his shoulder. She was kneeling beside him again, this time holding out a wooden cup. He accepted it with slightly shaky hands but drained the cool water greedily, pausing only to rinse it over his pasty tongue before swallowing the last gulp. He felt the water slide down his throat and imagined it washing through his parched body.

The water refreshed him somewhat, and his eyes followed the woman as she spooned something from the stone pot and brought him a steaming bowl. "Alteg," she said softly, and smiled. It was a smile completely free of guile or selfishness, and seemed to radiate from a temperament incapable of cruelty.

Kepa tried to return the smile but it showed itself as a grimace.

She offered him a spoonful of stew, which he opened his mouth to accept with little hesitation. The rich broth was crowded with small chunks of fowl, which Kepa guessed to be goose, and spiced with the sweetness of berries. He was surprised to detect even the flavor of salt. As his tongue savored the stew he decided he couldn't have eaten anything so appealing in months. With his face awash with appreciation, he said, "This is delicious." This his hosts easily understood and the old man nodded encouragement as the next spoon was lifted.

When the last spoonful had disappeared Kepa would gladly have accepted more but he refrained from asking. He had no idea how well supplied these people were. Perhaps they were very poor. But his offering of stew was soon followed by a tea with a slight cucumber flavor. The first sip was so potent that it gave him a moment's pause, but he quickly realized his concerns made little sense. Surely they would not try to save him and then offer him something harmful. Not wishing to insult his hosts, he emptied the cup. With the tang of the drink still tingling his tongue he wondered what properties the herbal concoction might have held, and hoped that it would somehow lessen the pain in his head and leg.

This line of conjecture shifted abruptly, however, when the young woman set the cup aside and unceremoniously lifted back the fur that covered him. Seemingly unaware of Kepa's sudden discomfort at being so blatantly exposed before three strangers, two of them women, his observers gathered around to thoroughly inspect him. With murmurs of concern and speculation the outer bandages around his splint were loosened. This was done very gently to avoid jarring his ankle, which Kepa could see was extremely swollen. He watched the young woman touch the area with utmost care. Using gestures, she showed Kepa that the ankle had been dislocated from his leg. She then indicated that she had pushed it back into place and that the splints would hold it in position.

Dislocated, then, rather than broken. But badly dislocated. As she conscientiously rebound his lower leg, Kepa could find no fault with her methods and his gratitude for her efforts grew.

When the bandaging had been accomplished, to his surprise the young woman bent low over his ankle and blew lightly upon it. She repeated this strange action three times, each time following it with the recitation of a chant. The fourth occurrence seemed to mark the conclusion of the young woman's ministrations, but before the fur could be replaced over Kepa, the old woman pointed unabashedly at his chest and then at his groin and made comments of evident approval, to which the old man grunted in emphatic agreement. The young woman looked thoughtfully back at Kepa's face without offering a comment.

During much of these last activities Kepa had stared through his half-closed eyes at the smoke hole in the top of the hut and kept his expression as blank as possible. Although he was normally far from modest about the natural workings of his or any other body, these conditions and customs were far from normal to him. He endured the blowing and the gesticulation with all the stoicism he could rally but this lengthening effort was drawing down his small store of strength like water seeping from a cracked jug. By the time they'd finally resettled his covers he felt hollow, and he wanted nothing so much as to be left in peace.

Thankfully, the others now backed away and only the young woman reappeared at his shoulder, her gaze resting soothingly upon him. "Atlasmit," she said again, and momentarily closed her own eyes to show her meaning.

Weakly, he realized that he had not yet asked her to get word of his presence to his people, but sleep was tugging at him insistently. *In a few moments*, he thought dimly, *I will ask her to tell them.* He murmured, "Yes, I will rest a while."

He saw the young woman rise to her feet, pick something out from among her baskets, and take hold of the drum suspended from a pole. In a soft dual-toned melody she began to sing, striking the thin drum with a carved implement in time with her chanting. To Kepa's ears her phrases seemed to circle back upon themselves, following a hypnotic path. She took small steps from side to side in a subtle dance that matched the cadence of the drum, her voice shifting with the movements of her body. Kepa soon lost his ability to watch or listen, and his heavy eyelids fell.

Her song gently guided him as he drifted beyond wakefulness. He thought of Gotzon, picturing him with absolute clarity, and silently spoke to him. *These people have snatched me from death, little brother. Perhaps it will be a while longer before I join you.* His mind roamed farther until it came to rest upon the image of the young woman who danced and sang above him. She was lovely and kind, and she was doing her best to heal him. Perhaps, when her song ended, she would undress and lie beside him again. He wanted to feel her softness and her warmth. This consoling thought escorted him into the beckoning depths of slumber.

Beneath the furs Kepa stirred. This time he was forced to abandon sleep because of his complaining bladder rather than his stomach. The young woman came to him and, quickly assessing his condition, handed him an empty container made from an internal organ of some large animal. She busied herself among her baskets while Kepa made use of the supple bottle, then took it from him with no sign of embarrassment or squeamishness. *She has treated others before me*, he thought. When she left the hut to empty the container, Kepa pushed himself to a sitting position and attempted to reassess his physical condition. His head, while still aching without mercy, felt a little clearer. His leg throbbed a measure lighter than before.

His caretaker soon returned carrying an armload of wood. She set this down by the entrance and came to him to examine his leg. Once the bandage had again been removed, he thought he could see a reduction in the swelling. Still, he'd be nearly useless aboard ship for a while, four or five weeks perhaps.

As he was covering his legs once more the old man and woman entered the hut, this time accompanied by a young boy no older than six years. The round-faced, sturdy child watched Kepa with absorption and sat in awed silence with the old ones while Kepa accepted fresh portions of water, food, and tea. After finishing these offerings, he felt sufficiently fortified to attempt a new session of manual communication with his hosts.

"Please," he said, "I must ask you something." With slow deliberation he gestured to indicate his coming to the hut and the overhead passing of the sun. He held up first one finger then two, and gave them an inquiring look. When he received no reply he repeated his hand signals with slight variations twice more before the old man made a declaration of recognition and moved closer.

With confidence the old native raised four fingers. Kepa paled. Four days! He'd been here *four days*! His gaze darted around the hut. "Where are my clothes?" He threw off his fur cover and struggled to maneuver his legs beneath him only to be jarred by an explosion of pain so intense that he let out a deep-throated cry. The young woman hurriedly reached out for Kepa and called beseechingly, but it was the old man who caught him as he fell.

Four days. The ship could sail before I reach her. Kepa again demanded his clothes even as he recognized his request was hopeless. He couldn't even stand. Then these people would have to send word for him. "Do they know I am here, the other whalers?"

45

he asked aloud while trying to control his panic enough to signal this question manually.

The old man seemed to understand. Locking eyes with Kepa, he raised his hands and carefully demonstrated the sun traversing the sky once, and a ship, his ship, sailing away. He motioned for Kepa to lie down, to stay with them.

One day? Yesterday? My ship sailed, yesterday? No. Kepa sat very still. His mind faltered then froze as he faced the realization, *They've left me behind. They think I am dead.*

The old man must have left him briefly because he reappeared in front of Kepa's glazed, stricken eyes. He held up a thin, fur-wrapped bundle. Kepa's arms felt too heavy to lift. He stared dumbly and did not move. But the old man, his expression growing fearful, offered the bundle again. Forcing himself to take it, Kepa rested it in his lap. When he failed to unwrap the thing, the old man moved aside the covering with reverence, careful not to touch what it protected.

Kepa looked down. There in his lap rested a metal harpoon shank. Barely aware of his actions, Kepa took it in his hands and turned it slowly. Five inches below the tip, just beneath the black-smith's personal mark, a familiar stamped impression stared back at him. It was a bird's wing, created to replicate the birthmark on his neck. He was holding his own harpoon.

Kepa's shoulders began to tremble as a sardonic laughter rose from the core of his weakened frame. It burst from him, sharp and bitter. Much to the concern of the native adults and the confused apprehension of the child, Kepa's outburst grew louder and more turbulent until it possessed him entirely. The woman called to him pleadingly but her voice couldn't reach him. Then, abruptly, the laughter ceased. With another glance at the harpoon his mouth twisted downward as his eyes squeezed shut. His chest convulsed once, then repeatedly, releasing a storm of tears. Sobs of self-condemnation and desolation now took hold of Kepa more ruthlessly than the laughter had.

His ship was gone. His only family member was gone. His world was gone. All that had been left to him was one harpoon, to remind him of everything that had been lost and to mock him for his failures.

He had no strength left to fight his emotions and they held him captive for what seemed a long time. When exhaustion finally quieted his weeping he became vaguely aware that his older caregivers had left the hut, taking the child with them. The woman remained, silently watchful.

Raw and depleted, Kepa lowered his body and buried himself beneath his furs. Feebly, he cursed whatever compassionate impulse had caused the savages to pull him from the sea. He lay motionless, helpless to do anything but await the arrival of fate's next whim.

Achaku

6

Ten months, perhaps a year. If Kepa could just survive until next summer, more ships might come to bear him home. After hours of mental wrestling and finally calling upon his last reserve of tenacity, he'd clutched at this conclusion. But it had ultimately been his promise to Urdin, his vow never to court his own death, that had fortified his resolve and forced him to accept nourishment the third time it was offered. By then, the sun was setting.

He'd slept fitfully through a seemingly endless night and with the coming of morning the woman approached him, again offering a filled cup and warm bowl. He'd just finished his tea and was now listening to the noises from outside the curved wall of the hut, wondering how many others lived in this encampment. The sniffing and an occasional yip of a dog accented the human sounds. A group of children raced by squealing with laughter but they were hushed by a woman's voice.

Acutely aware that he was at the mercy of these natives, Kepa regretted the abysmal start he'd made with them. Even if he couldn't muster gratitude for his rescue, he was still in their debt for the many kindnesses they'd performed. His injury and abandonment were inadequate excuses for his behavior yesterday. It had been unmanly and unappreciative of him and he was shamed by the memory.

What must these people think of him after his complete loss of restraint? So far they'd given no sign of their disapproval, yet how could they not feel some measure of condemnation toward him?

As the early light crept deeper into the hut the old man, who had not spoken since Kepa's awakening, moved to sit cross-legged just outside the open door flap and began to whittle the forked end of a long stick. Now and then he paused in his carving to absently pat the head of a small, shorthaired, reddish dog lying beside him.

The young woman sat a few feet away, concentrating intently as she sewed red leather strings and small bones to a fist-sized leather pouch. The old woman and child were nowhere to be seen.

Furtively, Kepa studied the face of the young woman and wondered anew who she was, what she was. He'd seen the resemblance between her and the boy so he held little doubt that she was the child's mother, though she looked to be no older than nineteen or twenty. Was she a widow? No young man had shown himself. Remembering the feel of her body against his own, which he recalled too easily for his own peace of mind, Kepa was struck by the idea that she could be a prostitute. If widowed or disgraced, she might have little choice. Her serene nature did nothing to imply such a thing, he admitted to himself, but he knew little of prostitutes and even less of the customs of these people. If she made her living in such a manner, a payment of some kind would be expected for...for whatever had transpired between them when his judgment had been impaired. He couldn't quite decide whether he wanted to know what had taken place between them or not. In any event, remuneration would certainly be due for the medical care she'd given him, even in the absence of other services she might have provided.

It was time he showed his gratitude and began building a means of communication between them. He set his empty cup aside and cleared his throat. The woman stilled her hands and, when he beckoned her closer, set aside her task and came to him.

"I wish to thank you for your care," Kepa said, hoping his tone and gestures conveyed his meaning.

She listened and observed attentively, awaiting his next words.

Since he had only one possession, he picked up the harpoon shaft and held it out to her. "For you," he said.

Startled, the woman quickly got to her feet and backed away. She called out, "Ukumis, pachinata!"

The old man hurried inside and placed himself between Kepa and the woman. Thinking they misunderstood his intention, Kepa cautiously motioned the harpoon butt toward the woman and said, "For your daughter, for her care of me." Then, realizing he might have made a social blunder, Kepa extended his gift toward the man and said, "For all of you."

Uneasy yet apparently unwilling to offend Kepa, the old man

accepted the harpoon only after he'd found the fur it had been wrapped in previously and Kepa had set it within the folds. Rather than taking it to his own bedding, he laid it down within Kepa's reach. The native's insistent words, evidently meant to soothe and explain, left Kepa little choice but to let the matter of his gift rest.

"Please," he said, motioning for them both to sit down near him, "talk with me."

When they'd done as he'd asked, he pointed at the woman and asked her, "What is your name?" To make this query understood, however, he had to pat his chest and say, "Kepa," twice, then point again to the woman with a questioning gaze.

The old man nodded toward the woman and said in a tone of great respect, "Achaku."

The woman's gaze fell for a moment as if acknowledging an honor.

"Achaku," Kepa repeated, testing the resonance of the word.

The old man then touched his own chest and said, "Mihikin." He waved at a wolf skin suspended from one of the support poles. "Mihikin."

Ah, Wolf, thought Kepa, and he nodded.

Before they could proceed farther, the hide door was jerked roughly aside and a large man stormed into the hut, scattering Achaku and Mihikin apart and looming over all three of them with a condescending glare. With his first glance Kepa noted that he was impressively muscled. His shoulders were nearly as broad as Kepa's own and he was similar in height. Everything about the man's appearance declared a haughty pride. His bold face, elongated and angular, featured prominent cheekbones and a long, broad, straight nose. He wore nothing but a leather strip about nine inches in width that hung halfway down his thighs in front and back. This loincloth was suspended by a beaded leather belt from which hung a long stone knife with a wooden handle.

Achaku met the intruder's disdain calmly, which seemed only to stoke his anger. He barked a string of words that caused her to shift protectively toward Kepa. Unnoticed by the others, Kepa's hand had already inched within reach of his hidden harpoon. The native took a threatening step toward him but Mihikin hurriedly lifted his hands and spoke warningly, as if to remind him of potential consequences.

The contempt never left the man's face even as he hesitated, considering. Suddenly he flung his arms wide and shouted, demanding answers from Mihikin. Receiving what sounded like pacifying responses, he aimed hostile eyes at Kepa once more. Then he pivoted around and left them without another word.

In the aftermath of this visit Achaku and Mihikin sat with their eyes downcast for several uncomfortable moments. Kepa's head was pounding even harder now but his interest in his own survival had been fully awakened and he waited for some kind of explanation. Mihikin raised his arm, pointed toward the door, and said to Kepa, "unapama". With sign language he helped Kepa understand that the brute was actually Achaku's husband.

Good God, if he is her husband, no wonder the man is furious. Kepa glanced at Achaku but her expression told him nothing. She was caring for a stranger, an invalid, instead of her own mate, to say nothing of the more intimate interactions that may have taken place between them.

He should leave, now, but he could still scarcely tolerate the pain in his head and leg. He wouldn't last a day on his own. The sooner he could speak with these people and learn their ways, the sooner he could feed himself and live in a separate dwelling. He wouldn't be a burden, even a menace, to this woman any longer than necessary.

"Please," he said with newfound determination and the aid of his hands, "teach me your language."

Mihikin, after a brief discussion with Achaku and a grunt of agreement, patiently began to instruct Kepa, to reveal the world of his people through their words.

He started with descriptions of those who most closely touched his life, and Kepa soon discovered he'd been wrong about many of his initial assumptions. Mihikin's wife was called Liachita, which after many attempts to read Mihikin's hand signs Kepa concluded to mean something close to One-Who-Lightens-A-Burden. But she was not Achaku's mother nor was Mihikin the girl's father. In fact, Mihikin was Achaku's uncle, the brother of her mother. Both of Achaku's parents had, according to Mihikin's signing, passed into another world.

At this point in their lesson Liachita and the boy entered the hut, each carrying a bound animal bladder filled with water that Achaku took from them and hung from a pole. Mihikin pointed to the boy while saying to Kepa, "Nimu." The old man then beckoned the boy closer and spoke to him softly.

Touching his own chest, the child repeated, "Nimu," and kept his eyes on Kepa as he began to dance. Rather than performing the lively, turning, arms-high, heels-up steps of a Basque youngster, Nimu danced with utmost gravity, his steps small and low, his face composed and stoic. It was a dance of magic, or religion, somehow summoning, that matched the tempo of a private song playing within the boy's mind.

How remarkable, thought Kepa as he watched, that a child so young could show such spirituality. In Kepa's country, the boy would surely be selected for training to become a priest.

After a few moments the dancing ceased and Kepa, to be certain he'd understood correctly, repeated the word "Nimu" and then mimicked the action of a dancer with his hands. Mihikin's chin dipped once in confirmation.

Sitting down beside his great-uncle, the boy's features showed his fascination as the wounded visitor before him pointed to an object inside the hut, watched and listened to the explanation, and then pointed to another. Kepa could see that Nimu was evaluating him intently each time he worked to lock a new sound inside his memory. They were all evaluating him, as well they might.

Many of the finer points of Mihikin's definitions were beyond Kepa's immediate grasp but he soon began to pick up the basic rhythms and phonetics of the language. After trying to gather a few dozen words, he touched the beaded necklace resting on his chest and raised questioning eyes to Mihikin.

The old man contemplated for a moment before revealing that it had been made by Achaku and that it was very powerful. Perhaps, Kepa thought, glancing at Achaku, it was meant to heal him, or to protect him. He had taken time to examine it closely that morning, and saw that it depicted the wing of a bird much like the birthmark he bore on his neck. Kepa wanted to ask her about the purpose of the necklace but for some time his body had been protesting his exertions. He could no longer ignore his increasingly insistent need for rest. Seeming to read his mind, Achaku approached and soothingly encouraged him to lie down.

Once Kepa had tucked himself beneath the warm furs, Mihikin

moved toward his own robes across the hut and began rubbing a sanding stone back and forth over the concave top of the stick he'd been whittling earlier. Achaku returned to her sewing. This time, the boy was allowed to remain where he was, pondering Kepa's presence with the intelligent, searching eyes he'd inherited from his mother.

Very sleepily, his pain fading as his eyelids slowly shut, Kepa smiled over at him and murmured, "You need not fear me, little dancer. I will not eat you."

Nimu said something in response but Kepa couldn't understand his words. He was much too weary now to explore their meaning. It would have surprised him to know that the boy had said, "My mother and the spirits will watch over you. I, too, will do my part."

"Your eyes tell much, Achaku," Mihikin said softly, shaking his head in mild remonstration, "perhaps too much." He finished smoothing the roughness from the wooden crutch he'd been working on for Kepa and laid it down beside his sanding stone. "Saunuch is not a tolerant man. He will abandon you forever if he is pushed too far."

Achaku glanced at Kepa's sleeping form. "My husband will make his choices and I must make mine."

"I am long past my youth, and Nimu must be trained as he grows to manhood. It will be years before he can hunt large game."

Quietly, she said, "You would not wish me to ignore what the spirits have revealed."

Mihikin's brow furrowed with concern. "If your spirit or the Great Manitou has shown you that the newcomers are to touch our lives, this must be heeded. But are you sure you are meant to keep this man close beside you?"

"The coming of the people from across the great water has long been foretold to us. You are aware of the recent signs, my mother's brother. You watched him. Kepa and his followers hunt the mighty whales. You heard his music when darkness fell. And you know how he was rescued. In each of these things there is great power."

"He comes from wondrous people, strong people, but there is much we do not know about them. I fear that they may bring harm to us, to you."

"Do you think my dreams and the signs have been false?"

With a hint of shrewdness, he said, "As you are aware, Achaku, dreams are never false, only our interpretations of them."

"Then I can only believe that he was sent to us, and to me, for a purpose. I must heal him." Seeing the lingering worry on Mihikin's dear old face, Achaku added, "Saunuch has three other wives to care for him. And he will not risk the disfavor of the spirits by harming me or my son."

"His other wives are not like you. He will make trouble before he gives you up."

"Mihikin, will you teach Kepa more of our words?"

Mihikin glanced at Kepa and then at the wrapped harpoon. "There is much he does not know about our ways. He tried to give you his weapon."

"Perhaps," Achaku said contemplatively, "among his kind it is customary for a woman to accept a weapon from a man. I think he meant it to be a gift. It might have been better if I had taken it. We must make him welcome, even if we have to put some of our customs aside for a time."

Mihikin gave her an uncertain look, but went on. "There is much I would have him tell us about where he comes from and about his clan. But, yes, I will go on teaching him."

Achaku turned toward Liachita and Nimu, who had been quietly listening. "He will learn more quickly if we all teach him."

The old woman agreed to lend her services with a nod, the boy with a grin.

Upon awakening, Kepa found four intently focused faces staring at him. He'd barely rubbed the sleep from his eyes before his language lessons began anew, but the words already were coming too fast for him to keep up. Holding his hands out in surrender, he was able to slow down his enthusiastic instructors long enough to acquire a piece of tanned hide and some red dye from Achaku, and a thin stick that Mihikin sharpened for him. These instruments he intended to use to record the first words of a crude dictionary. Taking up his new writing implement and touching it to the dye, he gave them an encouraging wave to continue.

They all eyed his writing tools curiously, but Mihikin cleared his throat and motioned toward Nimu, saying, "Naapaas." Then he pointed to himself and to Kepa, and pantomimed a smaller version of their gender.

Nodding, Kepa bent over his leather parchment and began to write while verbalizing, "boy, napas".

At the first scratching of his crude quill upon the parchment four voices raised in speculation and query. They closed in around him to watch his careful last strokes and Kepa pointed out the sound of each letter. "See? N-a-p-a-s."

Captivated, Achaku's gaze moved from the paper to his face and back again. She reached down, held her finger below the word, and asked, "Napas?"

"Yes," said Kepa, pleased by her wonderment.

She sat back, and hushed words of awe passed between her and Mihikin.

"Woman?" Kepa asked Mihikin, pointing first at Liachita then at Achaku.

With a slight hesitation, as if he was uncertain as to the propriety of Kepa's writing, Mihikin answered, "Iskwa".

This too Kepa recorded with his improvised red ink. Additional words were offered slowly at first but then, as everyone joined in, with such increasing speed that Kepa had to ease the pace occasionally in order to capture every word.

When one long column of his parchment was filled Kepa thanked them all for their help and, much to the unspoken disappointment of his teachers, sat quietly with a fur wrapped over his shoulders to study on his own. Achaku soon interrupted him to attend to his digestive and medical needs.

Grateful as Kepa was for the newly exhibited devotion to his education, as the hours and then days passed by under a benevolent barrage of guidance, he couldn't help feeling as if he were being smothered by the close attention as well as his lack of physical activity. The hut seemed to shrink in around him until his restlessness began to rival his pain for dominance. He needed air and light and movement desperately but his clothing, which had been washed and returned to him, was inadequate to protect him from the dropping temperatures. Achaku had been working for days on warmer garments for him, after measuring his dimensions a time or two, but he hadn't found the courage to ask when they'd be finished.

Then one blessed morning Achaku came to him and, trying to hide her satisfaction, presented him with a complete set of leather clothing. One by one, he picked up his new leggings, loincloth, soft shoes, shirt, and a long, heavy coat. They were carefully sewn, and on the front of the shirt she'd painted a simple scene of men hunting a whale from a boat. Beside the scene, she'd replicated the same design of a bird's wing that she'd beaded with porcupine quills into the charm he wore around his neck.

"These are wonderful!" he declared in Basque before catching himself. Then, searching his memory for words in her language, he said, "You make…good-looking."

She smiled at his delight, and a little at his choice of words.

Kepa had never been more anxious to utilize a new gift. Sitting tall, he threw on the shirt and paused a moment to admire its wonderful fit. Then he lifted himself gingerly with the aid of the crutch and balanced on it and his one good foot. Much of the initial embarrassment he'd felt in Achaku's presence had drained away over the past week, yet he now stood fumbling with the loincloth, reluctant to ask for her help. But Achaku came to him without being asked, fitting the loincloth to his body as naturally as if she'd done it a hundred times before. She then helped him pull on his leggings, tying each of them to his waistband, and took a step back.

He saw it then, the slight shyness that had come over her, the hesitancy to meet his gaze. He felt pleased that she wasn't completely immune to his nearness. His awareness of her body, her voice, her touch was uncomfortably acute at times.

She raised her eyes at last and all that he'd been thinking passed between them. After a moment, she said needlessly, "You are dressed now."

"Yes."

"Would you like to see the camp?"

"Yes."

She helped him with his shoes but his long coat they left behind. It was for the colder times to come.

When Kepa stepped from the hut and into the unfiltered daylight he felt his cramped spirit lift and open like a limp flag unfurling in the breeze. He absorbed every sensation as the crisp, fresh air greeted his lungs and the bright sunshine warmed his cheeks. He paused there, just breathing, and let his gaze wander.

The camp rested on a slight rise just east of a small, scrub-lined river. Timbered hills rose within a stone's throw north of where he stood, and higher hills lay across a narrow valley that stretched southward. He wondered anew how far he was from the bay they'd named Aldapak, where he'd last seen his cousin and his men, but he tried to still such ponderings and to hold tightly to this moment under the sun.

Refocusing on the present, he saw that Achaku's wigwam was set a little apart from the other huts, perhaps twenty-five of them in all. From outside these dwellings people began to turn their heads and observe the limping stranger who had just appeared. As Kepa and Achaku slowly made their way between the lodges, people abandoned their hide tanning or meat drying or net mending to accumulate along their path. While the natives stared in silent wonder or chattered excitedly at their approach, Kepa noticed that they were a handsome people. Again he was struck by some of the similarities between this race and his own: the contours of the foreheads, the color and shape of the eyes, the tawny skin, the straight dark hair, the sturdy bodies. The most pronounced distinction seemed to be their lack of facial and body hair. He could see no whiskers on even the old men. A few of the males, evidently impervious to the cool weather, were shirtless, and none of them exhibited any chest hair.

The women held themselves back a little, whispering to one another with animation. Although many of them were attractive, he saw none who equaled Achaku in beauty.

A couple of the men began posing questions to Achaku but they were speaking so quickly that Kepa caught only a handful of their words. With such buzzing curiosity about him, he wondered, how had Achaku and Mihikin managed to keep the villagers from visiting their wigwam during his long days of immobility?

Although Kepa could not have known, during his first days of delirium several of the clan leaders had indeed come to inspect him. And they'd returned on more than one occasion. Much debate had taken place related to the nature of his future, or whether he should even be granted one. But today was the first opportunity for most of the natives to gaze upon the stranger Achaku had been protectively sheltering.

The women and children continued to keep a modest distance

from him but several men came quite near to scrutinize him fully. One stocky fellow was bold, or reckless, or generous enough to wish Kepa a loud and verbose welcome. The apparent acceptance of him by this gathering relieved him greatly, and he courteously acknowledged their reception with gestures and a few words from his limited vocabulary.

The throng greeted his fumbling attempts warmly, and moved right along with Achaku and Kepa as he crutched toward the heart of the village.

Even though the mood of Achaku's people was all he could have hoped for, he found himself scanning the group and wondering if her husband would suddenly appear with a lance braced or an arrow nocked. Rather than Saunuch, however, a slightly stooped man appeared ahead of them, wearing more fringe and quill beading on his clothing than anyone else Kepa had seen, and he looked to be several years older than Mihikin. For this man, the others moved aside respectfully. The women showed him particular courtesy, yet when he spoke to Achaku his manner held a touch of deference.

Achaku introduced him by saying to Kepa, "This is Wapitikwa, our wise leader."

Wapitikwa was several inches shorter than Kepa and his nose bore a deep scar across its wrinkled bridge. The old chieftain pointed to his own shirt, where the painting of a white caribou being pursued by hunters was displayed. Touching the caribou, he repeated with distinct pronunciation, "Wapitikwa."

After bowing slightly in acknowledgement Kepa's glance momentarily lowered to search the ground. He hobbled a few feet away, balanced precariously on his crutch as he bent down to pick up a rock, and returned to Wapitikwa. Laying a hand on his own chest, he said, "Kepa," and then he held out the rock.

The onlookers muttered a communal "ah", but Wapitikwa seemed to take particular interest in Kepa's name, weighing it carefully in his mind, considering its deepest meanings. At last he announced, "Kepa!" as if christening him anew. He offered a formal greeting and then seemed to voice sincere pleasure in the positive results of Achaku's care, the details of which Kepa understood only a little. What was perfectly clear to him, however, was that Wapitikwa would have said and asked a great deal more if they had been alone. The probing eyes of this aged chief were trying to read Kepa's character, his strengths, his intentions, and his potential for creating trouble or providing assistance. Kepa mused that Wapitikwa might well be every bit as wise as Achaku believed.

From the corner of his eye Kepa suddenly noticed Saunuch standing at the edge of the village, staring at him stormily. When their eyes met, Saunuch uncrossed his arms and strode forward with wide, determined steps. Voices stilled and bodies moved aside as he passed. Almost imperceptibly, Achaku took a small footstep closer to Kepa.

Using his good foot to stand to his full height, Kepa fleetingly wished that his harpoon were within reach. For protection only, he told himself. Protection for whom, he did not try to answer.

Saunuch pulled his glare away from Kepa and faced Wapitikwa, pretending to ignore his wife and the rest of the crowd. Stabbing a finger in Kepa's direction, Saunuch said in a sharp, demanding tone, "The time has come to force this stranger from our camp."

Wapitikwa's voice held a forced calm. "That would not be right. He is not yet strong enough to leave camp. For now, he is our guest."

"Look at him! The great whale hunter," he mocked. "He is helpless, a cripple. Where is his power now?"

Achaku tried to speak but Saunuch snapped, "Silence woman!"

Wapitikwa's voice sharpened slightly, "Under Achaku's care, he is healing quickly. When he is well —."

Waving an arm toward his wife, Saunuch shouted, "She wastes her power on him! She will only anger the Great Manitou." As several gasps escaped from the onlookers he turned to address the circle of stunned faces. "This man will bring evil upon us all. If you want to keep your children safe, he must be driven away."

Kepa understood the essence of these words if not the details. He scanned the crowd but only one or two seemed to heed Saunuch's threat. Most eyes shifted from Achaku to Wapitikwa.

"For now, Saunuch," their leader repeated with firm resolve, "he is our guest."

After a moment Saunuch turned his back on Wapitikwa to stare coldly, condemningly at the man who'd disrupted his life. But Kepa met his contempt with an iron gaze of his own, one that conveyed a spark of challenge rather than fear. Saunuch missed neither the defiance nor the dare. His face reflected an instant of surprise, even uneasiness, before his fists tightened. Then he lifted his head and barked a harsh, ridiculing laugh before he turned and stalked away.

Amid the unsettled muttering that broke out after Saunuch's departure Wapitikwa kept his expression blank, and he and most of the villagers soon drifted back toward their previous activities. Kepa and Achaku continued their slow walk through the encampment, their mood somber now. He asked himself why he'd been imprudent enough to provoke Saunuch as he had. It had been foolish, if not dangerous. He had no right to monopolize Saunuch's family, no right to cause him trouble. He didn't intend to stay here a day longer than necessary, so why hadn't he simply appeased this pompous savage?

And yet he knew the answer. Regardless of the temporary nature of his stay among them, regardless of their customs, he was galled by Saunuch's callous treatment of Achaku. She'd been very kind and taken considerate care of Kepa. It was only natural that he felt a sense of protectiveness toward her.

Still, in a few weeks he'd be well enough to provide for himself and she'd go back to Saunuch. The last thing she needed was for Kepa to worsen the strain between her and her husband.

Ways of the People

7

Late in the evening Kepa sat near the fire with his writing stick in hand and Mihikin patiently watching him record a few words. Achaku and Liachita had been called away to assist with the birth of a child, leaving the men to improve Kepa's linguistic skills on their own. They'd been working for only a few minutes when Nimu shyly sidled up beside Kepa, unrolled a small piece of hide wrapped around a pointed stick, and sat very still. He didn't ask, didn't even look up, he just waited for Kepa's reaction.

Musing, Kepa was taken back to a time when he was about Nimu's age, a time when, rather than making a silent request, he'd pleaded repeatedly to be taught. His uncle, a respected town scribe, had finally agreed to reveal the magic of Arabic letters. His father's brother, patient yet exacting, taught him well until Kepa was eight. Then the nightmare of the Black Plague had unleashed itself upon their town, taking the lives of Kepa's uncle, his father, and countless others. Those were days that tortured the hearts and souls of survivors as well as victims. Kepa, his mother, and brother had lived through the devastation but the scars they carried with them the remainder of their days ran bone deep.

The brutal memories were quickly forced aside and replaced with thoughts of his wise uncle and how his gift of letters had stoked Kepa's hunger for knowledge, eventually leading him into the study of medicine.

Four years after his father's death Kepa had taken a portion of his inheritance and traveled to far away Toledo to study medical practices and theories of the great Greek, Moor, and Jewish physicians of the past. Particularly, the written works of Az-Zahrawi fascinated him. They taught him much about the causes, symptoms, and treatment of diseases, the procedures of midwifery, and the preparation of drugs. He applied himself strenuously to absorb

every surgical technique, every method of treating wounds and setting bones. Kepa even explored the uses of potions to induce deep
sleep and to numb specific tissues. All this wondrous knowledge
had opened itself to him because his uncle had taught him how to
read and write.

Now, it pleased Kepa that the boy wished to learn the secrets of
the quill. Who could tell? Perhaps one day he would be a scribe
for all of his people.

"So, Little Dancer, you'd like to write too?" Kepa asked in
Basque. In Nimu's dialect, he said only, "Yes, Nimu."

The child could barely sit still as Kepa allowed him to dip his
stick into the dye and then hold it momentarily suspended over the
hide. "Nimu," Kepa said, and spelled it out on the boy's parchment.
"Now you," he instructed, pointing to the blank space beneath the
word.

Touching his stick's point to the parchment, Nimu painstakingly
scrawled a wobbly N.

"Good!" Kepa encouraged, and nodded for him to continue.

"Kepa," Mihikin said softly, and Kepa was surprised to find an
apprehensive look on the old man's face.

"Your power, it might be too strong for a child, even one such
as Nimu. To teach him these things, the signs of your spirit, is to
share secrets he has not earned and does not understand. It could
be dangerous."

Still unsure of some of Mihikin's words, Kepa asked, "It could
harm Nimu?"

"Each man's spirit must guide him along his own path. Nimu is
very young, but he has shown signs of being favored by the Great
Manitou. His dreams are clear and strong. They will reveal the
symbols of his inner strength and show him how to live. One day
his dreams may be as powerful as his mother's."

"But how can," he sought the right words, "my word signs harm
his dreams?"

"The Great Manitou could be displeased and keep the dreams
from coming to him. Then they could no longer guide him. We
have never seen your kind of power, Kepa. We do not know what
it might bring to us."

Thoughtfully, Kepa said, "Power comes from God, you call
Great Manitou. My word signs could help Nimu, someday."

Mihikin considered this as he slowly rubbed his hands over the fire to warm them. "Perhaps, but we should talk with Achaku of this. She is the spirit leader of our people. She is very wise."

Kepa stared at him in dismay. Achaku, a holy woman! Good heavens, and he'd first guessed her to be a prostitute. He grew uncomfortable as he recalled the times he'd wondered if she would come and lie beside him again in the darkness. She never had, not since he'd gained consciousness. In fact, each night she'd waited until he was asleep before undressing and lying down in her own robes. Every morning she had already clothed herself and started performing her chores before he'd awakened. And she was a holy woman. What must that mean to them?

She must surely be a woman of special status among this clan. He realized that this role might also explain how she was able to usurp her husband's authority, overlooking his displeasure while she cared for Kepa.

To Mihikin, he said, "Yes, we will talk with Achaku."

With this pronouncement Nimu lowered his head in disappointment but he muttered no word of protest.

"Nimu," said Kepa, "will you tell me about your dreams?"

The boy looked for permission from his great-uncle, who said, "Kepa wishes to know how our dreams help us, Nimu. The spirits will not be offended by your answering this."

"May I tell him of mother's dream, the dream of his coming to us?"

"That is for your mother to tell, if she wishes. Share only your dreams, and the long-told stories of our people."

"First," Kepa said to Nimu, "tell me more about the Great Manitou."

Kepa listened, fascinated and attentive, as Nimu's clear, young voice wove the tale of how the Great Manitou created the world and all the spirits: the spirit of the sun and the moon, the spirits of the stars, forests, rivers, men, bears, caribou, beavers, fish, bushes, rocks, and every other thing. The boy explained that the Great Manitou rules the spirit masters of all living things except men, for he himself is their benevolent master. Specific spirit masters govern the destinies of each animal by communicating with their spirits.

Nimu paused when his mother and Liachita entered. Setting

down her baskets, Achaku told them with a pleased, tired smile, "Wapisu has a fine son."

When the women had settled themselves, Nimu needed little encouragement to continue.

"The Great Manitou wants human beings to respect every creature. To do otherwise causes a man to fall out of favor with the Great Manitou." Nimu stopped his well-learned recitation to say to Kepa in a tone close to veneration, "You must have pleased Manitou greatly."

Kepa asked, "Why do you say this?"

"During your hunts the spirit master of the whales directs them to you, and they allow themselves to be killed. For a creature such as a whale to offer himself to a man, that man must have great courage and great virtue. Such a man helps his family and his people survive. I saw you do this two times, while watching with my mother."

When Kepa glanced at Achaku, her face was turned downward and she did not look up at him. He wondered how many times she'd watched him, and what she'd seen. Directing his attention back to the boy, he asked, "The whales wish us to kill them?"

"They yield their lives because their manitou instructs them to do this." Nimu added, "Such things happen when a hunter's actions are so close to the wishes of the Great Manitou that he is an example for others to follow."

Inwardly, Kepa balked at this. Now he could feel Achaku's gaze upon him, felt it like a fire's heat, but he said, "I am only a man, Nimu."

By the expression on the young upturned face, Kepa could see that this statement had done nothing to lower Nimu's opinion of him. The boy merely shifted the subject slightly by nodding toward Mihikin and saying, "My grandmother's brother has been a mighty hunter since his youth, and he has killed a caribou and a moose each winter of his life, even last winter when moose were scarce."

Mihikin and Achaku smiled gently at the boy. "Nimu," his mother said, "it is time for sleep."

"There is much more to tell, Mother," Nimu said quietly.

"And there will be more days in which to tell it," she countered.

Reluctantly, he moved to his furs, undressed, and nestled

beneath the coverings, but his eyes remained on Kepa. Mihikin and Liachita soon found their own furs and Kepa, wide awake, sat beside the fire wholly aware of Achaku's graceful movements as she banked the fire for the night.

Rather than going to her sleeping robes, she came to sit beside him in the near darkness. "You are learning quickly to speak in our tongue."

"I have good teachers."

"And your leg grows stronger each day."

"Yes, but I have eaten your food and accepted your care. It must be a burden for you."

"We have plenty of food. It causes us no hardship to feed one more."

Kepa had spent hours considering how he might compensate Achaku and her family for their care, but it would still be weeks before he could use his leg effectively. As soon as he was able to do so, providing meat for them might be an acceptable means of payment. Knowing what a bounty of meat one whale could provide, he'd considered whaling but only briefly. He could make a wooden shaft to fit his harpoon, but he had no trained men, no boat, no ropes, and no iron with which to make a lance, louchet, or flensing tools, so this option was set aside. That left hunting forest animals or fishing, and he had neither nets, his crossbow, nor a longbow.

And there was the looming challenge of Saunuch. Would the man reclaim his wife and son before Kepa's debt could be repaid? Kepa knew he should remove himself from their affairs as soon as he could. Yet the words that came from his mouth as he sat beside the fire with Achaku were, "If I can use Mihikin's tools, I can make a bow, and perhaps hunt with him for your family."

Achaku sat very still. "If that is what you wish."

"Is there another way I can help you?"

She hesitated, then said, "Will you teach Nimu to make your word signs?"

Hearing Mihikin softly snoring, Kepa said, "Mihikin told me it may be bad for the boy."

"Mihikin has not seen what I have seen." This was said softly, without the least bravado or doubt.

"Things you've seen in your dreams?"

"Yes."

"Things about me?"

"About you and others, Kepa."

"Will you tell me about these dreams?"

She seemed to consider carefully before answering. "The amulet you wear, that design came to me in a dream. I saw a man with that mark riding in a boat that floated upon the sea like a giant brown swan."

Picking up the neck charm, he scanned the burgundy image against a field of light brown. "A man with my birthmark in a boat like a brown swan," he muttered. "When did you dream this?"

"The night before I saw you come into the bay."

Kepa stared at her in amazement. "The night *before*? You *saw* us arrive?" Thinking back to the ship's anchorage, he suddenly remembered. "It was you we saw, standing on the hill? And there was a child. Nimu?"

"I told him about my dream. He wanted to be with me when I greeted you. I was called, Kepa, to be there when you arrived. But there were many men, so I waited. Now you are here."

And there it was, there in the depth of her eyes and the softness of her mouth, visible even in the soft glow of the banked embers, an absolute openness and acceptance of whoever and whatever he was.

Seeing it scared the hell out of him. Then, inwardly cursing himself for cowardice, he asked, "Did your dream show you why you were to meet me?"

She held his gaze for a long moment before drawing it away. "It is very late now," she said. "One day, I will tell you more." Standing, she went to her sleeping place and removed her shoes. With her back to him she unfastened and set aside her belt and then gracefully and unhurriedly slipped her dress off over her head.

Kepa could not have looked away if he'd tried, and he didn't try. She turned to face him and slowly lowered her flawless body to her furs. Rolling onto her side, away from him, she pulled her covering up over her shoulder.

For a half-hour Kepa remained by the fire, knowing she was not his, knowing it was far better that she was not, but the memory of her silhouette haunted him without remorse. Somehow, at last, he found the strength to make his way to his own bedding. Sleep was no more than an elusive stranger to him that night.

The following day Kepa left his bedding earlier than usual and managed to dress himself. He quickly ate the food Achaku offered to him, exchanging little conversation with her or Liachita. Hoping some fresh air would clear his thoughts, he grabbed his crutch and limped outside.

The fox-colored dog that stood no taller than a man's knee let out one short bark when Kepa appeared, but was quickly hushed by a word from Mihikin. As the dog stared intelligently back at him, Kepa wondered how it had lost the top half of its left ear, leaving only the right tip to point upward. The old man and the boy were studying the sky, absorbed by the wisps of clouds flowing out across the expanse of blue like newly combed tresses.

"Winter will come soon," Mihikin pronounced. "The geese are beginning to leave. It will not be long before we follow them."

"Where will you go?"

"South and west, deep into the forest where we will find moose and caribou."

"When?"

"Before the new moon, perhaps. Achaku and Wapitikwa will tell us when the time is right." Mihikin looked at Kepa inquisitively. "You spoke out in your sleep last night, Kepa. Did you have a strong dream?"

Kepa stiffened slightly. He did not recall a dream, but he was uneasy about what, or whom it might have touched upon. "What did I say?"

"You spoke in your people's words, which are strange to me, but one word you said three times. It was 'Arima'." Mihikin waited but Kepa looked at the ground said nothing, so he returned his attention to the sky.

"Some things, a man does not wish to talk about," Kepa said.

Mihikin nodded. "A woman, then?" When Kepa's face showed his surprise at the old man's perceptiveness, Mihikin smiled. "You spoke the word as only a man does when he calls the name of his favorite wife. She must be a good woman."

"She was."

The male voices fell silent as Achaku emerged from the wigwam.

Finding his words first, Kepa surprised them all by announcing, "I want to visit my old camp. How far is it from here?"

"A half day's walk," said Mihikin.

"Will one of you direct me to it?"

Achaku answered, "The path is not an easy one and your leg has not yet healed."

"When will it be strong enough?"

"Ten or twelve days perhaps. But why do you wish to go, when your people have left that place?"

How could he explain it well to her when he couldn't adequately describe the reasons to himself? Finally, he said, "I want to see what they left behind. And there may be graves that will tell me if any men died in the last whale hunt. I wish to know."

"Yes," said Achaku with understanding, "it is right that you should know. If they have left this world you can honor their spirits. I will go with you, Kepa, when you are ready." She reached out and touched his hand, a light, fleeting touch, and said, "There is another place I will show you, not far from your old camp. It is where you were rescued. Tell me, what do you remember of that day, after you fell into the water?"

Closing his eyes for a moment, wishing she hadn't asked him to remember, images came back to Kepa, and he said, "I remember pain, and cold, and darkness, and fear. Then, I remember surrendering my body to God. Of the rescue I remember nothing."

"Then you do not know," she said, and glanced at Mihikin.

"I know only that your people pulled me out."

She shook her head, and then assured him, "When we reach the spot we will talk more of that time."

"Mihikin and Nimu," said Kepa, "will you walk with me?"

Mihikin rose creakily to his feet. "I will come. Nimu must check his snares."

And so the two set out, the torn-eared mutt Kepa called Tracker prancing at Mihikin's side, on what was to become a part of their daily routine.

As the fall days passed, they walked farther and farther from Achaku's hut together, becoming a familiar sight to the villagers and drawing less attention with each outing. Mihikin was diligent in his speech instruction as they meandered well beyond the village, and Kepa's diction and vocabulary improved at a comparable pace with his health.

Kepa noticed that whenever possible Mihikin avoided taking

paths that increased their chances of meeting Saunuch. But on the occasions they did encounter Achaku's husband, with his brows lowered and his arms tightened, Mihikin agilely steered the two younger men apart.

No amount of query would draw further information from Achaku about why she wanted to return to the place of his rescue. She must have convinced the other members of her family to keep her secret as well, since even Nimu would avoid answering Kepa's questions, saying only, "Soon my mother will take you. It will be better if you can see for yourself."

One morning when the rest of Achaku's family was away, she unbound Kepa's splint bandages and examined his leg more thoroughly than usual. Sitting back, she smiled and said, "Your leg has become strong again. There is no more need for the splints."

With a satisfied sigh Kepa stretched out his foot and wiggled his toes. "Thank God," he said in Basque, agreeing with her but still reluctant to reveal his own medical knowledge. Then he thanked Achaku in her language. "Does this mean I can visit my old camp site?"

"In a few days we will go."

He noticed her manner changing subtly as her hands stilled, and she said tentatively, "The time has come when you can take pleasure in a woman again."

Kepa was so amazed by this declaration that he stammered over his first word. "I have no woman."

"But," she faltered, clearly confused, "you have had women before?"

"Yes, of course, I mean…I have." Kepa silently cursed himself for his verbal fumbling.

Achaku's gaze was searching. "Do you have wives, in the land you come from? Mihikin said, he thought…"

"My people take only one wife."

"And your wife lives across the great water?"

He forced the words to come. "No, I no longer have a wife. She died."

A quiet hush seemed to breathe over them as Achaku studied Kepa's features. "I see that this woman was very much in your heart. You still mourn her death."

How strangely uncomplicated the statement, yet how cruelly

difficult the event and its aftermath. The words now came against his will. "She died almost two years ago, but she died because of me."

"Then, this is the burden your spirit carries," Achaku said, as if a long dwelt upon question had just been answered. "How did you cause her death?"

"I... I was a healer, as you are." He saw her surprise but continued. "I should have saved her, Achaku, her and our child she was carrying." Unconsciously, one large hand moved to his belly as his words faded.

"Tell me," Achaku said.

When he found his voice, his tone had dropped to a rough whisper, as if recollecting each of the memories had taken the strength from his lungs. "That night there was a terrible storm. I was treating a woman who was going blind, and my wife came to her house to bring the family soup. She, Arima, she was very kind." He felt his chest continue to tighten. "We talked, and she went out in the rain again. Our house was not far away. As she walked home the wind grew so strong that it blew a tree onto her path. I found her trapped beneath it. She was wet and cold. I freed her, but her leg was broken. I carried her home and was tending to her leg when she started bleeding. I did not even know she was pregnant. We had been hoping..." His eyes stared unseeing at his hands, remembering that night with brutal clarity. "She lay there, so weak and pale, and she said to me, 'I was going to tell you about the baby tonight.' Those words, they were the last words she ever spoke."

He shut his eyes and had to pull a full breath into his constricted lungs. "I could not stop the bleeding. I did not save her, or the child we'd prayed for."

Bitterness seeped into his voice as his eyes rose to meet Achaku's. "My village had praised me as a great doctor, and I let Arima bleed to death in our own bed."

His head dropped to his hands, and he rubbed his eyes over and over, trying to erase the memories of the night that had drained his soul just as the blood had drained from Arima's body.

This was the first time he'd spoken of her death to anyone. He'd intended never to speak of it. He'd even forbidden his brother and his cousin to mention her. And as his breathing began to calm he wondered, why now? Why had he managed to relive her death in the presence of this kind young woman from a strange world? Or was it that simple? Was it her kindness, so much like Arima's in its way, that had moved him to speak?

"Kepa."

His face lifted slowly.

"You blame yourself, but it was not you. We have no power over the time or place that is chosen for a spirit to travel the ghost road. It was the Great Manitou who called your wife to the stars. When He calls, a spirit knows it is only right to obey. People have died while I cared for them too. Healers must accept such things as the will of Manitou."

Kepa suddenly cried out, "I am no longer a healer, do you hear me! Perhaps I never was!"

Unflinchingly, she asked, "Did you not cure others?" When he failed to answer, she said, "A healer is chosen, Kepa. That honor, that gift is too great to be set aside even when we are touched by deep sadness."

She watched his face soften slightly but his lips remained tight.

"I should not have shouted at you," he said.

She saw that she had not convinced him, saw his pain. Reaching out, she caressed his cheek above the line of his beard. "Will you let me comfort you? Another's touch can sometimes help heal a heart."

Her meaning could not be mistaken, and Kepa found himself tempted by her proposal. Achaku's lithe body had caused him too many moments of uneasiness during the days, too many restless nights, and it had been a long time since he'd reveled in a woman's embrace. He had been with only one woman since his wife's death, a widow six years his senior who'd come to him looking for security and permanence. He could provide neither, yet twice he'd let his despair and loneliness overtake him and he'd accepted what her body granted. Then he'd sailed away from her, away from everything, aboard *La Magdalena*.

"Your offer is generous, Achaku, but your husband—"

She didn't let him finish. "It is our custom, at times, to please others in such a way. A husband often offers his wife to a visiting friend to make him feel welcome."

"A husband loans his wife to another?"

At the astonishment in his voice she lowered her hand from his cheek. "Yes, willingly."

"And when she is returned to him, the couple goes on as before?"

"Kepa, the husband is pleased that his wife has obeyed him and that he has proven himself to be a good host. Usually, the wife is happy for the change."

"Change indeed," Kepa muttered with a measure of indignation. "Even so, Saunuch would never offer you to me. He sees me as his enemy."

"In this, now, I may choose."

"Saunuch would be a fool to give you that choice. If you were mine, I would never..." He stopped himself, knowing a few hours of passion might bring untold misfortune to her, and death to him. To strengthen his own resolve, he said, "Achaku, such things are very different with my people. In my world a man weds only one woman and she must never give herself to another, not as long as he lives. I would not be condemned for killing any man who bedded my wife."

Achaku was stunned. "You would kill a man for such a thing?"

Kepa's dark gaze answered for him.

"But," Achaku asked hesitantly, "if you may have only one wife, can you marry another if she leaves this world?"

"I want no wife, not ever again."

She sat very still, her eyes searching his. At last she said, "The wound in your leg was easy to see. The one in your heart runs much deeper. In time, perhaps that too will heal."

"Listen to me," Kepa's tone sharpened as he took hold of her shoulders, "that part of me is dead. Dead!" Seeing her flinch, he fought for control as he released her. More steadily, he said, "I am grateful for all you have done, Achaku, and to lay with you would give me much pleasure, but that is all, pleasure. And if Saunuch discovered us he might cause you great hardship."

"I do not fear Saunuch's anger, and I want nothing from you that you do not wish to give."

"Then understand that there can be nothing binding between us. When my ship comes again, I will leave this place. On this, I will not change my mind."

72

She lifted her chin very slightly, suddenly looking almost queenly with her composed dignity. "You will come to see what binds us, Kepa, before your ship comes again."

She stood and moved to the wigwam's entrance. There she paused, turning back and saying softly, "Perhaps you are right to be cautious of Saunuch. He is angry that he is no longer my husband."

Before Kepa could react to what she had just said, she was gone.

A Forge's Yield

8

If Achaku's announcement that she was no longer a married woman had not been fully explained, its effects soon became evident. Kepa left the wigwam moments after Achaku with the hope of catching up to her but had taken only a few tentative steps on his unsplinted leg when Mihikin, little Nimu, and Tracker emerged from the forest and hurried over to greet him. Leaving Mihikin's side, Tracker trotted to a stop between Kepa and Nimu, his wagging tail slapping against the man's leg as the boy held up three dead rabbits by their ears.

Glancing behind them in an unsuccessful attempt to spot Achaku, Kepa said distractedly to the boy, "They will make a fine meal, Nimu."

Solemnly but with pride, Nimu said, "My grandmother's brother and I are the hunters for our family now."

That gained Kepa's full attention. With Saunuch no longer sharing the fruits of his hunts, the family now risked hunger, even starvation if game became scarce. Kepa wondered what he might have brought upon these people? To Mihikin and Nimu, he said, "My leg is nearly healed. Soon I will hunt beside you."

"Good," said Mihikin, resting the butt of his hunting spear on the ground.

But with this single word, spoken with such relief and approval, Kepa felt the weight of what he had just implied. Hurriedly, he tried to clarify his meaning. "I must tell you, as I told Achaku, that I will leave when my ship returns with the warm weather." He tried not to heed the small inner voice saying that when he left them Mihikin would be another year older and the boy would still be too young to carry the burden of his family's survival. What if Saunuch would not take Achaku back as his wife?

The old man laid a weathered brown hand on Kepa's shoulder

and said, "Whatever happens then, we must trust in our spirits and in the Great Manitou."

Kepa did not respond to these last words. He'd just spotted Saunuch bearing down on them, his eyes fastened on Kepa, his body as tight as a squall-stretched sail. Pulling his charging strides to a sudden halt just inches from Kepa's chest, Saunuch spat out, "No man steals what is mine!"

Kepa neither moved nor spoke, but his glare flared to match the intensity of Saunuch's and his muscles coiled. Tracker let out a low growl and took a measured step toward Saunuch, but Mihikin silenced his dog with a sharp motion of his hand.

"Saunuch," Mihikin said quickly, consolingly, but this only turned Saunuch's anger toward him.

"You, old man, you do nothing while a woman of your own blood turns away from her people!"

Tracker growled more menacingly this time and Nimu took hold of the scruff of his neck. A few villagers had begun to gather near them and, at Saunuch's accusation, protesting words broke from one or two.

"Achaku's dreams—," Mihikin tried again.

"Do not speak to me of her dreams! A wife should dream for her husband, for her people, not for a crippled stranger who begs among us!"

For the first time Saunuch noticed Nimu, clutching his rabbits in his right hand and Tracker's scruff in his left. He sneered at the boy. "Hah! You think such meat will keep you through the cold times?" He suddenly bent back his hand and slapped Nimu's right arm with such force that it flung the rabbits several yards away and knocked the boy sideways. Tracker lunged at Saunuch but the dog was met by a sharp kick to its ribs that sent it tumbling after the boy. As Saunuch turned toward his son Kepa grabbed his sleeve but the native spun back with his stone knife drawn. Kepa leaped backward, his darting gaze seeking any form of weapon. The first one he spotted was Mihikin's spear but before he could grab for it the old man sprang forward and planted his body between the two younger men with the lance's point aimed at Saunuch's heart.

In a voice of forced calm but deadly command, Mihikin said, "No, Saunuch. Achaku has made her choice. She and Nimu no longer belong to you. Go back to your other wives and children."

Saunuch's hand darted toward the spear but Mihikin was quicker. He'd been a great hunter and his instincts and reflexes still remembered how to deal with a wounded animal. He jerked the spear out of reach and brought it back to the base of Saunuch's neck as quickly as a striking snake, stilling him abruptly.

Mihikin, his voice as sharp as the clash of metal, said, "It is finished, Saunuch."

Very slowly, Saunuch stepped back and then swept the onlookers with threatening eyes until they came to rest on Kepa. "No, Mihikin," he said, as if making a vow, "this will not be finished until he is dead or driven from our clan."

Not until Saunuch had turned and walked straight and tall into the cover of the trees did Kepa drop the sturdy club he'd seized from the woodpile beside the wigwam. The small crowd that had gathered was already dispersing. Nimu had regained his feet and stood with his head down where he had fallen, again holding onto Tracker's fur. He released the dog, retrieved his rabbits, and came to Mihikin. As his great-uncle put an arm across the boy's shoulders, Kepa said to them both. "Perhaps it would be a good thing if I return to the bay."

Mihikin and Nimu looked up at him in surprise. "You were meant to come to us, Kepa," Mihikin said. "Saunuch cannot control the spirits. No man can. They tell us our true course, and they told Achaku of your coming." He saw Kepa's doubt and went on. "At the bay the icy wind will come soon and the water will freeze. Then, very little will survive. But now, while the weather is still mild, we will hunt and fish near the sea. You can visit the bay again. After that we will go southwest, deep into the forest where the moose and caribou have offered themselves to us since time began. They will sustain us during the snows, but worthy hunters are always needed. It would please me greatly if you would stay with us."

"Then," said Kepa resignedly, "I will need weapons. I should have started making them sooner. Will you help me?"

Nimu sighed with relief and Mihikin smiled. "I will get my tools."

After Kepa emerged from the wigwam with his wrapped harpoon shank, a digging spade, a large piece of old leather, and an empty water pouch, Mihikin slung his tool pouch over his shoulder and they set out with Nimu and Tracker walking happily between them. His ankle was only slightly tender as they walked along, and it seemed to improve as they progressed. The stabbing headaches that had assaulted him since his first awakening had grown fewer and fewer during the past weeks. Now they came very seldom.

Their small party made its way to a stone-strewn ledge overhanging the river that Kepa had discovered on an earlier hike. Trying to explain his intention created many questions along the way but Kepa answered few of them in much detail. Upon their arrival he finally said, "Gather a pile of stones the size of my open hand and another pile of dried grass, and then place them here beneath the ledge. I will show you."

Kepa set to work digging a round, shallow hole while the stones were being collected. When it was completed to his satisfaction, he headed for the river with the spade, hide, and water pouch. As he had hoped when he'd first found the spot, with a little digging into the riverbank he extracted a good supply of gritty brown clay. This he piled onto the hide and dragged it back to the overhang. Carefully placing and securing the loaded hide in a rounded indenture between several large rocks, he mixed the clay with water and dry grass until it had gained the consistency of a workable mortar.

Next he selected stones from the impressive pile Nimu and Mihikin had accumulated and began placing them around the hole he'd dug. He intended to assemble a round, open-topped oven four-feet across and two-feet deep, resembling the surrounds that had fed the tryworks fires at the rendering station, but now it was iron rather than whale blubber he hoped to melt down. He called upon every memory he'd acquired while watching the ship's mason and blacksmith at work. Having never been more than an observer of these crafts, he was far from certain he'd be able to make the fire hot enough to be effective, or the forge strong enough to keep from bursting apart once the heat had reached its highest temperature.

Still, he felt he must try, and he must risk the loss of his only weapon for the creation of several more suitable ones. He was determined to never again be caught without a knife within his reach. And once he possessed hunting tools he could help insure the survival of himself and those who were now in his temporary care.

Scouting the area until he found a broad flat stick to serve as a

77

trowel, he picked up the first stone. While he mortared, set, and scraped, mortared, set, and scraped, Mihikin patiently instructed Nimu in the art of shaping arrow shafts, stopping often to allow them both to examine the progress of Kepa's strange project.

Tracker contentedly darted after squirrels as the men attended to their tasks and, finally catching one, proudly ambled over to Mihikin and laid it at his feet. "Today, Tracker," Mihikin told him fondly, "you may eat what you have killed," and tossed the squirrel back to him.

The murmur of the river, Mihikin's gently melodic voice, and the occasional honking of geese migrating overhead kept Kepa in good company as he worked. His long-idle muscles began to ache but he welcomed the discomfort, knowing it was the price to be paid for rebuilding his strength. The sun's warmth found him through the limbs of the trees, adding to the satisfaction of doing something of purpose after his extended incapacitation.

At last Kepa settled the last rock firmly into position, stood up, his hands and forearms caked with drying clay, and scrutinized the product of his labor. It looked tight enough, he thought, but would it hold?

Despite having shown his companions how to complete his project, Kepa realized how little he'd explained about its purpose when Mihikin asked politely. "What will you cook, Kepa, in your stone pit?"

"It is my hope that it will hold a fire strong enough to melt down my weapon so I can form it into smaller ones."

Mihikin tried to hide his uneasiness. "Your weapon is very strong. You ask much magic from rocks and earth. Should you not offer a song to their spirits and to the Great Manitou for such a favor?"

A prayer. Mihikin was asking him for a prayer. It seemed to Kepa that a lifetime had passed since he'd last prayed for a favor. But Mihikin and Nimu were waiting expectantly, so he said, "Perhaps you are right." He thought for a moment, recalling a song he had known since childhood, and then he raised his face and sang in a deep, wavering voice that strengthened as the words flowed. He sang the words in Basque, which his companions could not follow, but his praise to the glory of God and his request for His strength and mercy seemed to be understood by them just the same.

He found himself feeling the words and he closed his eyes as he voiced the final verse.

When Kepa finished and opened his eyes, Mihikin said with great feeling, "Your song is strange and beautiful, Kepa. In all my long life I have never heard such a thing."

"Manitou surely has heard you," Nimu said to Kepa, as much in awe as his great-uncle, but his young mind turned more quickly to the new possibilities before them. "What kind of weapons will you make?"

"First, a small flat surface, then the head of a mallet, and a—" he searched for a word to explain a file, "a smoothing tool, and then a knife. If enough material remains, I'll also make the parts for a special bow and arrow, and spear points. But, Nimu, I am unskilled at this. It may not work."

"Manitou will help you," Nimu said with unassailable faith.

"All we can do now is wait until the clay dries. Tomorrow we will see."

The following morning, much to Kepa's relief and Nimu's delight, the clay showed very little cracking and the stones had not shifted. To draw the remaining moisture from the clay they built a small fire in the forge and, that evening, a slightly larger blaze. On the third day, after finding no ill effects from an even more substantial fire, Kepa decided it was time to fully test the strength of his masonry.

Gathering enough wood to roast a large caribou, they fed the forge, watching and listening anxiously until it held a huge bed of coals that breathed and glowed like the living thing Mihikin believed it to be. When the heat grew to its greatest intensity a few chunks of mortar popped loose from the forge with sudden explosions, scattering the fire-tenders as they dodged the small missiles. When they cautiously returned to their posts, however, they could see that the forge stood solidly intact.

Finally, Nimu asked with barely contained eagerness, "Is it time?"

Kepa turned to him and smiled resignedly. "As my people say, one may recover lost possessions but never lost time. Hand me the harpoon, Nimu."

They all huddled closer to the forge, ready to leap for cover again at any sign or sound of trouble, but all was still. Folding a scrap of the hide he'd brought with him, Kepa used it to pick up his harpoon shank and swing its tip above the coals, but then he hesitated. As the embers glowed red beneath the outstretched metal point, Kepa suddenly realized that his hands held more than a weapon. It was a symbol of his people, of their courage and ingenuity and fortitude and tenacity. And he was about to destroy it for the slim chance that he could make other tools. His mind flashed to the possible hunger they all faced this winter, and he had to remind himself for the tenth time that men could not hunt an enormous whale with a single harpoon.

No, he must accept the risk he was taking.

Very slowly, his hand shaking ever so slightly, he lowered his harpoon until its tip rested upon the gleaming coals and they all held their breaths. As they stared, their nerves tightening, Kepa counted silently to thirty. No one moved or spoke. Nimu let a small whimper escape. Kepa lifted the weapon out of the fire and pressed the point of the triangular head against a rock of the forge's wall, but it did not move. He pressed harder and still it held its shape. Nothing.

The faces of his two companions worked to remain stoic but Kepa could feel their sympathetic disappointment.

With greater determination he shoved the harpoon deep within the coals, determined to let it rest there much longer. He forced himself to wait several minutes, then a few more. When Kepa finally eased the iron shank free of the coals, Mihikin let out an expletive of unknown origin and Nimu cried, "It's color, Kepa! Look!" And indeed the color of the head had brightened to a radiant orange. Before it could cool, Kepa quickly pushed it against the side of the forge and leaned his weight down hard. The edge yielded slightly, bending with the angle of his pressure. Hardly daring to believe, he again immersed the harpoon in the embers, waited, drew it out, and pressed the edge the other way. It moved. It was working! Breathing hard, Kepa once more brought the harpoon point to a radiating crimson and, using a flat stone and Mihikin's knife and spear, worked off the tip and shaped it into a crude arrowhead. They stared at it as it began to cool.

Sudden shouts of exultation broke from them all and rang through the forest. Tracker set off a chorus of barking as Kepa grabbed Nimu, tossed him into the air, and caught him as the boy laughed jubilantly. Slapping his chest in triumph, Mihikin grinned and improvised a little shuffling dance step. Then, with Nimu now perched atop one of Kepa's shoulders, the two grown men clasped each other's forearms warmly.

"I thank you both for your help," said Kepa.

Still smiling, Mihikin said, "I share your joy, Kepa. The fire must have approved of your plans."

"It does seem willing to help make me my tools," Kepa conceded, "but I have much work yet to do."

Little did he know how true these words would prove themselves to be.

Although Mihikin and Nimu came for short visits over the next few days, sweat and frustration were Kepa's most constant cohorts. The iron now seemed to take on its own personality, one that rejoiced in thwarting every new attempt to shape it into a workable surface, a mallet head, and a file. Basque curses sporadically startled the forest's creatures as Kepa singed his fingers and blistered his patience. It soon became an all out battle between Kepa and the metal, and the evidence ultimately validated that he was the more determined of the two.

When at last his first three implements were finished, Kepa began to shape his knife. Using the knowledge he'd so painfully garnered, he worked this special tool with almost loving care. He toiled for ten straight hours, pausing only to drink from the stream, until he finally accepted the small imperfections of his eight-inch blade and deemed it satisfactory. Then he picked up a clean cloth and began to polish its surface.

As the clouds overhead began to darken he scooted farther under the shelter of the overhang and sat with his back against the rock wall beneath it. He lifted his new blade and asked the silence, "Well, Gotzon, what do you think? Once I complete the handle I will be able to defend myself with something more deadly than my fists, eh?" It had been a long time since he'd spoken to his dead brother and he felt remiss about this. "I hope you are fairing well. Here, these people treat me with great kindness. You would like them." He smiled a little even as his eyes stung, imagining his big-hearted brother warmly embracing Achaku's family, and yet he regretted that it could never happen. "Yes, you would like them."

A cold rain began to fall. Gathering up his tools, Kepa went to the river to wash off his hands and headed back to the camp.

Upon entering the wigwam he slid out of his moccasins, pulled off his wet shirt and leggings, and hung them on a leather line strung between two lodge poles. Wearing only his loincloth he sat before the fire, realizing with mild surprise how natural it was becoming to sit nearly naked among these people. Nimu scooted close beside him, adoration on his upturned face, and Kepa asked the boy, then Mihikin, then Liachita about their activities that day.

Achaku, who'd been spooning out their food while she watched and listened, handed around their bowls then came to him and silently reached for his right hand. Her small pouch of medicinal salve rested between them as she closely examined his blisters. The icy water of the river had relieved some of the burning, but they still stung. With her gentle fingers she spread the salve over his skin.

They had seen little of each other over the past several days. Mihikin had explained Achaku's failure to visit his forge by saying she'd been working on projects of her own. In the evenings she had served Kepa food and tended to his clothing, dutifully but almost wordlessly, and she went to her sleeping robes alone. He studied her now as she treated his fingers one at a time, enjoying her touch and nearness.

When she'd finished, Kepa pulled a fur over his shoulders and said, "They feel much better. Thank you."

She nodded in acknowledgment and was about to draw away when Kepa said, "I would like to show you what I made today." She, Nimu, Mihikin, and Liachita all leaned in closer as Kepa unwrapped his knife blade from a leather rag. When it appeared a collective "ahhhh" arose from the group.

"Tomorrow I will make a handle for it," said Kepa, very pleased with their reactions. Certain that the women would not wish to finger the weapon, he held it up to Mihikin.

The old man took the blade in his outstretched hands as if it were as fragile as an eggshell. After scrutinizing its shape and weight he tested first the point and then the edge against his leathery thumb, drawing a small bead of blood. He handed it back to Kepa saying, "It is a weapon of much power, mightier than any I have known."

Nimu was staring at the knife longingly but dared not ask to touch it. Kepa handed it to him carefully, and said, "Mihikin has already shown us its sharpness. There is no need for you to do the same."

Even more reverently than Mihikin had done Nimu held the knife and slowly turned it over, fascinated by the play of the fire's reflection along its gleaming edge. When he handed it back to its owner, his eyes glowed with amazement and gratitude.

Achaku softly offered, "If you wish, I would be happy to make a sheath for your fine knife."

"That is kind of you, Achaku. That would please me greatly."

"Kepa," said Liachita, her eyes hopeful, "Mihikin has told me of your song to Manitou. Is it a song you may sing in the presence of women?"

"Yes, Liachita. It is a holy song, and it is sung by all the men and women of my village."

She asked with surprise, "You share such sacred songs with one another?"

"They are for all to sing. In my land, an individual does not keep a song for himself alone. "

"How generous your people must be," Liachita said with much feeling, "to share their songs, their spirit power with one another."

"We believe such power is stronger when it is shared."

"Mihikin has said your music is a wondrous thing. After you have eaten, will you sing for us?"

Kepa thought of his txistu that had been left in his cave, and wished he had the instrument with him now. Surely his cousin had taken it with him aboard *La Magdalena*. "I will sing in my language. In the days to come I will learn to sing it in yours, then I will teach you."

Liachita bowed her head slightly. "We would be honored."

"Achaku," said Kepa, "my leg is strong again. I would like to travel to the coast after my knife is finished."

"In two days from now many villagers will go there to fish and hunt. We will go with them."

Nimu squirmed and nudged Mihikin, who set down his bowl, got to his feet, and rummaged through his belongings. He returned with a long bundle. Presenting it to Kepa, he said, "We too have been busy these past days. We thought these things would be useful to you."

Kepa opened the folds of leather to find a newly made quiver, bow, and handful of arrows. They had been lovingly crafted. Each piece, even each arrow, bore an image of a whale, and near it rested the symbol of Kepa's birthmark. Looking up at Mihikin through tear-blurred eyes, Kepa was about to speak when Achaku reached from behind her back and laid a newly made leather pouch in front of his crossed legs.

"This too, is for you," she said.

Kepa felt his throat constrict even tighter. And Liachita had said *his* people were generous. After admiring the workmanship of the pouch he opened it to find two rounded pieces of flint like the ones Achaku used to start her fires, two thin beaded bands with tie strings at the ends, and a coil of braided sinew that had been dyed red and decorated with large curved teeth. He raised a grateful yet puzzled gaze.

"They are a game carrying string and leg charms," said Mihikin.

From Kepa's expression it was clear that he didn't understand their significance, so Mihikin explained, "Sometimes beavers show themselves along our route to the bay. If one of them allows you to kill him, you can show your respect for his spirit by carrying it home tied with such a beautiful string. His spirit will then allow your future hunts to be successful, knowing you are an honorable man in need of nourishment. The leg bands will also bring you luck in your hunts. As you can see, they bear the symbol of their powerful owner."

"Ah," Kepa said, noting the three small whales beaded into each band, and then carefully replacing the contents of the pouch. He met Mihikin's eyes, and then Achaku's. "I am humbled by your open hearts. With whatever strength I have, I will help feed and protect this family while I remain with you."

Mihikin assured him, "You are one of us, Kepa, for as long as you wish. You have become like a son to me."

"Then, if I may ask one thing more of you, Mihikin, will you teach me to shoot the bow you have made?"

"I would do so, happily, but Achaku is a far better shot than I am now."

"Achaku?" His eyes darted to her. "But I thought women were forbidden to touch weapons."

Achaku told him patiently, "Our men believe that if a woman

touches their weapons their power will diminish. So I have my own weapons, and the spirits have visited my dreams many times to guide me on hunts. The teeth that decorate your carrying string came from a beaver I hunted."

"Then, will you teach me, Achaku?"

She nodded, and Nimu beamed up at him, saying, "With mother's help, you'll soon be hunting a great bear!"

Having only an indistinct idea of what a great bear might be, Kepa confidently agreed.

Graves and Wonders

9

"Wait, Achaku. Leave that one where it is."

She was about to extract the last of seven tightly grouped arrows from the tree stump Kepa had been using for target practice. Turning back to him, she asked, "Why?"

"It is time I tested the balance of my knife," he said, pulling his blade from the sheath Achaku had given to him that morning. To add his own small contribution to the craftsmanship she and her family had invested in this and his other new possessions, he'd taken the time to carve two small whales into the butt of its handle.

Achaku asked hesitantly, "You mean to aim for the arrow? You do not have many arrows, Kepa."

With a subtle smile, he said, "You have too much faith in my aim."

"Your aim has been very true," she said, stepping away from the stump. "You have mastered your bow in less than two days."

"This bow is much like the one I have used since I was a boy. I had only to learn its ways. Achaku," he paused, noting her position, "it would be safer if you moved a little farther away." When she had complied he lifted his knife. Gripping the handle firmly and trying to remember the technique Gotzon and he had used years earlier with their mother's borrowed kitchen knife, he focused determinedly and threw it at the stump.

With a startled yelp, Achaku dove sideways as the knife flew wide of its mark and passed closer to her than the target.

Kepa cried out, "Achaku!" as he ran toward her. She was standing up and brushing the dirt and leaves from her clothes by the time he reached her. Taking one look at his appalled expression, hearing his stuttered apology, she started to laugh. She covered her mouth with her hands but the laughter bubbled out from behind them before she could quell it.

He couldn't help smiling ruefully. "I tried to warn you."

Her laughter settled into a grin. "Perhaps the arrow is as safe as you thought, at least until you have had more practice."

"Yes, and it would please me if you would stand closer to my side now, out of danger."

They walked back to Kepa's starting point and he tried again. After thirty-seven more throws and only a few minor cuts in Kepa's right hand, the knife finally imbedded itself close enough to the arrow to seriously endanger it. Satisfied at last, Kepa said, "That is enough for today. The wind is growing stronger." The clouds were darkening and lowering as well, and Kepa hoped whatever rains they released would not be heavy enough to deter their departure for the coast the following morning.

He retrieved his knife, wiped it clean on a patch of moss, and was about to sheath it when Achaku asked, "May I hold it?" Kepa knew she was asking much more than that. She wished to know whether Kepa trusted that his own power was strong enough not to be weakened by hers. Unwilling even to consider that Achaku would try to cause him harm, even if he believed in spiritual powers as she did, he handed her his knife without hesitation.

They stood side by side as she examined its character closely, her fingers and eyes seeming to measure a hidden essence concealed within the iron and wood. At last she said, "No knife in our land could have sustained itself through even ten of your throws, Kepa. This is a companion to trust and guard well."

"I must sharpen it now. I will join you at the wigwam soon."

After she had left him Kepa used his file and a sanding stone to bring out the blade's sharpest edge. He then walked to the river and took from a small pouch tied at his waist a concoction Mihikin had given him. It was a mixture of grease and herbs, although which herbs he did not know. Its creation had been kept as secret as the ritual Kepa was about to perform.

Slowly, with only a small, quiet pool to serve as a mirror, Kepa lifted his blade to his throat and sliced off the first strands of his bushy beard. As he continued to carefully work the sharp edge, he couldn't help wishing he possessed enough iron to make a razor, but at least his knife could serve this purpose occasionally. By the time he'd finished, to his surprise, he saw that he'd inflicted only three nicks to mar the smoothness of his complexion. Studying his reflection in the water, the skin that had been covered by his beard now looked starkly pale beneath his sun-browned upper cheeks. He sheathed his blade and stood hesitating, wondering what reaction his new face might stir up. There was only one way to find out, so he turned and headed back to the village

People stared and several women covered their smiles with their hands as he made his way through the circuit of lodges. As he approached Achaku's wigwam Tracker let out one loud yip before catching Kepa's scent and wagging his tail with exuberance. Petting the dog for longer than usual, still slightly apprehensive about his reception, Kepa's fortitude wavered. Then, mentally nudging himself, he ducked his head and entered the wigwam.

Nimu, who'd been holding up his writing parchment for Achaku's inspection, leaped to his feet and let the skin drop from his fingers. Achaku grabbed her son's arm, intending to pull him away from the stranger who'd just appeared when she realized who it was. Her eyes grew huge and she let out a soft, "Oh!" Liachita, who must have been let into the secret by her husband, and Mihikin sat upon their robes chuckling heartily.

"But," said Nimu, apparently disappointed, "you look less like a bear now."

Achaku's eyes never left Kepa's face. "The forest has enough bears, my son."

Nimu said pleadingly, "But you must not cut off the hair on your chest."

Smiling at this, Kepa said, "I promise you that I will not."

At this, they all gathered close enough to touch Kepa's naked jaw, Achaku's hands lingering a bit longer than the others'.

That evening as the clouds loosed a light but icy rain, they all packed for the next morning's journey. It didn't take Kepa long to gather his few possessions, so he began helping Achaku prepare and store what food they might need. When nearly everything had been made ready Achaku pulled from a basket a thin leather satchel that Kepa had never seen. On its surface was painted the image of a whale, but this one bore the recognizable white and black markings of an orca. When Kepa asked her to tell him about this image of the animal spirit, Achaku said, "It would be better to wait until another time." He could see that she was tired after the long day and he did not press her.

After the others had fallen asleep he lay awake listening to the night sounds of the quieting camp and the nearby forest, wondering what he would find the next day once they reached their destination. He tried to prepare himself, knowing he must accept whatever had been left behind after the ship's departure. The remnants might tell him nothing at all, but they might tell a story of their final days that would add great sadness to his long wait for their return.

And, fervently, he hoped that Gotzon's grave had been left undisturbed.

Morning frost was glittering upon the ground and around the needles of the trees when Kepa left the wigwam, but it melted away as dawn's light touched it. He stood in his warm coat with the comforting weight of his new knife sheathed at his belt. Scanning the thirty or so men, women, and children gathered before their lodges, he saw no sign of Saunuch. He must be hunting, Kepa concluded, and the thought of the long walk through the hilly forests and meadows took on a significantly lighter aspect.

Earlier that morning Kepa had helped bundle and tie their supplies onto a large caribou hide stretched between two thin poles that had been angled closer together at one end. Achaku now came to stand by his side, and they both awaited the signal to begin dragging this conveyance, a travois, behind them. Liachita, standing at the door of the wigwam with a large robe pulled over her head and shoulders, had chosen to stay behind to help a young mother care for her newly born infant. She stood waiting for them to set out.

Taking his position with his family at the head of the line, Wapitikwa lifted his arm to signal them forward and led the clan toward the river along a well-worn path. In addition to the many travois, some of the men traveling with them carried canoes. Everyone in the procession seemed happy to be embarking on the day's journey. Tracker, trotting beside Mihikin, occasionally darted from the trail to investigate a promising scent.

Kepa watched the rays of the sun filter toward them through the thin clouds as if it were striving to touch their faces. The scents of wood smoke and cooking meat receded as they waded the river and continued along a less noticeable trail. They started up the rise of the first hill and entered the cover of trees, where small speckled thrushes and red-crested warblers sang out from the boughs overhead, heralding their passing.

Nimu insisted on relieving Achaku of the burden of the travois from time to time, and Kepa could see that she let him in order to uphold his pride rather than out of weariness.

Kepa's leg served him well during the six-hour hike, his ankle beginning to ache only after they'd reached the edge of the trees overlooking the bay. And then there were other aches to deal with. Although he had told himself he harbored no hope that any of his men had remained behind, as he gazed down at the soulless site below him his heart sank at the absoluteness of his abandonment.

The sea's surface was spotted with breaching, spouting, diving whales but not a single boat. His eyes lingered on the empty section of water off the island's northern shore where his ship had lay at anchor. It already seemed long ago that he had walked her decks. Then he searched for Gotzon's grave but it was blocked from his view by the small hill at the southeast end of the island. With a heavy heart he descended the hill to level ground.

As women began to set up their hide wigwams and men and children carried nets to the shore, Achaku surprised Kepa by staying his hand as he reached for the last bundles from their travois. "Those we will need," she said. "We will not camp here tonight, Kepa."

"No?"

"The provisions for Mihikin and Nimu have already been unloaded. They will lodge and fish here with friends. When you are ready to leave, the two of us will take our belongings and camp in a special place."

He kept himself from voicing the questions that came to his mind, accepting that she had valid reasons for this. Instead, he said, "I must go to the island first."

She nodded her understanding and watched him walk toward the water.

At Kepa's request, two men agreed to take him across the bay. They soon had their canoe afloat and were pushing off from shore. He sat in the middle of the sleek craft and immediately picked up the cadence of the other paddlers. With each stroke he felt his nerves twist a little tighter. What he was hoping for, or fearing, he did not probe.

A pod of six Right whales lazed in the shallows not far from their approaching port side. As the canoe neared them the five adults, females, circled the young calf in their midst, forming a protective ring with their flukes pointing outward. Kepa had seen this shielding maneuver before and knew the mother and her companions would not hesitate to crush the canoe if it drew too close. But today he had no interest in disturbing their group and he turned his gaze to the island just ahead.

He leaped into the shallow water before the canoe had stopped moving and searched the shoreline only in passing as he strode toward Gotzon's gravesite. Kepa heard his two companions break out in excited speculation and glanced back to see them examining a short length of discarded hemp rope. His pace did not slow again until he came to the rise overlooking the cemetery, and then he halted abruptly. Gotzon's grave lay intact, the three large rocks they'd rolled over his body and his wooden markers resting just as they had when he'd last seen them. But Gotzon and the whaler killed while Kepa was still with them no longer slumbered alone. A large grave with four markers lay several feet from Gotzon's. Kepa forced his feet to move forward and he descended the small rise with slow, deliberate steps.

When he drew near enough, he leaned down and read the names on the two closest markers and let out a painful sigh. They were men from Bakar's boat. Good, good men. He read the names again. They must have died during that doomed hunt that had tossed Kepa out of his chalupa. He stepped toward the next marker and let his eyes trail to the third name. Slowly, heavily he dropped to his knees onto the rock-strewn ground.

Zorion's name brought tears to Kepa's eyes. Todor, his friend of many years, had buried his thirteen-year-old son in this cold, forlorn ground. Dutiful, brave, uncomplaining Zorion. So, manhood had been stolen from him. Was it during a hunt? Had he died that same day? Oh, God, had Zorion jumped into the water to save him? No, not that, Kepa's mind recoiled from the thought. He couldn't let himself believe that the boy had lost his life because of him, and yet he knew it was something Zorion might do. It took an effort, but he shifted to his side and moved his gaze toward the last new grave marker.

This stood closest to Gotzon's, and it was the only one he'd expected and feared. It read, "Kepa de Mendieta".

He was gripped by a clammy, unnatural sensation, staring at his own grave, knowing everyone who'd ever loved him believed him lost forever. He pictured Urdin standing here, weeping at the very spot where he now knelt. Kepa's heart clenched to think of the pain it must have brought his cousin, and poor old Paulo, and Captain de Perea, and the others. He wished he could tell them he was here, he was alive. But wishes were of no use to him anymore.

His knees dragged themselves toward Gotzon's grave. He sat down at the edge of the mounded dirt. "Hello, my brother." He took in a couple of breaths. Motioning his head toward the other graves, he asked softly, "Are they with you?" He reached out and traced the face of the grave marker as he said, "I pray it is so. It would be better if you had each other's company." His voice cracked a little. "You always wanted a son. Now, you can care for Zorion. You can comfort one another." His hand lowered to his side, knowing that the sounds of waves crashing, whales spouting, and gulls crying would be the only responses he would hear. His eyes began to spill their watery burden.

Almost without intention, he found himself singing the prayer he'd been teaching Achaku and her family. With tears slowly falling and his voice faltering time and again, he sat in the chilly breeze that swept over the graves and sang the hymn three times.

When he'd finished, he sighed deeply and said, his voice hoarse now, "I hope you are at peace, Gotzon, truly at peace. You are with me always."

He rose unsteadily to his feet and turned. The two men who had rowed him ashore sat a respectful distance away, waiting patiently for his return. Wiping his eyes with the back of his hands, Kepa climbed down the path to join them. Along their way back to the canoe the three men stopped when Kepa spotted a three-inch patch of beaten copper wedged beneath a rock, the remains of a burst try-works kettle. At least this misfortune took no lives, he thought.

Carefully but unsuccessfully, he scouted the vicinity for any other remnants that might be of use. While the other two men explored a wider area for treasures Kepa made his way to his old cave. It was empty of any trace of him. He hadn't really expected to find his txistu, but in this too he'd still held to a flicker of hope.

Remembering the nights spent in the cave, his mind gradually returned to the night to come and he wondered why Achaku had planned for the two of them to camp in a separate place. What was she intending, and how would he respond? As he made his way back toward the canoe he spotted what appeared to be iron sticking out of the sand. Pulling it free he found the cracked head of a flensing spade. *This,* he said to himself as he held it up, *this will give me parts for a crossbow, and perhaps some arrow tips.*

His visit to the island left him somber as he pushed off from its shore, but his eyes and attention were now pointed ahead rather than behind.

The overcast sky darkened the water near their feet to a midnight blue and the encircling hills to a deep gray-green. Standing on the pebbles just above the water line, Achaku studied Kepa carefully as she asked, "Do you remember anything of this place?"

"No, nothing."

They had trailed their lightened travois to the slight rise just above them and set up their wigwam. It had surprised Kepa to discover how close this hidden cove lay to Aldapak. Although out of sight from the larger bay, the smaller inlet was located just around its eastern periphery. He must have been hauled here by the whale and then crawled ashore. He recalled how foggy it had been the day he'd been yanked from his boat, and understood more fully why the whalers had believed him dead. They had seen little of his disappearance and nothing of his rescue.

"Were you here that day, Achaku? Did you help pull me out?"

"I was here, but I found you ashore."

"Were you here alone?"

A slight smile touched her mouth and a knowing shine in her eyes. "There were no other people. This is a holy place for me. It is where my power comes from."

Kepa looked with deeper interest around the cove, noting nothing exceptional.

Seeing his lack of understanding, she said, reaching out to take his hand, "Come to the sea with me."

He let her guide him, welcoming the warmth of her hand in his.

When they had seated themselves on a flat boulder resting halfway in the water Achaku sat very still and closed her eyes. Softly, she sang a supplication to the Great Manitou. Swaying slightly as she chanted, her eyes still shut, she asked for the return of her guardian. When the song ended she opened her eyes and sat motionless, watching the waves roll in. After several minutes, during which Kepa held himself still and silent at her side, she reached into the pouch with the orca emblem and withdrew a hand-made whistle. Leaning over the edge of the boulder and placing the whistle just above the water's surface, she blew a long, sharp call. She repeated the call twice, waiting and concentrating after each call.

At last she looked up at Kepa and said, "We must be patient. Will you keep watch while I make our fire?"

Kepa considered asking, Keep watch for what? but he was beginning to feel a little apprehensive about Achaku's religious calling. He merely nodded and obeyed as she hiked back to their wigwam.

As it always had, the sea drew Kepa's focus farther and farther from shore. He called to his mind countless images of people and events that had touched his life as he'd traveled the many miles across its vastness. But even now he shied from recalling the storm that had killed Gotzon. Beyond this memory he let his mind wander, let his muscles relax.

Gulls squawked and reeled above him, lifting his gaze. The clouds were beginning to thin and shift to the south, providing hope for a clear evening. He realized that Achaku was standing beside him again, this time with a net and a basket in her hands.

"Fresh fish will make a fine meal for us," she said.

They climbed a small rise that dropped off sharply toward the water and looked down into the crystal waters. After studying the schools of cod for a few moments, Achaku and Kepa each wrapped a securing line around one of their hands and cast the small, weighted net from shore. They let it sink a few feet, watched the cod swim over it, and then gently hauled it back. Three yard-long fish flapped in its webbing, their dappled gray-brown sides flashing in the filtered sunlight.

"Ha!" said Kepa, "there has never been a land with better fishing. How many more shall we catch?" He held the top of the gathered net open to allow Achaku to pull out the codfish and place them in her basket.

"Perhaps one more," she said, warmed to see his enthusiasm. "We need not catch any to take back to the bay. There will be fish already drying when we rejoin the others. What they catch will feed our camp for many days."

"My people preserve cod so that it lasts for many moons."

"How is that possible?"

"We soak them in…" he did not know the word for salt, "something before we dry them. A seasoning that looks like clear, fine sand. Once or twice I have tasted this seasoning in the food you prepare."

"Siwitakin?"

"Yes, perhaps, you'll have to show me to be certain. Do you have much siwitakin nearby?"

"No, it comes from far to the south, across the seaway and ten to thirteen days travel on foot. We carry only small amounts and use it sparingly."

Kepa nodded. "If we visit there, this place to the south, I will show you how to cure a great supply of codfish that will last through a winter. The siwitakin would also be useful to my people when they return."

Almost apologetically, she said, "It is kind of you to offer us such knowledge, but it has never been our way to store a great deal of food. To do so might show a lack of faith in the animal spirits who provide for us."

Kepa was trying to think of a way to convince her to accept his offer, and was about to toss the net back into the water when he suddenly stiffened and shouted out, "Great God!" He took one unsteady step, lost his footing, and almost slipped into the water. Scrambling back up to Achaku, he sputtered, "It's that devil fish!" He gawked from her, standing expectantly beside him, to the orca swimming not twenty feet from shore. "I thought you might have been trying to call one of them, I just never believed one would come!"

"Not just any of them came, Kepa. This one has been my spirit friend for years." She was already heading for the beach with the basket so Kepa grabbed up the tangled net and quickly followed. Disbelieving his eyes, Kepa was further startled when he realized that he was gaping at the very same orca that had plagued him and his whalers since their arrival. "That one stole the whales we hunted," he finally accused.

"I watched you both several times, you and him. He and his pod ate only the tongues, did they not?"

"The tongues are the best piece of whale meat, and he stole many from us."

Achaku now spoke softly, trying to ease the effect of her next words. "Kepa, he also saved your life, as he saved mine when I was twelve years old."

"Saved my... what?"

"It was not me who brought you from the water, Kepa, nor any other human. As I said, I found you ashore, but I am certain he was the one that lifted you to the surface and bore you here."

He stared at her, incredulous.

"Mihikin has no doubt either," she went on. "He saw this orca we call White Fin do the same for me when I fell from a canoe in rough waters. I was already taking a step onto the star road, my breath had left me, and he brought me up from the deep water. Mihikin and several others pulled me from the shallows where he left me and I began to breathe again. Just as you did."

Vague, ghostly images of Kepa's near drowning came eerily back to him. He remembered giving up, even welcoming the end of his struggles, and then he'd felt himself being lifted from the depths. Lifted by...? Could it have been this devil fish? "But, but you did not see him save me?"

Achaku took hold of his arm and said, "He was close to shore when I found you, Kepa, guarding you until I arrived."

Saved by a small whale, while he was trying to kill a large one? "Great God," he said again. This time it was only a whisper. Still reeling, he barely noticed that Achaku was walking to the boulder they had rested upon earlier. When he saw her lean out with a fish in her hands, saw the orca swimming very close to her, he let out a startled cry and ran toward her. Seizing her by the shoulders, he pulled her back sharply.

"Achaku!" he barked, his heart beating wildly. "He'll tear off your arm! Or he'll pull you in!"

Trying to be tolerant, Achaku said evenly, "Kepa, he is my

guardian, and yours. He will not harm me. I ask you not to interfere."

"He is a whale, a killer! We have both seen him attack a sixty-foot Right whale."

"Have you seen him or any of his kind harm a human?"

That gave him a moment's pause, long enough for Achaku to continue. "You have killed too, as all hunters must. We kill to survive. But, we must not harm our close brothers, whether they are our own kind or they take the form of other animals. White Fin has shown us much favor and he is wise and powerful."

Kepa released her shoulders and took a step back, his disquiet growing with each of her claims.

"You wanted me to tell you about my dreams, Kepa," she said, almost pleading, "and how you and I are bound together. Your coming was foretold to me. I knew not only that you would come, but how. Perhaps it was White Fin's manitou that sent me the dream. In it, he was here and he lifted a man from the sea that bore the mark you wear on your neck."

He shook his head, his mouth suddenly dry. "How can any of this be true?"

She did not answer him. Instead she returned to the boulder, and this time he didn't stop her. He watched, astonished, as she held out a codfish until the orca was three feet in front of her and then she tossed it into its open mouth. The orca swam slowly in a small circle, then came back to receive another fish. Finally, the whale drew close enough for Achaku to reach out and touch the tip of its nose with her outstretched hand. The orca remained very still, as if welcoming the touch.

For several heartbeats Achaku and the orca held their contact. Then they parted slowly, reluctantly. Not until the orca had left her and glided out of view around the rim of the inlet did Achaku turn back to Kepa.

He stood in stunned disbelief yet unable to erase the images his own eyes had etched forever upon his mind. Could this whale have saved him, intentionally saved him? Was it comprehensible that this kind of bond could exist between two such different creatures? Or, did Achaku have the astounding power to make all of this come to pass? Yes, it must be her. The proof had unfolded when the orca responded to her call and returned her touch.

She came and stood beside him again, a small and lovely young woman whose face revealed her every emotion. Now he felt a little afraid of her. Concerned by his troubled expression she reached out to touch him. The gesture, however, reminded Kepa of her contact with the whale and he drew back. Her eyes then tried to comfort him, but a question took dominance in his mind and repeated itself insistently.

How can what just happened be anything but a dream?

One Woman's Magic

10

The earthy aromas of stewing cod and silverweed roots prompted a loud growl from Kepa's empty stomach. Yet as Achaku ladled out his hot meal he couldn't help following her movements with his eyes and wondering if she had used some of her magic while concocting the soup.

"What do you wish to ask me, Kepa?"

His spoon halted halfway to his mouth, then returned to his bowl. "You even seem to read my thoughts. How can you have such powers?"

"Whatever power I have is a gift, one that I do not fully understand. Why White Fin chose me I can not guess."

"Why would he have saved me, a whale hunter?"

He saw her hesitate before responding, but the answer was already in her gaze. "It may have been so that I would find you."

"You mean, that I was saved for you?"

Her forehead creased with uncertainty. "Kepa, why we were meant to meet one another I do not know. My dream showed me this inlet and you lying on the shore in need of help. I came here the next day, and later that day I saw your people arrive at the bay. I returned many times, and I was there when you fell from your canoe. I ran here, knowing this is where you would surface, and I arrived here just as you crawled ashore."

"And yet you are sure that the orca rescued me?"

"Although I did not see him do so, in my dream I saw him lift you from the water just as he lifted me long ago. And he was still there when I ran to you. It seemed that he had only been waiting for me."

Kepa shook his head, still awed by her story. "I have never heard of such a magical thing, Achaku. And you seem to have caused it. In my country, they would call you a witch."

"Is a witch a bad thing?"

The worry in her voice cautioned him and he said for her sake, "It is a person who fills others with wonder."

This brought a relieved smile. "I am only a woman with wonderful friends."

Kepa touched the amulet that rested upon his chest. "When did you make this for me?"

"The day after I dreamed of you. I knew you would wear it one day. White Fin's manitou is very strong, and will speak to the spirits of the animals you wish to hunt. They will come when you need them."

"Your hunting customs are very strange to me."

"You are learning quickly."

"Achaku, has your power helped your people in many ways?"

"That is hard to say. I try to honor the Great Manitou and other spirits in my care of our people. We have been spared famine, and terrible storms, and diseases for many years. Our hunting and gathering has gone well, but these blessings are due to the good conduct of our entire clan, or at least most of them. Not everyone seeks peace and cooperation."

She had filled her own bowl but had not yet tasted her food. Now she watched her carved bone spoon as it slowly stirred the chunks of stew around, saying, "Kepa, have you noticed that Saunuch did not come with our people to the bay?"

"Yes."

The spoon stopped and she looked up at him. "He stayed behind to purify his body and mind in the sweat lodge. He is preparing himself for a bear hunt. Mihikin told me Saunuch intends to fast for days. When we return, he may ask you to join him in the hunt."

Kepa had by now heard several grand descriptions of this animal and he had seen the skin of a black bear hanging outside a wigwam. Impressive as it was, he could not imagine that the bearer of such a skin could be more formidable than a whale. He feared the thought of a bear hunt little. "It will take only a day or two to complete my weapons. If Saunuch asks me, I will join him."

"Men have been killed on such hunts, and he may place you in greater danger than is necessary. You must be very watchful of him."

"I will be watchful. You need not worry."

100

"Good," she said with some relief. "Eat now."

This was encouragement enough, and Kepa ate his fill.

After their bowls had been emptied, Achaku pulled a long, thin leather strip from among her things and held it up. "Do you know what this is?"

"I have seen you use it as a game with Nimu."

"Yes, it is a game string. It gives us many hours of amusement on long winter nights. Would you like me to show you how to play?"

"I would."

Tying the ends in a knot, she began to weave the large loop between her fingers until she had created something resembling an oblong spider web. "Now, pinch the strings where they cross, then lift your fingers up and around the outer strings and bring them up through the center."

He tried, and ended up with his thumbs and pointer fingers entangled. Achaku delicately held back her grin. "Try again," she coaxed.

The next few attempts went better and better until he began to successfully analyze the play of the strings intersections, guessing future configurations beforehand. But soon he became aware of a subtle change in Achaku's manner. Her hands moved ever more slowly, enticingly around the string. After each new changing of the string her eyes found and held him for a little longer and with a little more intensity. Finally she took another turn, her hands moving with slow graceful beckoning, and when she eased the string into its new design she held it very close to her chest. She held it motionless and waited for him to reach out. He looked up to meet the intensity of her eyes, rich and brown and fathomless. There was no demand there, no expectation, just hopeful invitation. His hand slowly lowered without taking the string.

He asked her, "Can you work your magic on me too, then?"

Her voice was low. "Even if I could, I would not have you come to me by magic. I would have you come willingly, as a man who wants what a woman can give." She set aside the string and moved close to him, her face inches from his.

Lord, she was alluring, but he had to ask. "Achaku, did Saunuch share you with other men?"

"He did not. He might have been afraid that it could weaken

my powers. But if he had tried, I would have refused. My position with our people gives me that right."

This assertion pleased Kepa more than he would have admitted. He touched her cheek as he leaned forward and softly brought his lips to hers. She drew back only inches, a look of subtle surprise in her eyes.

"It is called a kiss," he told her. "Is this not one of your customs?"

"It is strange to me, but very pleasant. Will you touch me with another kiss?"

Kepa held her cheeks in both hands now and pulled her gently nearer, letting the kiss lengthen and deepen. When he at last forced himself to ease back, Achaku responded by wrapping her arms around his neck and whispering, "More, Kepa."

Whatever restraint he'd been trying to maintain was dispelled by these two words. His arms encircled her small frame and pressed it to his, and every fiber and chemical of his body responded. His mouth devoured hers while his hands moved lower and took possession of her buttocks. He heard her softly moan and a moment later felt her hands fumbling for the ties of his leggings. They pulled apart only long enough to get to their feet and rid each other of clothing. As she stood naked before Kepa, he drew a breath and stared at her beauty. When she reached out to him he took her hands and held them to his chest, allowing a tremor of caution to reach him. "If there is a child, Achaku…"

"He will be cherished, always. You need not fear for his welfare." She wanted no further objections. She lay down upon the furs and held out her arms. Kepa did not keep her waiting.

All thoughts of consequences left him as he gave his senses and urges full indulgence, letting his hands and mouth roam at will, relishing the taste and feel of her, remembering the power, the magnificence of lovemaking. Emboldened by her responding passion and need, he nevertheless tried to maintain an unhurried pace. But now he found her to be even more impatient than he. Her body urged him on and he allowed himself to answer. As they came together and moved with a rhythm as old as mankind, Achaku muttered his name in a sensual chant. At last, at last Kepa and she cried out together.

Their movements eased and stilled. They held each other amid a tangled heap of furs, and Achaku found the strength to lift her hand and caress his bicep. As their heartbeats calmed and their skin cooled, Kepa pulled a fur over them. Lying in each other's arms, they listened to the fire's quiet muttering, the gulls' calling from the shore, the wind's intermittent thrumming against the wigwam.

After several minutes had passed Achaku turned her face to Kepa and said, "Never have I known a joining such as we have shared."

Kepa couldn't help smiling. "It must be your magic."

"No," she said, "if it was a matter of magic I could call upon, I would have known such pleasure many times before now."

He chuckled at this and she moved to lie on top of him. "Will you show me again?"

When she began to shift seductively against him, he willingly complied.

This time he did not hurry, and he taught her much of what she would from that day forward refer to as his magic. But even as their bodies gave and took all that could be exchanged, Achaku felt Kepa holding something of himself back. It was in the words left unspoken, the intimate looks avoided. *In time*, she told herself, *he will heal. He will let himself love another.*

Later that night, when Kepa thought Achaku was asleep, he took up his coat and crept from her side to walk alone in the cold moonlight. She let him go without asking to join him, sensing that he needed to talk to his ghosts.

White Fin did not return the following day, but Achaku took Kepa in her arms again, and reveled in the man her guardian had brought to her.

The camp was already being packed up when Achaku and Kepa rejoined the others, and they just had time to admire the baskets filled with Mihikin's successful catch before strapping them tightly closed. They set out, dogs darting back and forth beside the trail, children laughing and racing, and adults chatting about the day ahead. Heavily laden with dried cod, the travois dug into the trail as they began to climb.

Kepa noticed that an unusual number of speculative glances were turned in his direction, but only Nimu voiced his curiosity concerning what had happened to them at the inlet. He showered

Kepa with questions about the orca's visit. Not until every detail had been relayed did the boy sigh and say, "I hope to see White Fin one day." Achaku laid a hand on Nimu's shoulder, signaling him to silence for a time.

They had walked another half-mile when an excited murmur came down the line, announcing the sighting of beaver sign, and Nimu began to dance with anticipation. Before he could ask, Mihikin stilled him with, "It is not yet your time to hunt beaver, Nimu. Kepa and I will go."

Nimu's face fell.

Remembering how his own father had appeased him at such times when he was young, Kepa gently challenged Nimu. "Are you strong enough to carry the travois with your mother? It is a heavy load with all of this fish."

Stretching a bit taller, Nimu nodded with confidence.

"You are growing to be a fine young man," Kepa said. "Watch over your mother while we are away." He knew that others would lend a hand if the boy tired, and with luck he would rejoin them before long.

As the main group resumed its march up the same trail, Kepa, Mihikin and five other hunters split off and prepared themselves for the hunt. Following Mihikin's lead, Kepa tied his beautifully beaded leg charms just below his knees. He moved his neck charm to the outside of his jacket then, as Achaku had taught him, he sang a short hunting song giving tribute to the beaver.

Mihikin informed him solemnly, "Since neither of us has dreamed of beavers lately, we can only hope their manitou favors us today."

When all were ready the hunters started up several paths, their various dogs leading the ways. Sounds of the other teams of hunters faded and Kepa found himself remembering the first day he'd set foot on this land, the day he'd spotted the beaver-hewn tree stumps and thought he'd stumbled upon evidence of a human encampment. How long ago that seemed, yet he could so clearly recall how he and his men had jumped at the sound of the beaver tail slapping the water. Tracker's sudden howl jerked Kepa from his thoughts and he and Mihikin took off after the dog.

The two men broke into a small clearing just as Tracker was cutting off a pair of beavers scrambling toward a stream. Tracker kept up a chorus of barking as he darted back and forth between the two large beavers, herding them away from their escape route.

Mihikin fell to one knee and shouted to Kepa as he reached for an arrow, "Take the one to the west!" Kepa already had an arrow nocked in his bow and he let the dart fly. His beaver fell an instant before the one struck by Mihikin's arrow.

Mihikin hooted aloud and turned to Kepa with wide, shining eyes. He let out one satisfied bark of laughter, his eyebrows raised high on his forehead.

Smiling, Kepa said, "You look surprised, my friend."

Slightly chagrined, Mihikin admitted, "When a man is used to casting a weapon as heavy as your iron spear and killing an animal as mighty as a whale, it is a wonder he can also shoot an arrow with such skill. And remember, neither of us dreamed of this encounter so our luck has been rare. I should not have doubted your power. Come, we must show our gratitude."

He drew from his hunting pouch the red game carrying string designed to secure this particular animal, and Kepa did the same. Achaku had only had time to make Kepa one carrying string and he now wondered fleetingly how she'd known to make it for a beaver. They quickly wrapped the strings around their shoulders and hurried over to draw Tracker away from the beaver carcasses. Kepa saw that his arrow had pierced the beaver through the neck, Mihikin's through his rodent's cheek, so both of them had managed to avoid piercing the core of the hide.

With reverence Mihikin knelt down beside his kill and sang a short song of thanks. While he demonstrated to Kepa how to secure his beaver with the carrying string, tying one forepaw and one hind leg to form a kind of pack, he spoke in a grave voice that Kepa suspected was meant to inform the beavers as much as to educate his companion.

"We will honor the spirits of these fine creatures by skinning them with great respect. Their meat will be prepared with care and eaten from a special wooden bowl. No dog will touch their bones. That would be very offensive to the beavers. We will clean their skulls and hang them in the branches of a birch tree so they may still look upon this world. Their shoulder blades will be used to foretell of future hunts, and other bones will be returned to the waters of a river. Their teeth will adorn our clothing and pouches, or will be finely ground to make medicine. By these actions the beavers will know our appreciation and agree to be born again, remaining friends with us always."

Before hoisting the beaver's body to his back, Kepa's hand gently caressed the shimmering brown fur, still soft and warm beneath his palm.

There was no mention of seeking other beavers to kill. To Mihikin, he and Kepa had been generously granted the lives of two admirable animals. This was more than enough.

What a strange, marvelous people, Kepa thought as they took to the trail once again, the weight of his beaver solid and somehow comforting against his back.

Predator
11

It became clear to Kepa that the fishing trip to the coast had depleted Mihikin's strength somewhat when the older man reluctantly declined to return with Nimu and him to the forge. "This morning, I will rest," was all he said. It was a wise precaution, Kepa decided. The clan would be setting out tomorrow for their winter campsites and the journey would take a number of days.

Just the day before, Mihikin had repeated Achaku's warning to Kepa that at the first sign of a bear Saunuch would choose his hunters and go after it. So Kepa was determined to finish the metal parts of his crossbow by this evening.

He and the boy set out under a cloudless sky that seemed to expand the brilliance of the open spaces they crossed and add sharpness to the chill bite in the air. Tracker and Nimu frisked playfully along the path ahead, and Kepa was glad to have their lively company. When they arrived at the now familiar site they built an intense fire from the wood they'd stacked the day before, and soon Kepa was concentrating deeply on shaping a portion of his flensing spade into a triggering mechanism. He worked for a long time before finally setting the piece aside. Standing and stretching his kinked back, he noticed how quiet Nimu had become. He studied the boy's far-away look and asked, "Is something troubling you, Nimu?"

Patting Tracker's head and keeping his gaze away from Kepa's, he replied, "The bear hunt. I fear something will go wrong."

Trying to reassure the boy by teasing him, Kepa said lightly, "You have so little trust in my hunting abilities?" He immediately regretted this bantering approach.

Nimu, turned his pained expression toward him, saying, "Oh no, Kepa! I have great, great respect for you."

"Then tell me why you are troubled? Have you dreamed about the hunt?" After hearing of Achaku's dreams and witnessing White Fin's arrival at the inlet, the whole notion that some people's dreams could foretell the future had taken on a new believability to Kepa.

But Nimu was saying, "I have had no such dream, and that is good. But it would bring my heart great sadness if harm came to you."

Kepa laid aside his tools and motioned the boy nearer. When Nimu sat close beside him Kepa placed his arm around the small pair of shoulders and pulled his amulet from beneath his shirt. "I wear this to protect me, Nimu. You know your mother made it. We must have faith in her power and mine."

The boy nodded but Kepa saw that the concern had not left his face.

"I pray to my God for protection too. Would you like me to tell you about my God, and the faith of my people?"

"Oh, yes. I would be happy to hear of those things."

"We believe that God, the Great Manitou, sent his own son to earth many years ago. His son, and great men before him, taught us how to pray and how to live. As you believe, if we live by such honorable rules, after we die we will rise to a heavenly world and live there forever."

Nimu's eyes glowed with fascination. "Are your rules much like ours?"

"Some, yes."

"Will you teach me?"

"I will gladly teach you. You have been learning your letters well. I will show you how to write ten of our holy rules, called commandments. But our most important rule is the most simple. It is to love others as God loves us, even our enemies."

The boy's brows furrowed at this. "How can a man love his enemies?"

Kepa smiled. "I also struggle with that rule. Yet we must try to help all in need and never be cruel to others, even if they have done us harm."

Shaking his head thoughtfully, Nimu said, "Saunuch taught me that a man may even take the life of another if the idea comes to him in a dream. He said the world belongs to the strongest. He would never follow your rules."

"He is not alone. Many men of my own kind turn away from them, and I fail them far too often."

"But you keep trying?"

"Yes, Nimu, I do."

"Then I wish to try also."

"That, my boy, pleases me deeply."

Nimu's young face beamed up at him, his fears seemingly forgotten.

"Now," said Kepa, tussling Nimu's hair before drawing away, "go check your rabbit snares while I finish my last pieces."

"Come, Tracker," Nimu called as he bounded away, and Kepa watched the two take to the trail that led toward the bend in the river.

The first snow of the season, little more than a dusting, fell during the third night of their migration into the forest. By mid-morning of the following day just enough whiteness remained on the ground to reveal the ominous prints of the creature that had crossed their chosen path less than an hour before them. Kepa heard barking up ahead that was quickly hushed and then human murmuring as it rumbled down the halting line of travelers. He and Mihikin left their loads and hurried forward with their weapons ready.

Though Kepa had heard stories about bears, which Achaku's people revered above all other animals, seeing the evidence before him sent a chill up the back of his neck and into his scalp. The prints were 12-inches long, and must have been made by a creature twice the size of the one whose skin Kepa had seen hanging in the village.

Saunuch, Wapitikwa, and a group of other men fell silent as they stood over the prints. Based on their expressions, none of them had ever seen anything to equal the beast that had come this way.

It was Mihikin who voiced what all of them were thinking. "It must be a great bear." When all gazes turned to him, he added with reluctance, "I have seen only one bear that could leave such a print, many years ago."

This produced admiring mutterings from the men, none of whom could match this claim.

Wapitikwa's face showed his surprise. "You have been with our clan since your marriage, and I have never heard you speak of this. Such a story would have given us much to think about."

"It is not a story that brings comfort or pride, and it is not one that is easy to tell."

They waited expectantly, so with an effort he went on. "I had lived through just fourteen summers. I was hunting beaver with my father and two other men when the great bear surprised us. We all fired upon him but our arrows did him little harm. He...he tore the head off of one of our men before he left us alone."

Kepa watched the stunned expressions around him, knowing it was the desecration of the body, barring the man's peaceful entrance into the next world, that shocked them more than the death.

"Four men could not kill the bear?" Wapitikwa asked.

Mihikin let his eyes linger on their leader for a moment. "We tried but failed. We shot nine arrows into his body. They seemed to inflict no injury at all, but they encouraged his rage. There was no fear in him, no show of pain. He was the fiercest creature I have ever seen. He took his vengeance out on the closest of our hunters." Closing his eyes for a moment, apparently trying to diminish the horror of the memory, Mihikin opened them again and told the rest of his tale. "After he had killed him, he stood over his body and looked at the three of us who were still alive. It felt as though he meant to remember our faces. Then, he turned away and we carried our friend back to camp."

Mihikin needed a bracing breath before issuing a warning. "The might and cunning of this animal is beyond my understanding. He has the strength of twenty men."

A hush of uneasiness held them all until Saunuch said, "I have prepared for this hunt for many days, and I have dreamed that the bear would give his life up to my bow."

Without challenge, Wapitikwa asked, "Are you sure it is this bear you saw in your dream?"

"It must be. Now, who will hunt with me?"

The hesitation was short-lived. "I will come," said Kepa.

Amid the surprised expressions, Saunuch frowned and said to

the others, "Will you let this outsider shame the rest of you? Where is your courage?"

Two others stepped forward. Then two more.

"Six of us," said Saunuch. "That is a good-sized party. Get whatever weapons and supplies you will need."

Maintaining as unworried an expression as he could, Wapitikwa said, "The rest of us will follow this trail to the next river and set up camp. All of you," he said, his eyes touching on Kepa's, "return to us safely."

Not even Mihikin had noticed that Nimu had been watching this gathering from behind a nearby tree. As Kepa went to prepare what he intended to take with him, Nimu hurried to his mother's side and told her he was going to travel farther back in the line for awhile. The family of his closest friend was there, Achaku knew, so she found nothing suspicious about his announcement. She nodded distractedly as she watched Kepa don his hunting talismans and then lift his pack to his shoulder. Without taking her gaze from the hunters as they took up the bear's trail, she called to her son, "Stay close in line." But Nimu had already snatched up his small bow and quiver and dashed away.

They were getting closer to the bear. Kepa could tell this by the freshness of the tracks and by the growing sense of fear in the men. He'd been jogging along in the third position until several minutes ago when Saunuch halted ahead and motioned him forward. Seeing Saunuch's sharp hand movement and his look that said, "Go on ahead, if you dare," Kepa took the lead. Saunuch had then fallen back to the end of the line.

Kepa tried to match the nearly soundless tread of the natives, tried to keep his heart from pounding unevenly. Though he guessed his sense of smell was not as keen as that of his companions, he tested the gentle breeze often for any clue it might give. His eyes swept the thickly timbered area surrounding him and his ears strained for any snap of a twig or rustle of a bough, but nothing stirred. The trees began to thin a little as they approached a small clearing. Perhaps they would soon catch sight of the bear.

When the sound came it was nothing like what they'd been

anticipating. A child's scream erupted from Kepa's left. "He's charging, Kepa! Behind you!"

Kepa spun toward the voice and spotted Nimu releasing an arrow aimed at a monster of fur and teeth that was bearing down on the men. In the instants it took Kepa to load his crossbow, his mind grasped what one glimpse of the bear had revealed: the thickness of its reddish brown pelt, the height of its humped shoulders, the immensity of its roaring head. Each of the five other hunters had leaped toward the nearest tree and lifted his bow. But just as Kepa too was about to fire, Saunuch stepped before the bear and blocked his shot. Five arrows hit the beast straight on but it didn't even alter its stride. Kepa jumped sideways, fighting for a clear shot. He found it only when the bear was ten feet from Saunuch. He fired his iron-tipped dart and saw it strike the bear's huge right shoulder. The bruin stumbled, but only for a moment. Pushing off with its uninjured front leg, taking a second round of arrows from the long bows as it rose to its full eight-foot height, it swiped at Saunuch with such force that the hunter was flung twenty-five feet and crashed into Nimu who had been racing to his father's aid.

As the remaining native hunters released more arrows Kepa loaded and fired again, his bolt piercing the bruin's hide just below its sternum as it spun toward another man. Erupting with a thunderous growl, it clawed at the dart embedded to its fletching. The bear swung its long outstretched claws toward the nearest hunters but the men leaped out of reach. Enraged, snarling, and bleeding from many wounds, the bear fell to its three paws and tried to take a step. Its right shoulder collapsed beneath its weight and it tumbled onto its face. But it swiftly pushed upward again and lifted itself to stand on its hind feet. Before it could advance it was met by five grimly waiting archers. Four of their arrows hit the bear's abdomen and it lurched a step forward. Kepa took careful aim as the bear stood swaying twenty feet in front of him. His finger eased off the trigger release and a bolt burst from his crossbow, piercing the bear's left eye with an abrupt *thunk*. The towering creature fell backward and crashed to the ground.

As the beast lay unmoving, yet guarded by the other hunters, Kepa ran to where Nimu had fallen. Saunuch lay face down on top of the boy. Neither moved. "Please, not the boy," Kepa said in Basque, his throat clogging and his hands beginning to tremble.

Carefully rolling Saunuch to Nimu's side Kepa saw that both were covered with blood. It took only a glance to see that Saunuch's midsection had been sliced open, baring his lower ribs and inner organs, yet he was still breathing. Nimu stirred and opened his eyes as Kepa quickly scanned his small body and found that his right arm lay in an unnatural position at the elbow. The upper bone had chipped, broken away from the lower bone, and torn through the skin. Where the joint had once held the bones together, these two pieces were now three inches apart.

Nimu tried to lift his head, but Kepa said. "Lie quiet, Nimu."

"The great bear?" whispered the child.

"He's dead, my brave boy. Your warning likely saved at least one life, and your arrow was the first to strike him."

"My arrow?"

"Yes, Nimu." Kepa watched the small eyes close and whispered a prayer of gratitude as unconsciousness again took possession of the child.

The other hunters were gathering around them now, taking in the scene. One of them asked, "Will the boy live?" They must have already concluded that Saunuch would surely die from such a ghastly wound.

Kepa did not answer.

He'd sworn never to practice medicine again, never to take the life or health of another into his own bloodied hands. And yet there was no time to send someone for Achaku. There was only one way Saunuch had a chance to survive and one possibility for Nimu to regain the use of his arm, small as those chances were. Kepa stared at Saunuch for a moment that stretched into another. Only a fool would try to save a man who'd meant to see him killed. His gaze returned to Nimu, his young face pale and his breathing shallow. He pictured Achaku's eyes looking down upon her boy.

A gut-deep anguished cry escaped Kepa as he slammed his fist against the ground, startling the men near him.

"Bring me my pack," he ordered angrily. When no one moved, he took a deep breath and said more calmly, "I am a healer among my people. I will need one man to help me."

The youngest of the hunters agreed to assist Kepa and hurried to get his pack. Another man crouched down beside him and said, "Kepa, it was your arrows that killed the great bear. You must be the one to thank him."

Now that his decision had been made, Kepa was impatient to begin. "That can wait."

Concern entered the hunter's voice. "To wait would show disrespect. This mighty bear sacrificed his life for you, for all of us. Such ingratitude could bring much misfortune on our people."

Kepa saw that they would accept no delay. "All right, but someone must build a fire here, and bring water."

Returning to the carcass, Kepa was again awed by the imposing size of the animal on the ground. Following the respectful instructions of the others, Kepa sang a short chant of thanks as he circled the body several times with dancing steps. He then placed a piece of dried meat in the bear's mouth. This rite seemed to satisfy his companions and they allowed him to return to the wounded members of their party.

Still fighting his own fears, Kepa began to work on Saunuch first. With no medicines at hand and no time to search for herbs, he could do nothing more than cleanse the wound, repack the protruding organs into their cavity, and sew Saunuch's muscles and skin closed with thin sinew. The young hunter who'd volunteered to help Kepa proved to be an able assistant despite his inexperience, and the operation was performed with few pauses. Kepa sat back and looked at the rows of stitches across Saunuch's belly, knowing it was probable that the wound would become corrupted and a fever would kill him. Well, Kepa had done what he could.

With tense apprehension he turned his attentions to Nimu. Upon close inspection he saw that the tendons and flesh of the boy's arm were not as badly torn as he'd feared. Although the bone chip was not large, whether the elbow would ever knit itself together and regain its full motion was doubtful. At the first painful pressure, Nimu uttered a small, breathless cry but his eyes remained closed. Thankfully, he did not fully waken even when both men forced the bones back into place, or when the assistant held them tightly while Kepa stitched, or when the mended elbow was bound securely with smoothed sticks and a long leather bandage. At last Kepa sat back and wiped the sweat from his face.

He realized that two of the other hunters had been watching over them. Both nodded at him with approval, but Kepa knew all too well how futile his efforts might prove to be.

One of the hunters spoke up, "We sent Usuy to bring back others to carry our wounded and the great bear. Two travois have been built and his body has been prepared for the journey."

Kepa glanced over and was subtly surprised to see that the bear had not been skinned or butchered. Instead it had somehow been lifted whole and placed face up on a travois much larger than any he'd ever seen. The memory of the bear's ferocity and the present proof of its mass struck him anew. Guessing its weight to be at least eight hundred pounds, he hoped Usuy brought back a good number of men to help drag the heavy conveyance. The hunters' arrows still stuck out of the immense body like oversized porcupine quills, and Kepa caught a glimpse of a wide, decorative strap that someone had tied to its lower jaw.

On the ground beside the bear rested another travois that awaited the wounded. But as another hunter went with Kepa to carry this back to where he'd been tending his patients, he couldn't help thinking that no matter how carefully the bearers tried to pull it, Saunuch would not survive the return trek to the encampment.

Fortunately, nine men soon appeared to help haul their loads along the woodland path. And Achaku walked with them.

When she spotted Nimu on the travois ahead she broke from her place in line and ran to him, her expression rigidly composed until she knelt down beside her son. Her relief at seeing him alive dampened her eyes and caused her fingers to tremble as they touched his face, lightly brushing his cheek to confirm that he was still breathing and warm, and with her. She drew her hand away and lifted the fur that covered him aside. Careful not to disturb the binding, she inspected his injured arm. After covering him again she turned her head toward Kepa, who stood a few feet away, and for a long moment their gazes embraced one another. Neither spoke. Neither needed to.

Steadier now, she removed a cup from her shoulder-pack and filled it with liquid from a small pouch. This she held to Nimu's lips and coaxed him to drink a few swallows. His eyes held hers unsteadily while he drank, then closed as if too heavy to remain open. After resettling the cover, Achaku leaned forward and let her forehead touch that of her sleeping son.

Moving to the other side of the travois, she examined Saunuch's stitches. They were sewn in neat and even rows. Around the red, foot-long lines, the area was already swelling badly. Saunuch's body was warm to her touch with a building fever. Pouring a brew from another pouch into her cup, she managed to get Saunuch to swallow only a few drops before he turned his head away.

When she finished her ministrations she stood up and walked to Kepa. She said, "My heart is so grateful," and her face showed that she knew what it had cost him to try to save them.

He touched her hand briefly, feeling very weary. "We must get them back. Will you watch over them while we travel?"

Without further delay they took their positions.

Against the suggestions of several men, who felt the crossbow hunter should walk proudly beside the great bear, Kepa insisted on taking up one of the poles of the travois that carried Nimu and Saunuch. Glancing back often at the boy, Kepa saw him wake fitfully several times. Whenever a jolt or bump sent a surge of pain through his arm Nimu bit his lip to keep from crying out. Achaku soothed him with her presence, singing softly to the spirits as they walked along.

Bear Feast

12

The heavily burdened travois bearers were still a half-mile from camp when they encountered people who had been worriedly awaiting their arrival. Mihikin was among the first to spot them. While the old man hurried directly to Kepa and Achaku, a great chorus of awed exclamations arose around the hunting party as more and more natives gathered to catch a glimpse of what lay on the large travois. The noise grew ever louder as they entered the encampment and lowered the mighty bear to the ground. Voices were already rising to proclaim the courage of the hunters as Achaku carried her son away and Kepa helped Saunuch's wives move him to his wigwam. Mihikin then accompanied Kepa to their own tent.

By the time they entered, Achaku had already settled Nimu beside a warm fire. Liachita hovered close, her old eyes fearful for the child. Kepa sat down beside Nimu and watched his face, his breathing. To his worried family, he said. "We did not know he had followed us. To be so small and to follow a group of men hunting that creature… As the bear charged us from behind, Nimu shouted a warning and we were able to fire at the beast before he attacked." He shook his head, still amazed. "I have never heard of such courage in one this young."

They had already heard the account, passed along to them from the messenger sent to camp to gather men, but from Kepa's lips it brought an even deeper sense of pride.

Achaku approached him, knelt down, wrapped her arms around his neck, and pressed her cheek against his. He folded her in his embrace and just breathed in and out.

After a few moments, Mihikin said, "Kepa, there is much that must be done now that you have killed this bear."

"Many of us killed it, and Nimu's arrow was the first to strike it."

"Was it not your arrow that pierced its brain? All who helped you will be honored for their bravery and skill, but you must accept your role. The bear surrendered himself to you."

Weariness crept into his voice. "What must I do?"

"I will show you. Come with me. Wait, you will need your mallet."

As they left their lodging and headed toward the gathering crowd, Mihikin gave hurried instructions to the bear hunter along the way. Near the far edge of the camp Kepa noticed a dozen women completing the construction of a wigwam at least five-times the normal size. This, Mihikin explained, was for the feast during which Kepa was to act as host. Listening to Mihikin's list of essential behaviors and duties, Kepa deeply wished this role had fallen to someone else.

"Most of the clan will be invited to the feast," Mihikin said.

"Why not everyone?"

"Unmarried young women and married women who have not borne children must never look directly upon Short Tail. They are not yet worthy of so great an honor. To do so might harm their health or the health of others." It was not until then that Kepa realized that most of the younger women were nowhere in sight.

The people parted as Mihikin led him to the bear, where the other hunters stood protectively over their prize. Kepa momentarily struggled with the thought that many in his homeland would consider the rites he was about to perform to be acts of sacrilege. But here and now, he had little choice.

As Mihikin had directed him to do, Kepa approached the massive head and laid his hand on the fletching end of his arrow protruding from the eye socket. In a loud, clear voice, he said, "I thank Grandfather Bear for placing himself within reach of my arrow and the arrows of the other hunters who faced his might. We will show him our gratitude by honoring him in an abundant feast."

A chorus of salutations went up around him.

Taking a wide strip of leather from Mihikin's outstretched hand, he wrapped it around the bruin's head as a blindfold. He then unsheathed his knife and carefully sliced off the bear's right ear, and then the left. Holding them up, he deviated from the custom of keeping these trophies by announcing, "I will give one of these ears and a claw to young Nimu, who became a brave hunter today, and the same to Saunuch because he led the hunt."

Mihikin's craggy features lit with surprise and pleasure as shouts of approval at such generosity burst from the onlookers.

Mutterings of praise were still dying away as Kepa and the other men and boys stepped back, temporarily surrendering the bear to the mothers in the crowd. The honorary name given to the bear by Mihikin became more meaningful when Kepa saw how diligently the women skinned around the tail and kept it attached to the rest of the hide. Even this appendage evidently had some significance to these people.

After the wide, cumbersome fur was carefully pulled free of the carcass and taken away to prepare for tanning, the women lowered their eyes and left the area. Now the men set their coats aside and stepped in to butcher the remains, and during this activity, too, there were rituals to be observed. Kepa was very glad to have Mihikin beside him, subtly tutoring him in the proper ways of handling the meat.

While they worked, other men stood guard in a circle around them. Any dog that approached the carcass felt the sharp whack of a wooden lance shaft against its side or rump.

When all was ready every piece of gut, bone, tendon, and flesh was carried into the feast wigwam. The head was set on its side upon flat stones before Kepa. He glanced at Mihikin and received a nod, then pulled the mallet from his belt. Kneeling beside the head and bracing it firmly against the stones, he swung two well-aimed blows and knocked one canine tooth free of the upper jaw. He handed the tooth, well over two inches in length, to Mihikin and went to work on the other three canines. When all four had been extracted Kepa accepted them back from Mihikin, wiped their yellowed surfaces clean with a rag, and placed them in his hunting pouch.

"Now," he said, "I ask each of the hunters who shared in this kill to take a tooth and a claw."

The men did not hesitate. An unspoken understanding seemed to dictate who stepped forward first and it did not take long for the trophies to be reverently claimed. When Kepa showed no inclination of taking possession of the remaining teeth or claws, they were removed by the other hunters and presented to him.

At a signal from someone outside, Achaku entered and helped

oversee the frying of the guts and the stewing of the meat, but even she was not allowed to touch the sacred head. Wapitikwa had the honor of mounting the skull, still bearing its fur, on a spit and setting it to roast above the coals. Bones such as the patella, scapula, and leg bones were cleaned and set aside. Fragments that would not be used for tools were placed in one of the two fires set several feet apart in the center of the lodge.

Finally, there was no more that needed to be done but await the coming of the meal. Looking down at his bloody arms, Kepa suddenly felt very tired. He left the lodge and walked slowly to the river, his head lowered to discourage conversation with villagers wishing to speak of his heroic feat. When he reached the riverbank he stood still and stared at a group of rounded rocks that showed above the surface, the water churning around their bases. Watching the swirling liquid as it swept the rocks with one continuous flow, he thought of how the rocks would not move despite their constant washing. He had proven himself to be less steadfast in his determination. He had moved.

With all that had happened during the last few hours, Kepa's present weariness only enhanced his sense of having lost the fragile balance he'd clung to since he'd thrown aside his practice of medicine. Today he'd laid himself open for that crushing loss and pain again. He'd done it for Nimu, and yet his arm might never heal. If the boy could never hunt, never provide for a family, he might someday wish that Kepa had left him to die where he'd fallen.

Kepa did not want this responsibility for saving others, this fear of losing someone he cared about. And once he'd treated someone in need, he began to care about even the least admirable of his patients. All too often they couldn't be saved. The chances of Saunuch recovering were slim indeed. Perhaps it would be better if he didn't.

Knowing he was being unfair and cursing his weakness, he couldn't suppress a building resentment. He let his gaze fall.

The sloping river's edge was fringed with ice that glittered up at him in the fading light. The waters refrain of cascading, rushing, gurgling sounds called to his battered spirit in healing tones. He took off his coat and shirt, knelt beside the bank, and plunged his hands into the sandy riverbed. The water was so cold that his fingers were numb in moments. Using the sand as his only soap, he scrubbed and rinsed the blood and sweat away. His shoulders were shivering as he squeezed the water from his dark, shoulder-length hair. He rinsed the dirt and blood from the sleeves of his shirt, hurriedly put it and his coat back on, and headed toward Saunuch's lodge.

Inside, he found Achaku sitting beside her former husband, her eyes closed, her arms outstretched over his body, chanting in rhythm to a leather rattle in her hand. When she finished, Kepa moved beside her and removed the bandage to inspect Saunuch's wound. He then laid his hand over Saunuch's heart, measuring its strength and tempo, and touched his sweaty cheek to judge his warmth. His fever was raging.

For a while Kepa discussed with Achaku the medicinal herbs that might reduce the fever. She agreed to try the remedies he suggested.

During his visit, Saunuch's wives and children had watched Kepa closely, silently. When he glanced over at them he could see the fear and sadness on their faces. At a small exclamation from a wife who'd been watching Saunuch, Kepa turned back to him. Saunuch's eyes were half-open and resting intently on Achaku.

Giving himself a mental nudge, Kepa took the bear's ear from his pouch and pressed it into Saunuch's hand. "This is yours," he said. "You must live to tell the story of how you led the hunt for this great bear."

Weakly, Saunuch lifted it closer to his face for a moment before letting his hand drop to his coverings. His fevered eyes searched Kepa's briefly, flickered back to Achaku, and then closed. Sleep soon overtook him, relaxing his tortured body. His hand alone seemed to reject its need for rest. It continued to clutch the large, furred ear.

The succulent smell of roasted grizzly met Kepa before he'd drawn within fifty feet of the feast lodge. He hadn't eaten since that morning and his stomach rolled and grumbled. Beside him walked Nimu, his upright bearing that of a proper hunter despite his flushed cheeks and bandaged arm. Hung upon a red leather thong to rest against the front of his shirt, a bear claw shifted slightly from side to side with every step the boy took. In the short time available to her, Achaku also had managed to string the other claws and teeth into a fanned array, creating the necklace that spread across Kepa's expansive chest.

Wapitikwa and Mihikin entered the tent just ahead of Kepa, and the rest of the men arranged themselves according to their clan rank, which seemed to be based primarily on age. They sat in a large oval around the two fires. Tonight Kepa was seated in a place of distinction between Wapitikwa and Mihikin. Then the mothers and male children entered quietly and filled in the areas behind the men.

The roasted bear's skull had been placed on a birch-bark platter set just toward the center of the lodge within the stones circling the fire to his left. It faced the fire at the other end of the wigwam. Even with its charred fur and empty eye sockets, its size and fearsome shape were still enough to inspire admiration.

Once everyone was settled in, Wapitikwa cleared his throat roughly and gave a short speech of praise to the bear as his audience listened with rapt attention. Afterward he invited the hunters to rise to their feet and begin dancing. Kepa stood up along with the others, hoping his apprehension was adequately concealed. He had no idea what the penalty might be if he unknowingly disgraced this pagan ritual, but he didn't intend to find out. With Wapitikwa commanding their rhythm through a drum and his fluctuating voice, the dancers began to take shuffling, bobbing steps in a line that snaked into a figure eight around the two fires. Their shadows paraded as wavering black ghosts that danced around the wall and over the heads of the watchers and the sightless bear.

Kepa followed the simple pattern, treading easily enough and, once he'd deduced that this was as complicated as the dance was going to become, he began to relax a little. When Wapitikwa's song ended Kepa was encouraged by a nod from the chief to chant his own tale. Creating such a melody was not a serious challenge since only a few notes were needed to imitate the customs of the clan, and Kepa was able to improvise a few lyrics about Nimu's courage during the bear hunt as he danced. He repeated his verse several times, sensing that his words were clumsy and deficient, but from the corner of his eye he caught a glimpse of the boy's face and he knew the song had done what he'd intended.

As soon as Kepa's voice stilled, another hunter lifted his voice in song, and then another until each of the bear hunters had had his turn. Then, other men within the lodge stood and joined in the dance, each encouraged to sing his sacred strains. At last Wapitikwa struck his drum with a final loud boom, signaling the men to be seated once more.

Mihikin leaned over one of the huge, meat-filled, wooden bowls near the fire, picked up a spoon made from the shoulder blade of the bear they'd killed, and ladled bear fat into a smaller vessel. When nearly a gallon of grease had been scooped into the bowl it was passed to Kepa. Mihikin had told him earlier that eating large portions during the feast would show respect for the bear, yet even Kepa's empty stomach could not rush his hand as he lifted the spoon to his lips. The heat of the thick liquid alone was comforting and, to his relief, the taste was pleasant despite its richness. He smiled and those around him muttered and chuckled in satisfaction. Twice more he drained the spoon, and then handed the bowl to Wapitikwa.

The bowl of grease circled the men three times before Mihikin set it down, almost empty, and lifted the platter carrying the bear's head. He pulled back the skin and placed the meaty skull before Kepa. Having learned from Mihikin that anyone who dared to use a knife on the bear meat would commit a grave irreverence, Kepa used his fingers to pull a chunk of meat from the cheek and place it in his mouth. Its flavor rivaled the taste of roasted pork, and he needed no encouragement to take another large piece before passing the head along. As did the bowl, the platter circumnavigated the ring of men several times. The single exception to the custom restricting the consumption of the bear's head to the men was allowed when Mihikin ceremoniously gave a small portion of the meat to Nimu. He chewed his small bite with the greatest of humility and deference.

All four of the cooked bear's paws were presented to the oldest men of the group, and then a long fried sausage, made of intestine casings filled with fat, blood, and berries, made its appearance. Each man tore off whatever length was to his liking and ate it with great relish. As host, Kepa was obligated to take a longer portion than he would have done out of hunger or a craving for the flavor. So, although his stomach was already beginning to protest under the strain of the feasting, he managed to eat an eight-inch length of the sausage.

Yet there was a great deal more to come. Several bark trays, now piled high with steaming meat, were passed from man to man. From separate platters the women and children were at last offered their first opportunity to share in the bounty, but this included only the meat from the rear portion of the bear.

As the evening wore on and Kepa's belly stretched to previously unknown dimensions, his weariness grew heavier and heavier. Finally, he leaned toward Mihikin and asked, "When does the feasting end?"

Mihikin looked at him with mild amusement, then seemed to realize he'd omitted this detail in his explanation of the celebration. He smiled tolerantly and said, "It ends when the food is gone."

With a silent groan Kepa glanced at the piles of meat before him.

"If you are tired, sleep," said Mihikin. "When you awaken, eat."

Sleep? Kepa thought. *Sleep where?*

Then he spotted several feasters already curled up on the bough-covered ground, soundly sleeping despite the people talking and milling around them.

He looked over his shoulder in search of Achaku. Her soft smile reached out and touched him with the warmth of a caress. Before he could respond Nimu's head bumped against his shoulder, nodding in sleep. With care not to jostle his damaged arm, Kepa picked the boy up and carried him to his mother. Achaku took him in her arms and left the lodge with Liachita following close behind her.

Two Healers

13

After a day and a half of concentrated eating, the last morsel of the bear meat had finally been swallowed and the guests began to leave the feast lodge in the late morning. Others had drifted in and out as duties required, but it had been acceptable for Kepa to leave only to relieve pressing calls of nature and to check briefly on Nimu and Saunuch. On one trip to his wigwam, he'd managed to take a covered bowl of bear grease that he hoped to render into lamp oil.

Now, anxious to check on Nimu, Kepa hurried outside and welcomed the bright sun and cold air that met him. He closed his eyes and stood for a moment, breathing deeply to help clear his food-induced sluggishness. He strode forward, reveling in the stretch and pull of his muscles.

Achaku met him before he had reached their lodge. She had been excused from much of the feasting to tend to the injured. When she was close enough to hear him, Kepa asked, "How is Nimu?"

"Restless and in pain." She smiled ruefully. "He does not like the taste of the medicine that would make him more comfortable."

"I will talk to him." Then, expecting a negative response, he asked, "Is his father still alive?"

"Yes. He is very weak."

"I will go to him but not until I have seen Nimu."

She nodded and walked quietly beside him, their breath puffing clouds and their feet crunching small ice crystals along the path.

When they reached the wigwam Nimu brightened at the sight of Kepa, and he held very still while his arm was examined. With Achaku and Liachita looking on, Kepa finished his inspection and, keeping his face stern, said, "You must drink your mother's brews, young man, if you wish to get well."

Nimu's face fell a little but as Kepa loomed over him and watched intently, the boy emptied an entire cup of medicine. Kepa had to hide his empathy as Nimu's eyes squinted and his nose pinched at the pungency of the taste.

After the last gulping swallow, Nimu said, "Now I am well enough to go set muskrat snares with my friends."

Kepa noticed that the boy was carefully avoiding his mother's eyes. "Not yet, Nimu." Despite the crestfallen slump in his young patient's shoulders, Kepa felt he had to add, "If you do not follow the instruction of your mother and me, your arm may not mend well. It may be crooked and weak your whole life. What then? Your hunting would suffer greatly." Kepa feared this ultimate outcome even with the best efforts of all three of them, but he didn't want Nimu's youth and indomitable nature to reduce his small chances.

"Obeying a healer takes much courage and patience, Nimu. One who dreams and has hunted a great bear surely has such gifts."

"I will try."

"Then lie quietly while your mother and I go to visit your father."

"I wish to ask you something, about my father."

"Yes, Nimu," said Kepa, already rising.

"Will he die soon?"

Kepa had taken a step, but this question stopped him. He faced the boy again and squatted down near him. "It is likely that he will."

The boy's lower lip quivered for just a moment, but then firmly pressed against his upper lip. "Then my arm must heal. I must be able to hunt for my family."

The unspoken words, "when you go away," hung in the smoky air.

"We will do what we can," said Kepa, "and you will work harder than anyone to heal your arm when the time comes."

Liachita stayed with Nimu as the two healers left and made their way to Saunuch's wigwam.

The sour, fetid smell of infection assaulted them at the entrance. Saunuch did not stir as Kepa lifted aside the blankets and clothing and stared at the wound. A swelling the size of his open hand near the end of the longest row of stitches seemed to rise up at him. When Kepa touched the purplish-yellow bulge, Saunuch moaned. His skin was very warm under Kepa's gently probing fingers.

Sitting back and taking in the gauntness of Saunuch's crimson cheeks, Kepa asked Achaku, "When did he last eat?"

"He has refused everything but a little water."

Kepa soundlessly wondered, *How can he still be breathing?* He pointed to the infected region and said, "I must drain the swelling and wash the sickness out."

One of Saunuch's wives drew near with her head bowed and said to Kepa, "My husband has told me that he no longer wants healers to come to him. He has decided to travel the star trail."

Kepa's gaze circled the wigwam and took in the haunted faces staring back at him. Looking at the woman who had spoken, he said, "*I* have not decided that he should."

"But, if he—"

"Woman, do not tell me again what this man wants! I do not want to be here trying to save him, but I am! Now, all of you, leave us. Send four men here to hold him down."

As they hurriedly gathered up a few of their belongings and departed, Kepa said more calmly to Achaku, "I will need a poultice to cover the wound when I have finished."

Very weakly, a deep male voice reached them, saying, "Do not shout at my women, Bear Hunter."

Kepa quickly leaned over Saunuch. To his astonishment, the patient's mouth managed to cast the shadow of an ironic smile just before he closed his eyes again.

Well, damn him, thought Kepa. *Damn him!* "I will stop shouting," he said, "if you will eat."

"Why should I eat?" Saunuch asked in a whisper. "Why will you not let me die?"

"You must get strong again to care for your wives and children."

Saunuch's right eye cracked open and pinned Kepa with intensity. "You knew. You knew I wanted the bear to kill you."

Kepa gave no confirmation. "What we want is often taken beyond our reach."

"Beyond our reach. Yes. The strength of my spirit failed me on that hunt."

"Your strength will also be tested today, this time at the point of my knife. Do not let it fail you again."

Again the hint of a mocking smile flickered across Saunuch's face. "Use your magic knife, then. Cut out this illness if you can. I will not resist your efforts."

Together Kepa and Achaku chose the most promising herbs, and these were boiling in water by the time the four men entered the wigwam. One was Mihikin.

Kepa motioned them toward Saunuch's arms or legs, then drew his knife and thrust it into the coals of the fire. At Kepa's nod the men took hold of Saunuch. His eyes opened and scanned the faces around him. "No," he tried to say forcefully. "I do not need them."

"Hold him," Kepa ordered. He grabbed the handle of his knife and touched the tip to the distended skin. It ruptured immediately and began spilling blood-splotched puss. Wasting no time, Kepa pierced the rim of the opposite side of the mound. Saunuch's body tensed at each puncture and his lips clamped tightly, but he neither cried out nor struggled. Noting this, Kepa honored Saunuch's restraint by signaling the men to release their grips. But the four assistants stayed close by as Kepa pressed from the center of the swellings outward toward the incisions, working to empty the bulge fully. The guts beneath his fingers felt appropriately firm and properly positioned. Perhaps the corruption had not spread to deep inside.

Achaku knelt quietly beside him, wiping away the drainage as it trickled from the incisions.

When Kepa could draw no more from his cuts, he turned to ask her for the poultice. She was already holding it toward him on two outstretched sticks. It had cooled just enough for him to lift it and place in on Saunuch's belly. A slight wince was his only reaction. Kepa covered the poultice with another piece of leather, then lowered Saunuch's shirt and replaced his coverings. With words of thanks, Kepa told the four men that their help was no longer needed, and they left the wigwam with the exception of Mihikin.

"Saunuch," Kepa said, "you must eat now."

Saunuch looked intently at him and said, "Send back my women. They will feed me."

My women, thought Kepa. Achaku sat right beside Saunuch, and she did not seem to have been included in this group. Kepa wondered if, with this pronouncement, Saunuch was releasing any claim to her. It seemed that Mihikin had drawn the same conclusion when he cast a brief look of relief toward Achaku.

"I will send them to you," Kepa said, and then he, Achaku, and Mihikin left the wigwam.

Now Kepa wanted to sleep for two days. He had rested little during the feasting and his body and mind were growing heavy with fatigue.

As he often did, Mihikin seemed to be reading his intentions. "Kepa," said the old man, sounding weary as well. "After a bear feast there is one last duty that must performed by the hunter."

Knowing it was pointless to delay whatever Mihikin had in mind, Kepa followed him back to the feast lodge and Achaku separated from them. Once inside the huge wigwam the men meticulously cleaned and dried the bear's skull and painted red designs around the eye sockets and across its brow ridge with ochre. Mihikin directed him to a place that he'd previously prepared at the northern edge of camp, where they secured the skull to the end of a long pole and firmly anchored the other end into the ground. After stepping back, Kepa looked up and eyed the decorated skull on its perch.

"It is done," said Mihikin, brushing dirt from his hands. "From that high place, Short Tail will enjoy the changes of the seasons and all that occurs around him."

It might have been caused by the exhaustion, but Kepa was suddenly struck with the notion that his brother was looking down from the heavens and chuckling at him. And why should Gotzon not laugh? Here Kepa was, a Christian whaler, devoting all this careful attention to the bones of a dead animal. There seemed to be no end to these pagan customs, and no way to avoid them.

"This will be a holy place now," Mihikin was saying. "We will stand here again when the warm season comes."

On the other hand, Kepa's exhausted mind continued ruminating, his own belief that humans were the only creatures to possess spirits would seem just as incomprehensible to Mihikin as the need to placate a dead bear.

"The clan will be separating tomorrow," Mihikin informed him.

"Separating? Why?"

"Each family group will collect their toboggans from the cave that is a four-day journey from here. Then they will travel to their usual hunting grounds. The smaller groups can stay in one place longer since fewer animals are being hunted."

"What about Saunuch?"

"His wives and children, the families of his two sisters, and we will remain here until he is stronger. Or until he leaves us to travel the star road." He looked up one last time at the bear skull with satisfaction and took in a deep breath. "Come now," he said as he laid a hand on Kepa's arm, "I smell snow in the air. We must finish your snowshoes."

They began walking, Kepa keeping a slow pace to match the unhurried gait of Mihikin's stiffer joints. Feeling the chill slide down his spine, Kepa pulled his coat closer around his neck and wondered how he was going to survive the much more severe temperatures of the next few months. Mihikin, wearing no coat at all, didn't seem to feel the cold.

"Tell me, Kepa, does it snow a great deal in your land?"

"Seldom, and then very little."

"How strange," Mihikin murmured sympathetically.

Three days passed and still Saunuch did not die. Although Kepa repeatedly treated his infection, there were many hours that demanded little of his time. So he began to learn Achaku's many remedies and to collect plants from which he could create new ones. He also grew determined to impart much of his medical knowledge on to her, which she seemed only too happy to accept. She watched his demonstrations carefully and listened to every word he offered in instruction. Sometimes she minutely questioned the details he offered, and she often asked him to illustrate his techniques on a tanned hide so she would have them for the future.

With Kepa taking on the medical aspect of Saunuch's care, her treatment of him shifted to the spiritual side. Every day she sang and danced and played her drum over Saunuch, but her gods didn't seem to notice. She could see no improvement in his health.

Kepa did not share with her his belief that Saunuch's misery would linger until his death ended it. Also, he was beginning to fear that Nimu's arm was healing crookedly, yet he struggled with the decision to break and reset it.

On the fourth morning after the feast Kepa awakened to discover a foot of snow surrounding the wigwam and pushing in against its base. He opened the edge of the door and saw that the world had become alien to him. Peering out at the whiteness, he thought how different this land was from his home, and longed to be there. He'd have given a fortune at that moment to purchase one day in his cousin's house, warm and safe, surrounded by beloved Urdin and his family, sharing good wine and the food he'd savored since childhood. To lift a cup and trade half-true stories like cousins should, that would be worth treasures uncountable.

For a while he watched the snowfall as the rising wind built it into taller drifts around the wigwam. As they rose higher, the mounds of white seemed to close him in, trapping him. His old grief stirred to life. He let the flap fall closed and moved to the fire, keeping his face blank. When Mihikin left to check for animal tracks, Kepa did not go with him.

A ring of water from melting snow began to form at the rim of the wigwam and seep inward, causing Kepa and the others to shift nearer to the lodge's center. Water dripped from the smoke hole overhead, occasionally hissing as it hit the embers below.

Nimu's reaction to the snow was far different from Kepa's. The boy fidgeted and paced until he asked Achaku for the third time, "Why must I stay inside?"

"Nimu," she said, "you know your arm needs more time to heal."

In a rare show of petulance, he blurted, "But it may never work as it should! I don't want any more healing! I want to snowshoe! I am going out!"

Kepa flung aside the pouches of herbs he'd been sorting through and snapped, "Nimu! That's enough!"

Nimu halted halfway to the door.

"You heard your mother, now come here and let me look at your arm," Kepa snapped. Achaku and Liachita were staring at him uneasily, but when Nimu hesitated he ordered again, "Come here."

Nimu walked to him slowly, apprehensively. When Kepa reached out to Nimu, the boy pulled back slightly. This small movement struck Kepa like a slap. He suddenly recognized Nimu's fear, his own anger, and mentally shrank from both. *My God, what am I doing?*

He let his hand fall and shifted back, lowering his gaze and muttering, "No, no, let it be." After a moment he dropped his head to his hands and tried to breathe evenly.

He did not see Achaku approach her son and wrap an arm around his shoulders. He didn't see her head motion slightly toward Kepa as she spoke to Nimu. Yet with his eyes closed and his head down he heard her words. "Sometimes, when a wound seems too severe to ever heal, help must come from another. It is our duty to help those who have not found a way to cure themselves."

Nimu looked up at his mother with large, perceptive eyes, understanding her meaning. He went to Kepa and sat so close that their knees bumped. Gently, he laid his hand on Kepa's thigh.

Kepa felt the touch of the small hand, felt it all the way to his soul, and for a moment his throat refused to work. "I am sorry, Nimu," he said, lifting his face at last.

"Will you change my bandage, Kepa?"

The pressure of tears stung the edges of Kepa's eyes, and again he waited for the tightness in his throat to ease before speaking. He took in a breath. "Listen, Nimu. The wind has stopped. Perhaps we can go for a short walk." He glanced at Achaku and saw her nod. "Then we will tend to your arm."

Kepa gathered up the snowshoes, dressed in his warmest clothing, and dug the snow away from the door. Soon the wigwam flap fell closed behind him and Nimu.

Bending over a pair of Mihikin's worn moccasins with a bone needle in her hand, Liachita said softly to Achaku, "I have never known a wiser woman."

Skyward Lights

14

Snowflakes fell lightly from the windless sky, dancing cheerily as they descended. Kepa's hood and shoulders were dusted with them. This relatively mild evening would likely bring an end to the storm that had settled another thick blanket of white over the world.

During their trek toward the cave he was discovering many of the countless personalities of snow and was beginning to acquire a grudging respect for its dominating beauty. He'd become so comfortable walking in snowshoes that he often broke the trail for the four families, as he was doing now. Because of his exertions his coat hung open in the front, brushing the tops of his knees as they lifted and fell with every step into ten-inches of new snow. Each exhale puffed from his mouth in a wisp that dissipated over his shoulder as he marched. Tracker walked just behind him, a position the dog would take up for a while before roaming back to check on Mihikin. From behind, Kepa could hear the shuffling of twenty-four sets of snowshoes, short phrases of soft conversation, the snow-muffled hissing of the travois poles, and the occasional sneeze or growl of a dog.

Despite being told that the first heavy snowfall always enticed bears into a season-long sleep, his memories of the grizzly attack were still vivid enough to prompt him to repeatedly scan the area surrounding them. He kept his watch vigilant and his crossbow slung over his shoulder within easy reach.

Saunuch, exhibiting a newly found determination to remain among them, had gradually gained enough strength to stumble along in the middle of the line for an hour or so each day. No amount of coaxing, reasoning, or demanding could dissuade the invalid from these daily ploddings. Someone, frequently Kepa, would then have to fall back and help strap Saunuch's thin and exhausted frame back onto a travois. Frustrated but powerless, short of knocking the stubborn native unconscious, Kepa watched out for him with a grudging eye, convinced that Saunuch's hiking could well use up whatever vigor he had managed to store.

At least it would be easier to haul him, and their less troublesome loads, after they'd reached the cache of toboggans. That morning Mihikin had told Kepa that they should arrive at the cave well before dark. The sun was already sinking behind the treetops ahead of them so it shouldn't be much farther.

He glanced back, caught Nimu's eye, and smiled to encourage him on. The boy waved back with his good arm but his expression and his tread were heavy with exhaustion. His broken arm was slung to his chest beneath his coat, making the balance on snowshoes a challenge, yet he'd insisted on walking the entire way. At just six years old the boy was a better patient than most men his physician had encountered. Still, Kepa had decided not to reset the break in Nimu's elbow and now he could only hope that it might one day fire a bow again.

"Kepa," Mihikin called out from behind, "the cave is just ahead."

Relieved at this news, Kepa halted and lifted his gaze to examine the high ridge before him. Unable to see any large indenture or cavity, he let one of Saunuch's brothers-in-law take the lead.

The cache turned out to be well concealed. It was reached by a broad but steeply winding path that ran halfway up the incline. Small trees had been cut and woven across the entrance and the snow had completed an effective screen. When the entrance had been cleared and their torches lit, Kepa entered a space much more vast and comfortable than he'd anticipated. It was large enough for all of them, their belongings, and their dogs, with a good deal of room to spare, saving them from having to erect wigwams in the dusky light.

While the men inspected their long-stored toboggans for any damage, the women lit fires in stone rings they'd used during countless visits to chase away the chill and cook their dinners. Kepa and Mihikin joined several others as they pulled toboggans outside, cut fresh young branches, hauled them back into the cave, and arranged them on the stone floor around their family's chosen hearth. They then covered the sweetly aromatic limbs with a layer of furs.

There was little privacy inside the cave but tonight most of its inhabitants didn't seem to mind. Relieved at their safe arrival and the absence of damage to their cache, the mood during their hot meal grew almost festive. Laughter rose from around the fires and children ate hurriedly before racing off to explore the cave's recesses, their dogs leaping and prancing about them. Nimu watched his half-siblings and cousins wistfully but did not join in their play. He appeared content enough to sit beside Kepa and pet Tracker's back as the dog pressed close against his small leg.

Kepa's body seemed to be adjusting to the low temperatures over the last few days, but he was still the first one to reach for his coat or a fur robe. As Mihikin began to discuss the finer points of toboggan construction with him, Kepa was the only person in the cave still wearing his coat. He gradually shifted a little closer to the fire while he listened, hoping its warmth would enable him to shed the heavy outer garment before long. He motioned Nimu to follow him as he edged forward and the boy willingly complied.

"When we reach our winter camp," Mihikin was saying, "I will help you make a toboggan of your own. We can also build a heavier sled for hauling game."

Kepa nodded in appreciation.

They were interrupted by the approach of the eldest of Saunuch's wives. She knelt down next to Achaku but spoke to Kepa. "Bear Hunter, my husband asks for you." When Achaku stood along with Kepa, the woman held out her hand and said, "No, Achaku. He wants only Kepa."

When Kepa reached Saunuch's hearth the women and children moved to the farther reaches of their fire's light, obviously having been ordered to give them privacy. Saunuch lay on his furs, his head propped up upon a rolled one. He motioned Kepa to sit close beside him.

"Are you in pain?"

"I am dying."

"How do you know this, Saunuch?"

"My gut stopped working days ago. Soon the pressure will kill me."

Kepa thought for a moment then reached into his medicine pouch, but Saunuch stilled him. "No. No more remedies. That is not why I called for you." He tried to hide a sudden grimace but failed. His voice lowered and he said, "When I die someone must care for my family." He was scrutinizing Kepa, waiting for a reaction.

"Which of your sisters' husbands—"

In a sharp hiss Saunuch said, "One is a fool and the other is an unlucky hunter. It must not be one of them. My family might starve." Saunuch's gaze that gripped Kepa was somehow both commanding and beseeching.

Kepa balked, astounded at what he suspected was coming. "Your people would never let a woman or child go hungry. The clan has many good hunters."

"None like you, none with your weapons, your power."

"Saunuch," Kepa said, still only half believing this demand, "I will not be here. I have made no secret of my intentions."

"Change your intentions! When I die my people will need you!"

Kepa firmed his jaw. "No."

Saunuch scowled fiercely in growing anger. "What kind of man would refuse such a request?"

"Listen, you stubborn savage. If you had intended to die you should have done so the day the bear attacked and saved us a lot of trouble. You will not die, not if I can help it! Do you hear?"

Saunuch merely glared back at him.

"Now," said Kepa as he pulled some herbs from his pouch, "I will make something that will awaken your bowels. They will be flowing by morning."

Saunuch snapped, "I will be dead by morning."

Before leaving his patient Kepa made certain that he'd drunk every drop of his concoction, to which he'd added just a little more purgative than might have been necessary.

Before dawn of the next day Saunuch rolled groaning from his furs and left the cave at a trot. When Kepa crossed his path soon afterward, Saunuch appeared much less stooped and pinch-faced than he had for some time. He stalked up to Kepa and accosted him with, "I should cut out your heart for giving me that poison. My anus is still on fire."

Unable to stop himself, Kepa grinned. "That means it worked perfectly."

To this, Saunuch found no response so he turned and paced away in measured steps.

With the snow-depth mounting Kepa knew they could not linger in the cave but he wished they could have enjoyed its solid, dry walls for a few more days. People were already beginning to load the toboggans, however, so he headed toward his hearth to help get their things in order. Achaku was tying up the last of their bundles but none of these had yet been lifted onto the sled. Mihikin and Nimu had their heads together and cast him a conspiratorial glance as Kepa drew nearer.

"Kepa," said Mihikin, "since you had not seen a toboggan before yesterday, you have never ridden one."

Suspicion sparked to life in Kepa's mind. "Ride one? I thought they were used for hauling."

"Not just for hauling," Nimu said. "They are good for sport as well. We race them at the clan gatherings."

"I see."

The boy asked hopefully, "Would you like to try it?"

Hesitating, Kepa glanced around. "Everyone is working. I should help."

One of Nimu's uncles overheard this and said a little too big-heartedly, "Go ahead, Kepa. We are in no hurry."

Standing with a robe folded over her arm, Achaku cast him a reassuring smile.

"I will ride a toboggan if Achaku rides with me."

Encouraging chatter and laughter gathered around them both as all work came to a standstill. Mihikin's toboggan was carried to the mouth of the cave and slid to the lip of the cliff. Nimu's uncle took the hauling rope and waved Kepa and Achaku forward.

Staring down at the aggressive slope below the entrance, Kepa began to have second thoughts but the crowd kept nudging them toward the toboggan. Even Achaku, though she was still smiling at his side, seemed to hesitate.

Saunuch shouted tauntingly from the back of the group, "Go on, Bear Hunter, go on."

"Wait now. Wait," Kepa said, intending to learn how the sled was controlled. But hands pushed him the last few steps, his legs straddled the sled, and his rump plopped down upon its wooden base. When the sled shifted beneath him he jerked his feet forward and planted his heels firmly in the snow to keep the toboggan still. He held the sled in place and cast an eye at the terrain below as Achaku nimbly seated herself in front of him. She gathered up the hauling rope tied to the head of the sled, and told him, "Hold this."

Wrapping his arms around her and grabbing the rope, he asked quickly, "How do you steer? Look at the trees on both sides of the—whoaaoo!"

A high screech from Achaku joined his yell as the sled was shoved forcefully from behind, leaped over the rim of the hill, and careened downward. Whoops and hollers followed after them from above as the toboggan gained speed.

A spray of snow shot skyward on both sides as Kepa's hands clutched the rope and his elbows squeezed Achaku's arms. Squinting to see through the flying snow and bracing his feet against the curled front of the sled, he felt the pounding in his chest. He let loose a laugh of pure exhilaration. They were racing, racing over the steep blanket of white. Before that moment Kepa had not imagined such a thrilling benefit from the white stuff that had caused him such discomfort.

Suddenly his grin froze and eyes widened as he realized how fast they were approaching the bottom of the hill, how quickly the opening in the trees was narrowing. They were too far to the left and drifting farther as they sped downward. Working on instinct, he leaned to the right and pulled on the rope but almost overturned the sled. He tried to slow the sled with his heels but it was like trying to anchor a ship in a gale. Achaku was tugging on the rope and shouting something but he couldn't catch her words.

They met the bottom of the hill at a breakneck speed that slowed very little, slashed by a bush and through the tree line. Kepa jerked Achaku backward to avoid a low-hanging branch. They managed to steer the slowing sled away from the next two trees but the third loomed too quick and broad to avoid. The toboggan crashed into the heavy trunk, throwing its riders in opposite directions.

Stunned for a moment, his eyes seeing sparkling lights, Kepa struggled to free himself from the deep snow and called out, "Achaku!" His eyes cleared as he frantically scanned the snow. There! She had landed face down and was weakly trying to lift herself. She was trembling, perhaps badly injured.

Kepa clawed and crawled his way over to her, calling her name. Gasping, he gently took hold of her shoulders and slowly turned her over. "Achaku, are you hurt?"

She was laughing so hard she couldn't speak. Laughing! He fell back in the snow and lay there, too relieved to move. After a moment he said, "Woman, you nearly scared the life out of me."

Trying to control herself, Achaku pulled in a few breaths and then rolled over on top of him. "How could I frighten a man who would take such a dangerous ride?"

Her hood had slid down her back and her hair was framed in white crystals, her smiling face glistening. Pulling her close, he kissed her. The response was warm and immediate. Their kiss deepened, their mouths questing hungrily until their bodies began to move together. Breathless, Kepa just managed to ease his lips from hers and look into her eyes. He chuckled low and soft, "Now, in the snow?"

Whatever her answer might have been, it was stolen from him by the approach of a pair of toboggan runners, and then another. These sleds had evidently avoided the trees because there had been no crashing sounds and their riders were calling out gustily for Achaku and Kepa.

With a regretful groan he yelled, "Here!" Yet he didn't rise until he had kissed her thoroughly once more.

The others met them as they were pulling the damaged toboggan away from the tree. Half of its curled lip had broken off and one of its slats was split.

After seeing that the two they'd been searching for were truly unharmed, the four rescuers took one look at the sled and burst out laughing.

Most of the way back up the hill Kepa was pummeled with good-natured harassment about his talent as a toboggan runner.

It took three weeks of trudging and fierce battles with two blizzards to reach their winter hunting grounds. Now that they were here, Kepa paused at the edge of a majestic lake and sighed in awe at the beauty of the site. The lake was frozen and snow-covered except for a wide half-circle where the river flowed into it. Across the bright, flat expanse the mountain range towered grandly before him, its high, jagged peaks in silhouettes of deepest blue against the white.

They were fortunate to have arrived on a clear day and they eagerly set to work building their winter wigwams before the next storm could catch them exposed. As they worked, Kepa was pleased to see that these new shelters would be sturdier than their summer lodgings had been. First, they removed the snow and then chipped and dredged a foot-deep oval from the hard ground. Following Mihikin's instructions, Kepa dug the edge of the hole at an outward slant and into this they braced and bent sturdy branches to form a rounded frame. The roof they lifted to a height a couple of feet taller than Kepa. Once they'd completed the frame they set large birch bark strips around the base until this covering stood six inches or so above ground level. Now the earth they'd removed from the ground was packed solidly against the bark, forming a seal against moisture and air. And finally they covered the rest of the structure with more birch bark, upon which poles were leaned to stabilize the wall further. The door had been set at the narrowest curve of the oval to allow for the largest and warmest sleeping area within.

After setting the final bracing pole, Kepa stood back, his face shiny with sweat, to admire the fruits of their labor. He clapped Mihikin on the shoulder and said, "It's a good house."

"Yes," Mihikin said, "now we must see if the game is as friendly as the weather today."

In less than an hour they were back with a beaver on each of their carrying strings. Kepa followed Mihikin into their warm wigwam, his weight and movement awakening the scent of six inches of balsam branch tips, and handed his catch to a proudly smiling Achaku.

The hours of daylight had been lengthening as the snow levels gradually deepened, and by the time darkness finally fell that evening Kepa was exhausted. Yet, tonight he felt restless. As the rest of the family settled under their covers Kepa said softly to Achaku, "Come outside with me."

She hesitated, her expression uneasy. "Kepa, you know the spirits walk at night."

"We will not go far from camp."

"But wolves might be hunting nearby."

"I will bring my crossbow," he said, knowing it was the spirits that frightened her more than the wolves.

Though Achaku was still apprehensive she allowed him to lead her through the door and into the blackening darkness. When they reached the edge of the encampment they indeed heard a wolf howl from across the lake, and Achaku paused again. Another answered from farther south.

"How is it, Kepa, that you have no fear of the spirits?"

"I do not believe they will harm us. Some kind spirits, my people call them saints, may even help us."

"Saints," she tested the word. "Kind spirits."

"At times, I speak to the spirit of my brother, Gotzon."

Her voice was steady but her face showed her surprise and concern. "My people do not speak to the dead. We seldom speak *of* the dead. Do you not fear that your brother will return to this place, angry that you have disturbed him?"

"I do not believe he can return, ever. If he could, and chose to, he would not be angry."

"When you speak to him, does he hear you?"

Kepa smiled, at himself more than at her question. "I like to think he does."

"But he has never answered you, not even in a dream?"

"When I see him in a dream he and I are young boys again." He sighed low and long. "Let us talk of other things now. Walk with me a short while." But they had taken only a few steps toward the lake when Kepa glanced up and sucked in his breath. Achaku grabbed his sleeve and huddled close. His large arm eased from her grip and circled her body protectively, but his eyes were transfixed on the sky.

Subtle at first but growing brighter, forms of blue, emerald, orange, and purple elongated and undulated above them, dominating most of the northern sky. Kepa asked breathlessly, "What is it, Achaku?"

"Spirit dancers," she whispered back, and clung even tighter to him.

"Have you seen them before?"

"Only twice."

She tugged at his coat. "We must go back." When he stood

rooted, utterly spellbound, she said more urgently, "Kepa, we must leave here."

"Why?" He pulled his eyes from the heavens to search her face. "What makes you think the lights will harm us?"

"They are spirits. We must not look at them."

"But why not? Perhaps we are meant to look." His gaze was drawn irresistibly back to the shifting colors. "They may dance above us so we will notice them. Perhaps one of those lights is Gotzon, sharing his dance with us. Stay with me and watch, Achaku."

That Kepa was fearless beneath the swaying lights gave Achaku the ability to remain sheltered there in his arms. At that moment, her wonder of him grew even stronger than her fear of the spirit dancers. She held on to him tightly and dared to lift her eyes again. This time, she let her awestruck gaze drink its fill.

They remained like that until Kepa felt her shivering and he realized that his feet had grown numb. Bending down, he lightly kissed her forehead and they headed back to the wigwam, both still held in the spell of the unworldly illumination.

Early the following morning, just before Kepa and Mihikin were about to set out in search of game, the old man closed the flap of his hunting pouch and asked, "Achaku, did you dream of our hunt last night?"

"Not of hunting. I dreamed of dancing lights, my mother's brother."

"Dancing lights? Spirits? Were they angry?"

"No, they were mating."

Kepa looked up at this and Mihikin grunted his surprise, "Mating spirits. What can this mean?"

"I think it is a good omen," said Achaku, "for your hunt and many other things."

"No dream came to me last night," Mihikin said ruefully. "They come less and less often now. Well, your dream encourages me. I am ready, Kepa."

Whether it was God's grace that delivered the dream to Achaku or just luck, Kepa had no way of telling. And it was possible that her dream had not really been a forbearer of good fortune, but Mihikin and he soon returned with a beaver, two otters, and a marten. When they neared camp with their catches in tow they met

Nimu and Achaku returning from an outing of their own. They too had been successful. Over Achaku's shoulder a pair of spruce grouse were tied. These they'd caught less than a mile away.

After praises were exchanged for the results of both hunts, Nimu was sent to deliver a grouse, the beaver, and an otter to Saunuch's family. But the boy appeared back at the wigwam with the beaver still in his possession.

Achaku sat plucking a grouse as Kepa and Mihikin skinned and gutted the fur bearing animals. They all looked up at Nimu with questioning glances.

"My father said that tomorrow he will hunt with his sisters' husbands, so they will not need as much meat in the days to come. He also said..."

"Yes, Nimu?" Mihikin asked.

"I am to say also that he needs no more medicine, that the healing performed by some is... worse than dying."

Kepa let out an appreciative chortle, and the others smiled. He bent down to Nimu's eye level. "And what do you think, young man?"

"You and my mother are the best healers in our clan, even if the treatments are sometimes unpleasant."

Kepa sobered somewhat. "I know it will be unpleasant for you but I must work your arm again tonight."

"Can I write afterward?"

It had become a reward for his brave tolerance. "For as long as you like."

"And then will you tell us a story about your ship?"

"Yes, my boy, but don't you ever tire of them?"

"I want to hear them all."

"Work first, then stories," said Kepa.

Achaku and Mihikin remained outside to finish their tasks as Nimu and Kepa went in. They both sat down near the fire and Kepa slowly unwound Nimu's bandage.

"Now, reach out toward me, Nimu."

The boy obeyed. Even extended as far as Nimu could force it, the arm would not straighten to its full length, making it difficult for the muscles to gain much strength. Kepa was determined to change that.

"All right then, take my fingers and hold them firmly." Very gently, Kepa pulled toward his own chest as his other hand put pressure on the bottom of Nimu's elbow. Nimu held his breath and grimaced but uttered no sound of protest.

The two of them were still stretching Nimu's arm several minutes later when Achaku and Mihikin entered, and they were too involved in their healing efforts to notice the glances of affection and approval that passed over their heads.

Sacrifice of Winter

15

Startled shouts and confused clamoring thrust Kepa to full wakefulness one early dawn. Flinging off his covers, yanking on his knee-high moccasins, belting on his coat, and grabbing his crossbow, he ran out the door certain the camp was under attack. He'd barely cleared the wigwam when he was nearly run down by the strangest looking four-legged creature he'd ever seen. Almost as tall as he, its long face and bulbous nose would have looked comical under different circumstances. He loaded his bow and started after it, watching back legs angled so sharply at the knee that he was amazed the beast could walk at all, let alone run. A cry from Mihikin of, "Kepa, she is coming!" spun him around in time to leap aside as a much larger version of the bizarre quadruped charged passed him. Instinct and training brought his bow up and he fired, but at that moment the huge animal stumbled in the snow and Kepa's arrow shot over it.

As the panicked calf turned back toward its mother another hunter's arrow struck the base of its neck. It staggered sideways, lost its footing, and fell thrashing through the side of a wigwam. Screams from women and children broke from inside but they quieted quickly when the pursuing hunter arrived and dispatched the wounded yearling with another arrow.

Kepa, Mihikin, and Saunuch were hurrying to cut the mother off before she could reach her calf. They lifted their bows almost in unison and let their arrows fly. The great head tossed as a guttural bawl burst from its mouth. It lowered its head as if intending to charge but a second round of arrows struck the top of its lowered neck. As the formidable head tossed back and forth the hunters gained a more lethal side position and fired a final round of arrows. The animal fell to its knees then sank slowly sideways, its heavy head falling last and imbedding itself in the snow. By the time the men reached the spot, the animal's kicks were subsiding and its eyes had begun to glaze.

Mihikin knelt beside it in the snow and laid a hand lovingly upon its shoulder. "Thank you, my sister," he said softly. "You and your calf will be remembered."

When Mihikin had sung his brief chant of thanks and moved back, Kepa stepped closer to retrieve his arrows. His hand stilled suddenly. He counted them again. "Mihikin, there are eleven arrows."

Mihikin turned, spotted what he had suspected he'd find, and let a smile crease his face. "We had another hunter."

Already following his gaze, Kepa stared in wonderment at Achaku. She was holding her bow in her lowered left arm, an arrow in her right hand.

"We told you she could hunt, Kepa," Mihikin said. "Had you forgotten?"

He had, or at least he'd never expected her to test her skills and risk her life against an animal that must have weighed seven times as much as she, and an angry animal mother at that.

Achaku walked past the men and approached the beast as Mihikin had done. Stroking it gently, almost reassuringly, she touched her forehead to its side and sang so softly that Kepa could not catch the words. Then she raised her hand and lovingly closed both of its shining brown eyes.

By then Nimu, Liachita, and most of the camp had gathered around. Achaku regained her feet and silently parted from them all, as if somehow saddened by the success of the hunt. Liachita watched her walk slowly back to their home with understanding eyes, but she remained with the men a while longer.

"There will be moose meat for many days!" Saunuch announced. After the many weeks of pain and resentment brought about by the bear hunt, he looked reborn standing over this kill. He had reproven himself as a hunter, as a man, this morning. Kepa found himself still amazed Saunuch was alive yet sincerely hoping that today would complete the man's recovery.

When a hide was brought forward and spread out beside the moose, Mihikin asked Saunuch to make the first cut of the butchering. Cooking fires were already being stirred to life.

146

"It is good to see a woman showing our men what a fine hunter she can be," said Liachita as she lifted a log from the pile inside the door and fed the fire. "Your aim is as fine as ever."

Achaku nodded to accept the compliment but kept methodically pulling porcupine quills from a pelt Kepa had brought her the day before.

For a while Liachita watched her work, then said in a tone of exaggerated casualness. "My mother used to tell me that moose meat was good for an unborn child."

This drew Achaku's gaze. She smiled knowingly, "I am not carrying a child."

"Oh? Then it might happen soon. You and Kepa seem to be trying very hard to start one. I don't sleep as soundly as I once did and my ears sometimes hear movements in the night."

The smile on Achaku's lips only broadened. "He is a strong, vigorous man."

"From the sounds of things, he is not the only one who is vigorous. He seems to please you greatly."

"He does, greatly."

They laughed at this, and Liachita went on. "Perhaps it is taking longer than usual to start a baby because his magic is so great."

"Yes, perhaps that is why."

"Do not be concerned. I believe a baby will come. And since a father's seed helps strengthen and nourish a baby in his mother's womb, your child will be robust indeed."

Now Achaku's smile faltered and she sat in meditative silence.

Liachita grew serious as well. "He still intends to go?"

"When the time comes."

"A man's plans sometimes change, my child. And our hopes are sometimes answered."

After feasting on moose meat that night the snores rising from beneath the sleeping robes that covered Mihikin and Liachita were louder than usual. Not far from the door Nimu and Tracker slept curled close together for warmth. Achaku and Kepa lay in each other's arms, drained from their lovemaking. Kepa's fingers ran softly up and down her arm as his lips brushed her head.

Contentment so profound swept over Kepa that he let out a long sigh.

Achaku whispered. "It was a good day, Kepa."

"A very good day."

"Are you happy here with my people?"

He hesitated long enough to consider his words. "Yes, for now." He wished he could see her face more clearly.

"My people could become your own."

"Our worlds are very different, Achaku. I have described my relatives, and customs, and village to you many times. I will return there. Can you understand this?"

She almost wished she couldn't. Yet she knew how she would feel if asked to leave her own people, even for him. They needed her, just as his people must need him. "I understand, Kepa."

"Can you accept it?"

"Yes, because I must."

"Do you want things to change between us?"

"Change? How?"

"Do you want me to stop sharing your sleeping robes?'

"Your body brings me joy. I do not want that to end."

A short silence fell between them before Kepa said thickly, "Do not fall in love with me, Achaku. Do not hope that I will stay. That hope will only bring you pain."

Her voice quivered slightly in the darkness. "Hope comes to life when it will. And it cannot be stilled through caution or desire." A tear escaped and rolled to her hand resting on Kepa's chest. "We cannot kill it even when we wish it gone."

Day by day Kepa developed a more tenacious admiration for the severe, stunning winterland surrounding him. After a bout with frostbite that left his knees numb for three weeks, he'd acknowledged the mastery with which the cold winds governed the land, and the dominance that this country held over mere humans.

As long as there was daylight, and there was plenty of that, the hands of Achaku's people were seldom idle. Game fell often to their archers and trappers. After chopping away ice from the river, it yielded many fish. Women and children occasionally returned to camp carrying a ptarmigan or spruce grouse home for dinner. Mihikin made good his promise to help Kepa build a toboggan, upon which he steadfastly refused to ride for sport. Mihikin had also taught him how to make snowshoes and animal hide stretching frames, as well as other useful tools.

The need for firewood was ongoing yet the women never complained when they set out for the woods with their toboggans and axes. The abundance of game produced a welcome supply of pelts, but each one needed to be scraped, treated, and stretched. These many tasks and the harshness of the season were hard on clothing, which required continuous fabrication and mending by the women.

Kepa's life beside the frozen lake marched to a bustling rhythm that enticed time to pass quickly. Yet he was surprised one day when Mihikin set down the fishing net he'd been repairing and said, "Soon, Kepa, we will leave for the gathering. I am growing hungry for caribou meat."

They had pulled old robes outside to sit upon while they worked under the afternoon sun. Kepa had been smoothing the handle of an axe with his file. "When will we go?"

"Six or seven days if the weather is calm."

Calm, thought Kepa, meaning the wind is not strong enough to freeze your lungs with every breath. It was still something of a mystery to Kepa how Mihikin knew when to do things such as moving the camp. He seemed to read the wind and sun as accurately as a ship's pilot read the stars with an astrolabe.

Mihikin went on. "Wapitikwa enjoys the flavor of caribou even more than I do, perhaps because he has been linked with its spirit since his first hunt."

Both men jerked their heads up when a frantic yell burst from the trees to their east. Kepa jumped to his feet and was reaching for his bow before he comprehended the words the woman was crying. "Liachita! She's fallen in the river!"

Without pausing to strap on his snowshoes, Kepa grabbed the net from Mihikin's lap and ran. The path before him was well trodden but icy. As he slipped and skidded forward he heard Mihikin following behind him as fast as he was able. Kepa dashed into the trees that crowded the rivers' bank, snow from the branches above spraying down on his head and face, his eyes darting.

There they were. Achaku and Nimu knelt on an icy ridge beside the swirling water, their arms clinging to Liachita's unconscious form. Achaku's wet clothing clung to her shaking body. "Kepa!" she cried through desperate tears, "help us!"

Kepa dropped the net and skidded on his knees to the edge of the water. Grabbing Liachita under her arms and lifting, it took all of his strength to pull the woman from the river's grasp. Mihikin reached them and threw his coat over Liachita. "Hold her!" Kepa tore off his coat and wrapped it over Achaku's shoulders, and then he took Liachita from Mihikin, clasped her tightly to his chest, and ran toward the wigwam. Struggling to keep his balance while cradling Liachita, he glanced down and saw that her head was bleeding.

The others rushed into the wigwam just behind Kepa but he'd already covered Liachita and was vigorously rubbing her arm. She wasn't breathing. He said tightly, his eyes on Liachita's face, "Help me, Mihikin. Rub her other arm." Achaku stood dripping next to him. "Get into warm clothes, Achaku. You too, Nimu, and stoke up the fire."

As the men massaged Liachita's icy skin, water spilled in an intermittent trickle from her mouth but she drew no breath. Kepa turned her over his arm and pushed down on her back, forcing a spew of water out, but still she did not inhale. Silently, Achaku appeared beside him in a dry shift but she was trembling viciously. "Nimu," Kepa barked, "wrap a robe around you and your mother. Keep her close to the fire." When her eyes searched his pleadingly, his expression said she could do nothing for Liachita. She must take care of herself and her son.

After several minutes without awakening the slightest stirring of life, after Kepa knew Liachita was gone, he and Mihikin kept rubbing. In the end it was Mihikin who released his wife's arm and sat back. He lowered his head and waited for Kepa to stop, but Kepa didn't stop. Mihikin's vacant eyes lifted as he muttered, "It is over, Kepa. She has taken the path." Kepa allowed his movements to slow but did not let go of her. Watching Kepa's tortured face, Mihikin reached over and took his hands, stilling them at last. Then he leaned over Liachita's body, took hold of her sleeping robe, and slowly pulled it up over her face.

Staring at Mihikin's desolate features, remembering the night he too had sat devastated beside the body of his beloved wife, Kepa said, "I am sorry, my friend."

Mihikin looked back at him, understanding, accepting whatever consolation their shared grief might offer.

Kepa crawled over to Nimu and Achaku. They were softly weeping together inside the folds of the heavy robe. He took off his damp shirt, gathered them both onto his lap, and wrapped another robe around them all.

While Mihikin sang farewell to a wife he'd known since the day of her birth, Kepa held Achaku and Nimu close, rocking them and trying to take away a measure of their pain.

Before dusk Liachita's bundled body was reverently placed on a toboggan and transported to the base of a huge spruce tree. The men of the camp used ropes and a ladder to lift it ten feet above the snow where they secured it to thick boughs.

Mihikin stayed beneath her resting place long after the others had drifted back to their lives, stayed until Achaku came and begged him to come inside. "She will dance in the sky now," she said quietly, her voice raw from weeping, "but it is not yet your time. We need you with us tonight."

Slowly, weakly he rose and they left the tree together.

There, Liachita would sleep until they moved her to the next camp, where she would again lie in the limbs of a tree. In the spring they would carry her back to her summer home where she could be buried in the ground that cradled the bones of her ancestors and friends.

The Gathering

16

Achaku's family and Kepa caused a growing rumble of excited speculation as they entered the bustling, sprawling tribal campground of the gathering clans. Shouting, pointing, waving natives seemed to appear from behind and within every wigwam. Mihikin and Kepa pulled the toboggan bearing Liachita's body in the last place of Achaku's family line but this sled didn't draw nearly the attention that Kepa did. In anticipation of their arrival he'd shaved his beard again and loosed his hair, which he often wore tied back in a short queue. These efforts, however, did little to help him achieve anonymity. It became clear that the news of his coming had preceded him when he heard calls of, "The whale hunter is here!" and "Look, the killer of the great bear!" People quickly grew so thick around him and Mihikin that they were forced to stop in their tracks.

Hands, most of them female, reached out to touch Kepa, pulling back his hood, stroking his hair, and caressing his face. Not wishing to start his encounter in this camp on a weak footing, Kepa tolerated their touching as stoically as he could manage. But his forbearance seemed only to embolden some of the more inquisitive women and they soon were exploring less visible parts of his body. When a young woman lifted the front of Kepa's coat and reached for his crotch he tried to sidle away but he was surrounded by bodies. Other groping fingers followed hers before he could tug down his coat and step back. When the questing arms did not give up their search his patience threatened to give way to his temper. It was Achaku and Mihikin who rescued him by easing closer to each side and motioning the onlookers back.

Kepa caught a moment of amusement flickering across Mihikin's face for the first time since Liachita's death, but one glance at Achaku revealed that the curious women had tested her tolerance.

As the evening shadows lengthened, Mihikin wove his way through perhaps a hundred wigwams and pointed out their designated spot. They had not even completed shoveling the snow from around a perimeter before other people arrived to offer them help, and in a little more than an hour their wigwam stood finished, their floor and beds were arranged, and a lively fire crackled in their hearth.

Kepa finally sat down with a long sigh, ready for a well-earned rest, but Mihikin said expectantly, "Kepa, we must meet the others while our meal is cooking."

"What others?"

"My relatives and friends. It will still be days before the rest of the clans arrive and the caribou hunt begins. There are many hunters who wish to know about you while there is time."

With his face hopeful, Nimu piped up, "May I come?"

"You must come. They will all want to meet the other great bear hunter."

Nimu let out a small whoop of joy.

It was clear to Kepa that their arrival had done much to rejuvenate Mihikin and subdue his grief. He didn't have the heart to disappoint either the old man or the boy.

"All right then," Kepa said, reaching for his coat and giving a small farewell wave to Achaku.

The men and Nimu had departed from the wigwam only moments before a middle-aged man, whose hawk nose extended so low it nearly touched his lip, and two young women interrupted Achaku's meal preparations. She knew the man, Mwakwa, only slightly but welcomed them all and motioned them to sit down.

They exchanged polite queries and responses before Mwakwa got to the point of his visit. "Word came to us of Mihikin's loss. Our hearts are heavy for him and we wish to help him find happiness again."

Achaku said, "Your intentions are very kind."

Mwakwa shifted as if to find a more comfortable place on the boughs to rest his buttocks but Achaku sensed that the man was nervous. Then Mwakwa said, "Mihikin is growing old but he still has much power and much esteem among our people. I have brought my two daughters to you because of your wisdom, and I ask that you tell me if either or both of them would make Mihikin happy."

Considering this request with the same degree of sincerity in which it was extended, Achaku looked over the girls more closely. They appeared to be healthy but neither was beautiful. One had crooked teeth but a shapely body and warm, inviting eyes. The other did not smile so her teeth could not be seen, but she was thinner and seemed much shier than her sister. Unlike their father's, their noses were of average size and well formed. Achaku guessed their ages to be thirteen and fifteen.

"This offer is generous, Mwakwa. A young wife might please Mihikin, but he has not spoken of a desire for one."

Encouraged, Mwakwa went on with enthusiasm. "Although it is our custom for the husband to live with the family of his new wife, I do not ask this of Mihikin. I have another daughter younger than these two." He glanced at the fire to avoid Achaku's eyes before saying, "I have heard that Kepa will leave us when the snows melt. When that day comes Mihikin should not be parted from you and your son, and my daughters can be of comfort to you." He looked at her now. "Many men will want you as their wife, Achaku. The man you choose will hunt with Mihikin to feed the women and children of this family. I have two sons, both good hunters. Either of them would be pleased to add you and your son to his family, but if you do not choose them, they will still help you if there is ever a need. Half of what they killed they would share with you."

Achaku's voice did not falter. "You have thought much about our welfare."

"I have. It is my hope that these daughters will bear Mihikin's children. Men even older than Mihikin have been known to produce a child. Such an offspring would bring honor and pride to my family. Do you think Mihikin can do this?"

"He has never had children, but he took only one wife. Their bond was very close. I can not tell whether Mihikin can father a child but I believe he is still able to try."

"You have had no dreams that show you his child?"

"No, but many things are kept hidden from me."

After reflecting on this confession for a moment, he said, "It is enough, Achaku. Will you consider my daughters?"

"I will speak with them and learn their natures."

"That is only right."

To the girls she said, "Come to me in the morning after the men have gone."

As they departed, Achaku began to hum contentedly as she turned back to her chores.

Her men returned a couple of hours later and hungrily ate their dinners while sharing news from around the camp. To all that was said Achaku listened attentively. Not until their tales had exhausted themselves did she nonchalantly say, "I had a visitor after you left."

Mihikin asked with mild interest, "Who was it?"

"Mwakwa brought his two young daughters here."

"Was he looking for me?"

"He wanted me to meet his daughters."

"Does he want you to train them as healers?"

"The girls do not wish to be healers. Mwakwa asked me to decide whether they would make suitable wives for you."

At Mihikin's startled stare, Kepa couldn't keep a grin from his face.

Achaku went right on, "He wanted to know if you would prefer one or both of them."

Mihikin blinked. "Two young wives? At my age?"

Kepa was softly chuckling now.

Achaku tried to take no notice of his levity and said, "Their father hoped you would be able to sire a child with each of them."

Noting Kepa's now quaking shoulders, Mihikin said with indignation, "Why do you laugh, Kepa. Do you think me incapable of such a thing?"

"No, no," Kepa sputtered, "you just seem a little fearful of the idea."

"Fearful! Of a couple of women? I am still able to please a female, or even two." He glowered at Kepa, who tried to hide his smile behind his hand, and turned to face Achaku. "What are they like, these women?"

Pleased that Mihikin had risen to his teasing challenge, Kepa pretended not to hang on Achaku's response by calling Nimu closer. He lit the fibrous wick protruding from a small, oval, stone he used as a lamp, filled the hollow with his carefully hoarded bear oil, and they brought out their writing instruments. For once, Nimu seemed less than enthusiastic about his lessons.

He leaned in close to Kepa and said quietly, "I want to listen."

"We can listen and write at the same time," said Kepa with a wink.

This they did. As Achaku answered numerous questions about the two girls, Kepa and Nimu scratched words on his crowded parchment, one of several they'd created, and eavesdropped. Every now and then they paused to listen closely and to trade a secretive grin.

Once the initial curiosity about Kepa's appearance and character had subsided, for which he was exceedingly grateful, it was Achaku whom the people continued to flock to. Her stature became even clearer to Kepa as she was beckoned to many lodges to give advice or perform her healing craft. It seemed that she would just return from such a visit only to be met by someone waiting to make arrangements for a wedding or a divination ritual meant to predict the future. Young and old, male and female appeared at their door to seek her services. On several occasions she called upon Kepa to assist her or to take the lead in a medical situation, and he willingly complied.

After meeting with Mihikin's prospective brides more than once, deciding at last that each would be fitting in her own way, Achaku arranged for the members of both families to come together for a meal the next evening so that Mihikin could scrutinize the girls himself.

The area around the camp had not yet been seriously thinned of game so Mihikin's bow was able to provide a young deer for their important gathering. He and Kepa hauled the deer home together but Mihikin left it in the care of his family and disappeared to visit friends until the meal was ready. Kepa chose not to tease Mihikin today. He had enough on his mind to make him nervous.

When the appointed time arrived everyone grouped in a large circle around the fire. Mwakwa's two wives and daughters helped Achaku serve the food while Kepa furtively observed Mihikin. He had to admire the old man's composure, or at least his appearance of composure. There was not a sign of apprehension visible on his wizened features. Whenever he spoke it was to exchange comfortable conversation, but it was always addressed to the girls' father rather than to them.

Nimu, on the other hand, seemed unable to sit still as he listened to every word and watched every movement of the visitors. Kepa became amused when he noticed that the boy's gaze returned repeatedly to the pretty little sister of Mihikin's intended brides, a girl close to Nimu's age. Achaku, Kepa saw, had detected her son's fascination as well. Meeting Kepa's gaze across the fire, her expression seemed to say, "Perhaps she will be his one day."

Mwakwa stretched in a slightly exaggerated manner and stood up rubbing his belly. "It was a good meal. My family will leave now but my older daughters will remain with Mihikin for awhile."

For the first time that evening Mihikin's self-possession faltered, although it was quickly restored.

Imitating Mwakwa's movements, Kepa now stretched and rose to his feet. "Achaku, Nimu, I feel like taking a walk. Come keep me company. Mihikin, we will be back before dark."

Without hesitation these three took up their coats and snowshoes and left Mihikin staring after them.

It was a lovely, clear evening, so lovely that Kepa didn't even feel the icy sting in the slight breeze. They chatted happily as they roamed the camp, meeting many who called them over to discuss the possibility of Mihikin taking a new wife. Upon seeing Achaku and Kepa, the entire village seemed to deduce what was going on in their wigwam. Several men even offered to place wagers with Kepa on the outcome of Mihikin's success with the two young women, which Kepa declined to accept. The light had nearly faded from the sky before they headed back the way they'd come.

When they arrived home Mihikin lay alone and still beneath his sleeping furs. The other three undressed quietly and nestled down for the night.

A little disappointed that he'd have to wait until morning to learn the outcome of the past two hours, Kepa soon let his thoughts be absorbed entirely by Achaku. Snuggling close to her, he was kissing her neck when he was suddenly stilled by Mihikin's voice.

"Achaku," he said in a formal tone, "you may arrange a wedding between me and both of Mwakwa's daughters. They are young and want children, so we will need a wigwam of our own."

"We will be glad to build one with you," Achaku said.

"And Kepa," said Mihikin with strong authority, "after tonight, there should be no more talk of my abilities with women."

He managed to respond solemnly, just. "You are right, Mihikin. Never again."

A satisfied grunt ended the conversation.

Mihikin was not the only inhabitant of Achaku's lodge to have his sexual inclinations tested at the clan gathering. As Kepa grew more closely acquainted with several hunters in the coming days, a few of them hospitably offered him the favors of their most appealing wives. From what Kepa was told, the women had no objections whatsoever.

Having no intention of subjecting himself or Achaku to whatever reciprocity might be expected when such overtures were extended, Kepa delicately declined. He gave as his excuse the likelihood of weakening his magic, and this they seemed to accept, most of them without offense. Before long their proposals subsided and the pastime of choice turned to the trading of possessions rather than wives. Extravagant prices were offered in exchange for Kepa's weapons. Even after he had let it be known that he meant to retain his belongings, however, men with ever-higher offers kept approaching him. One man's persistence flared to anger at Kepa's refusals and the deadlock nearly resulted in blows before calmer heads led the bargainer away. Although Kepa heard many outrageous offers, in the end he could only be persuaded to part with one iron arrowhead.

While this dealing and bartering was a fascinating diversion, Kepa spent much of his time hunting with Mihikin, or helping him and Achaku construct the groom's new wigwam.

Anticipation for the caribou hunt had been building around camp for some time, and when the last of the clans finally arrived all' agreed that the hunt would take place in two more days. Weapons were shaped and sharpened, gear was repaired, and sweat lodges were completed for the use of the hunters and holy leaders.

On the very afternoon that the day of the hunt was announced, Achaku greeted Kepa in front of their lodge by saying, "I have a gift for you. Come inside." Once there, she brought out a long braided cord adorned with tiny bones and dyed strips of leather. "It is your caribou carrying string. I meant to have it finished sooner but I have been busy with many things."

Kepa turned it in his hand and looked over its full length. She had devoted great care to its creation. "It bears your fine touch, Achaku. I am sure it will bring me good fortune. I am grateful." He reached out to her and kissed her. But when he would have done more she pulled back from him. "We must not, Kepa. I am preparing to enter the sweat lodge."

"Soon?"

She nodded.

"Tell me what will happen there."

"My body and spirit will be cleansed and strengthened. This will prepare me for a dream tonight. In the dream, I hope the caribou master will reveal himself. You can help me, if you will."

"Tell me what to do."

Within the hour Nimu and Kepa hauled a toboggan loaded with wood and several caribou bladders filled with water to the small, low, dome-shaped lodge at the center of camp. The snow had been removed from beneath and around it. Mihikin awaited them beside a large fire that was surrounded by a thick ring of rounded stones. Achaku approached the lodge and paused at the door. She removed her coat and moccasins, and handed them to Mihikin. Naked, she stepped inside carrying only her drum and striker.

Once the door had closed behind her, Mihikin and Kepa used flat sticks to pick up heated rocks and pass them through a small side opening. They moved at a quick and steady pace until steam began to rise from every gap in the lodge. And then Achaku's voice started to sing as her drum beat the first throbs of a rhythm both beckoning and haunting.

"Those are enough rocks for now," Mihikin whispered to Kepa. He picked up one of the water containers, pushed its mouth through the portal into the lodge, and began to trickle it over the stones below. A whoosh and hiss of steam sounded from inside, and Kepa saw a cloudy wisp curl up past the wall opening toward the curved ceiling.

Now they added more stones at a much slower rate, always followed by a tiny cascade of water. After Achaku had been singing for several minutes, Kepa bent lower and peered deep inside the lodge. At first he could just make out Achaku's form, then he perceived her more clearly, kneeling and sitting back on her calves, her eyes closed, her head tilted up, and her skin glistening in the dimness. She was magnificent, an apparition of mystical, feminine perfection. And then Mihikin was beside him again with another stone.

Perhaps an hour had passed, perhaps more, when the drumming and singing ceased. Mihikin took the last bladder of water and handed it into the lodge. Kepa heard Achaku using it to rinse her body. When she appeared at the door moments later, she slipped on her moccasins as Kepa wrapped her coat over her shoulder and they walked back to their wigwam. Her trance-like manner kept all of them silent as they made their way. *Tonight*, Kepa thought, *there is magic in the very air around us.*

Early the next morning, after they'd eaten, the hearth was completely cleared and they all inched nearer to the fire. Mihikin gently drew from his basket of belongings the scapula of a caribou. He surrendered this into Achaku's hands but she took it hesitantly.

She had been preoccupied since she'd awakened but Kepa could get her to tell him little of what was troubling her. "It might be wiser for you to read the bones today, my mother's brother," she said. "I did not dream of the caribou master last night."

Mihikin asked, "Did you feel the caribou masters presence with you in the sweat lodge?"

Her brow furrowed. "I felt something very strong but very strange. I am not sure what spirit was with me."

He studied her for a moment. "Still, your readings have never failed us, Achaku. It is you who should do it. Go on, my child."

Nodding once, Achaku pressed the joint end of the shoulder blade firmly into a split stick. She stoked the coals and stared into their glow for a moment before saying solemnly, "Brother fire, tell me where the caribou can be found so that our good men may have success in their hunt today."

Carefully, she placed the bone over the coals and left it there for several seconds. Kepa heard the bone make a thin cracking sound just before Achaku pulled it from the hearth.

As she and then Mihikin and Nimu leaned with fascination over the scapula Kepa could not help doing the same. He could see a few circular burned spots along one side and a short crack that wondered wavily between two of the rounded marks. Mystified, he heard Achaku announce as she pointed to a spot more oval than the

160

others, "This is our camp. This," she added, pointing to the crack, "is the creek that runs a half-mile south of us. That creek will lead you to the caribou."

Mihikin asked, "How far?"

"Eleven miles, or as far as fourteen."

Mihikin accepted the bone back from her and tucked it into his hunting pouch. "It will guide us well. We must go now."

Kepa could hear the restless shuffling of snowshoes and the deep voices of men gathering outside. He touched Achaku's cheek and gave Nimu's long hair a playful tug, saying, "I want no followers on this hunt, young man. You must stay in camp." Receiving an obedient bob of the head from the boy, Kepa ducked out the door.

If he could have described a perfect day in winter in this northern land it would have possessed the characteristics of this one. The sky held just three small clouds in the distant western horizon, the wind for once was utterly silent, and the early sun was casting a pink glow over the snow. He breathed in so deeply that his expanding chest stretched the leather of his shirt. He held it for a moment, maintaining with the breath his hold on this moment of beauty, bestowed by the enormous, open country surrounding him.

The hunters were already drawing into a tight circle to huddle with their heads close together, consulting each other about the omens that their spirit readers had discovered. Kepa joined the circle and listened to the talk, noting that each hunter seemed to be free to follow the guidance of whichever diviner he chose. Mihikin told them all of Achaku's reading and this was considered with much gravity. When the throng of men separated into several groups, eleven men joined Kepa and Mihikin. Mihikin said quietly to Kepa that this was because of their faith in Achaku but also because of their desire to hunt with the famed whale and bear killer. Kepa was only mildly surprised to see Saunuch among them.

Picking up their toboggan ropes, they moved out toward the creek Achaku had named and they followed its bank in a wordless single file. Kepa could feel the hunters' excitement building with each mile, felt his own stomach flutter with the thrill of anticipating the unknown. The eyes of the men in his party were never still and every beaver dam, fishing hole, otter den, and animal track along their path was studied and, he knew, tucked into memory for future use.

They'd walked, climbed, and slid for about seven miles over hilly terrain when Kepa noticed that Mihikin's pace was beginning to slow and his shoulders to slump with fatigue.

He called to him softly, "Mihikin, I would like to see the caribou bone again." They halted just below the crest of a knoll and the other hunters came up to study the scapula Mihikin pulled from his pouch once more.

Glancing from the bone, to the lower path, to the top of the hill, and back to the bone, Mihikin said, "It is hard to judge, but this curve might be just below us. If so, the caribou should be four or five miles ahead."

One of the men had been looking with distaste at Kepa's crossbow and he now pointed to it and said, "Why do you choose to carry so clumsy a weapon, Kepa? I have seen how long it takes to load it. My bow can fire three arrows for every one of yours."

Saunuch's voice broke in forcefully. "Have you not heard the stories of the great bear hunt? Kepa's bow was needed that day. It may be slower to load than our bows but it can kill when ours are not strong enough. Do not speak of things you do not understand."

Kepa stared at Saunuch, somewhat uncomfortable at hearing a speech made in his defense by an adversary. He wasn't sure he didn't prefer Saunuch's hostility.

The debate over weapons resumed, but before it could proceed much further they were all silenced by a low guttural sound that reached them from somewhere on the far side of the hill. In unison they scrambled up to the summit, legs churning, quivers bouncing, and snow flying. They crouched and then crawled the last few feet on their bellies, and peered over the top.

Whatever expectations Kepa might have held were obliterated with a single glance. His mouth hung slack as his mind took in the milling herd of, how many? Four, six, seven hundred caribou? He grabbed Mihikin's sleeve and shook it, and both men grinned at each other like fools. Mihikin mouthed the words, "Achaku knew."

Kepa wasn't about to remind him that he'd just interpreted her reading to mean the herd was still four or five miles away.

The caribou were spread out along the edges of an expansive valley. They were using their hooves to dig through the snow around the trees, perhaps feeding on lichen or moss that clung to the trunks and limbs. Most of the animals bore antlers, the larger ones rising and falling like grand curved bowsprits as their owners moved their heads. Staring at the antlers, the striking brown and tan bodies, and the proud ivory colored necks and shoulders, Kepa thought how perfectly they complement this country. And he was struck with the memory of the single caribou he and his whalers had killed on their first day ashore. That was a few months ago. A lifetime ago.

At Kepa's side Mihikin motioned the men back down the hillside, and in hushed voices they briefly discussed how best to approach the herd. When all was decided, Mihikin led them forward.

Descending and skirting the hill, Kepa glanced at the other men and saw hungry anticipation both on their faces and in the tight stealth of their movements. There was a little breeze now, but Mihikin kept them downwind of the caribou as they drew nearer. Wondering if it was his imagination, Kepa thought he could smell the combined breath of the roaming herd.

They left their toboggans behind a thicket and set arrows to their bows. With the use of hand signals Mihikin divided the hunting party into three groups. He, Kepa, and two others crept to a central position while the other men fanned out on both sides. At Mihikin's nod Kepa separated from him and, hunching low, skulked closer until the caribou were again in his sight.

He chose a large animal and angled toward it, moving slowly and keeping hidden behind the trees. His movements became even more measured. Right foot, pause and look, left foot, pause and look. As his muscles tightened, his breath shortened, and his back trickled sweat, his heart hammered more forcefully with each closing step.

When only a huge spruce tree stood between Kepa and his caribou, he halted and held himself still. He swallowed and attempted to quiet his pulse, wondering how his body could react to hunting caribou, hunting anything, with such ferocity after so many whale hunts. He'd taught himself to calm his face and control his actions, yet his organs still seemed disinclined to submit to any such discipline.

At some unfamiliar sound or glimpse of the men the caribou

suddenly became restless, lifting their heads with a jerk to listen and scent the air. Peering through branches, Kepa saw the great animal he'd selected paw the ground as if in protest of their presence.

Glancing to either side, he saw that the other men were watching Mihikin and awaiting his signal. A moment later the old hunter raised his hand and let it fall. Every hunter leaped from cover and let loose a tightly drawn arrow. Kepa aimed and fired, piercing his caribou just behind the shoulder. Before it collapsed he was already loading another dart.

As the first animals slumped to the ground the other caribou began to run, their big hooves splaying in the snow and their movements somehow setting off a strange clicking noise as they loped for the forest to the west. The last of the herd was racing past Kepa and he fired again. Another caribou fell to his crossbow. The last of the caribou disappeared into the shelter of the trees and Kepa turned toward the valley before him and scanned the snow. He counted twenty-eight dead caribou, enough meat to hold off the hunger of the entire camp for weeks.

Mihikin and the others were already approaching their kills to sing their thanks and praise. Kepa trod over to his first animal and knelt in the snow, admiring its beauty. His head bent low and the words seemed to come of their own will. "Dear Lord of all, for this day and for all the days you have watched over my survival, I am grateful. I thank you for letting us find these caribou to feed Achaku's people."

Though he could not know it, his prayer was similar in spirit to the others being offered on that snowy valley floor. He did not pause to reflect on how his bond with his God had changed greatly over the last months.

They entered the camp to cries of jubilation and congratulations, their toboggans piled high with caribou. Today the festivities would be especially meaningful and lasting. While the feast was being prepared all of the couples intending to marry, or in Mihikin's case, a triple, were gathered together in the center of the encampment.

The eldest holy man among them stood solemnly amid those to be wed and over a hundred people encircled them. The elder lifted his voice and called out, "These before us will spend the days to come as husbands and wives. Let us all help them live with kindness and helpfulness so that the Great Manitou will be pleased and bring good fortune to all of us." At this, the drums began to beat a slow, steady rhythm and voices lifted in a song of celebration.

Kepa's searching glance found Achaku standing not far from the ceremonial elder. She was drumming and singing, her features composed and unreadable. She began to dance in a large circle, stepping lightly with the rest of the moving crowd. Watching her still, Kepa wondered if she regretted that there had been no marriage observance for them, that there would never be one. She had not shown him any sign of lamentation because of this omission, yet didn't every woman value such a rite?

It held no surprise to Kepa that the feasting lasted well into the night, long after he was too sated to eat another bite of caribou meat, or fat, or marrow. As the hour grew very late he leaned close to Achaku and asked, "Are we to remain inside the ceremonial lodge until the last of the caribou is gone?"

To his great relief Achaku smiled and reassured him that much of the meat would be dried for other days. Soon afterward, they and most of the other celebrants left for their own wigwams.

As Mihikin and his two new brides separated from Kepa, Achaku, and Nimu to enter their new lodgings, Kepa grinned broadly and clapped Mihikin on the shoulder. "Sleep well, my friend."

Mihikin scowled at him in an attempt to hide his own apprehensions.

Dreams Fulfilled, Dreams Abandoned

17

"This crossbow is heavier than it looks, Nimu. Hold it firmly. Now, find a forked tree to brace the stock on." They stood at the edge of a small clearing, the snow deep and heavy in every direction. As a final reward for Nimu's work ethic and pain tolerance while regaining his arm's flexibility, Kepa was teaching him to shoot the crossbow. The boy's elbow could straighten nearly to its full extension at last and Kepa was extremely proud of his small patient.

A crowd had begun to collect around them while Kepa had fired the first demonstration shots. He'd anticipated this since they were not far from camp and the crossbow was still a curiosity to many of the hunters. He did nothing to dissuade the watchers. The more people who observed, the greater the esteem that might be earned by his young charge. He had very little doubt that Nimu had the ability to learn the secrets of his bow quickly, so there was not much risk of him bringing embarrassment upon the boy.

Once Nimu found a tree with a wide fork at his chest level he rested the crossbow upon it and Kepa strode to him on his snowshoes. "Have you chosen your target?"

"There, that dead tree leaning toward the west," he said, pointing.

Raising an eyebrow, Kepa, asked, "For your first shot? That tree is two hundred feet away,"

"I have seen you hit a target at five hundred feet," Nimu pointed out.

"That was sheer luck." Not wanting to discourage the lad, Kepa protested no further. "Go ahead then and try to load the arrow. The string is very tight, even for grown men." Nimu slipped out of his snowshoes and stamped down the snow at his feet, as he'd seen

Kepa do many times. He stepped into the leather stirrup with his right foot to pin the bow to the hard-packed snow beneath.

"Bend that front knee and lean forward a little," Kepa instructed. "Turn your shoulders toward me. Now pull the string up toward the nut." This notched disc of iron, secured by a sear and a locking cord, would hold the tightened string in place until the trigger was pulled.

Nimu grasped the string with hands spread a few inches apart and pulled upward. His arms, thighs, and buttocks strained as his face reddened but he couldn't bring the string up far enough to meet the nut. Kepa stepped in close and put his hands on the string just outside of Nimu's. They pulled together until the string was pinned in place.

Kepa bent down and placed Nimu's hands properly on the weapon and let him lift it to the tree's fork. "Brace the stock tight against your shoulder, Nimu. There. When you are ready, take a deep breath, keep your aim steady as you let it out, and release the trigger gently."

Staring down the bow's stock at his targeted tree, Nimu's tongue poked from the corner of his mouth and his eyes squinted in keen concentration.

Biting back a warning, Kepa realized too late that he'd failed to caution Nimu about the force of a crossbow's kick. The trigger released the arrow with a *thwick* and the bow bucked upward, jolting Nimu back a step and showering snow and small twigs down on the boy's ducking head and shoulders. Nimu shook himself to shed the downfall, looked up, and gaped as he stared straight ahead. "I hit it!" He danced a few bouncing steps before Kepa as the onlookers let out a whoop. "Do you see?"

"I see a crossbow arrow sticking out of that tree. It was fine shot, Nimu. Do you want to try again?"

"Oh, yes!"

The crowd grew larger and more animated as Nimu steadily emptied the quiver of arrows, and still he wanted to continue. Smiling, Kepa shook his head and said, "Enough for today. Look at your fingers." They were red and swollen with building blisters, caused from repeatedly drawing back the string. "There will be other days for practicing. We need to check your snares and see to our other duties before we can break camp tomorrow."

After retrieving the arrows they walked through the still milling throng. Hands reached out to pat Nimu's head or shoulder and
voices murmured words of approval as he walked by. The young
archer accepted their praise with unpretentious joy and grace.

As if to add to Nimu's happiness today, his snares, which had
been moved farther and farther upstream in search of game, provided a marten and a mink. This catch was a bounty worthy of gratitude in these dwindling days of the clan gathering. He and Kepa
made their way back to camp with light steps and high spirits.

Upon their return to the wigwam they found Mwakwa and one
of his wives talking with Achaku. Greetings were offered and Kepa
and Nimu sat down to listen as the strings of conversation were
picked up once again.

"The news we bring pleased us very much," said Mwakwa.
"We hope you are also pleased. And we have a favor to ask of you,
Achaku."

Achaku motioned for him to continue, but he nudged his wife
slightly. She said shyly, "Our young daughters did not leave
Mihikin's wigwam to join the other young women during their
moon times."

Kepa watched Achaku's surprised face, suspecting but not quite
sure what this implied.

"Both? He, he, so soon?" Achaku's hands came up and covered her smiling mouth, her eyes shining. "He has said nothing of
this."

"He may not know. My daughters had told no one until they
came to me today, but I have been watching them and I knew several days ago. This morning they came to ask many questions, as
daughters do. They each look at this as a great blessing."

Why that old stallion, thought Kepa. *He'll never let me tease
him again.*

Achaku said what her face already revealed, "Your news brings
me much joy." She savored this for moment and then remembered
to ask, "What favor do you wish?"

Mwakwa said, "We would have you name the infants when you
feel the time is right."

"That, too, would give me much joy." As if to convince herself
of its reality, its certainty, she murmured, "Mihikin's children will
be born in the fall."

Nimu had been gawking from one adult face to the other and had somehow managed to keep from interrupting his elders, but it was clear that this announcement had astounded him. Kepa had no doubt it would amaze many.

"We must go now," Mwakwa said, getting up. "It was good to talk of this with you."

After they'd gone, Kepa said, "We should invite Mihikin and his wives to eat with us tonight."

Achaku eagerly agreed but Nimu, still ruminating on Mihikin's upcoming fatherhood, merely nodded half-heartedly. At his mother's request to deliver the invitation her son silently left them. Kepa watched Nimu disappear out the door and wondered if he was worrying about being replaced in his great-uncle's heart by these new cousins. Partings of any kind were hard on a child, Kepa knew, and a spasm of guilt tugged at him with the knowledge that his own departure would add to Nimu's pain. To suppress this, he busied himself around the wigwam.

When their guests arrived they brought with them a congenial though unexpected addition. Mihikin sat down, his knees cracking, with a puppy in his arms. Reaching out to scratch its chin, Kepa guessed it to be two or three months old, so it could not have been one of Tracker's offspring. Still, the coloring was the only noticeable difference in features. This pup was tan rather than a fox red, and its belly was more cream than snow white.

"This animal is to be your companion, Nimu," Mihikin declared, and handed the pup to the delighted boy. "He shows signs of becoming a good friend and hunter. Tracker and I will help you train him."

Beaming, Nimu rubbed his cheek against the pup's soft head as it tried to lick his face. "It is a fine dog, and I will work hard to train him well. Does he have a name?"

"Not yet. You must find one for him."

The boy held the squirming pup at arm's length, studying him for a moment, then pronounced, "I will watch him closely. Then I will choose a name."

Mihikin smiled. "You are a wise boy, Nimu. Now, that meat smells good."

As Achaku filled and passed wooden bowls, she said, "Mwakwa came to visit today."

Both girls stiffened slightly and glanced at each other. Achaku's searching gaze went to each of them. No, they hadn't told him. First one and then the other gave a slight nod of her head.

"Oh?" Mihikin asked with mild concern while he chewed. "Is he well?"

"Mwakwa is very well," Achaku said, but her hesitation to continue drew Mihikin's full attention.

"What is it?"

"He told me of his happiness. Soon he will be a grandfather again."

"His son's wives are still nursing..." Mihikin's eyes grew wider as his hand stilled and his mouth fell open. He closed it and swallowed loudly. Looking from one wife to the other, he asked, "Who?"

They giggled and said almost in unison, "Both of us."

Mihikin's eyes darted to Achaku, needing verification.

Her hands were clasped together at her chest, her face aglow. "Their mother told me the same thing."

He swallowed again.

"You're to be a father, my mother's brother."

Tears welled and then slid from the old man's eyes and his chin fell to his chest. He took several ragged breaths and squeezed his eyes shut. When he could control his voice a little, he said, "Many, many years I have hoped for a child." He raised his creased, tear-streaked face and patted the cheek of one pleased young wife and then the next. "You are good women, good, good women."

All this time Kepa had been grinning like a well-fed wolf. "We are happy for you, Mihikin." He went over to Mihikin, clasped his hand, and nearly shook his arm off. "Very happy."

Smiling broadly now, Mihikin had rallied his emotions enough to quip, "You, you are the one who doubted such a thing."

"Not really, my friend. But so soon? You must have been very busy lately."

They all laughed heartily at this, then excited questions and speculations circled the wigwam like a zephyr. Occasionally every voice chimed in at the same time, producing another round of laughter. At last they each settled down to finish their meal, every bite tasting richer now that it was seasoned with Mihikin's joy.

After the last bite had been consumed, Mihikin said, "Kepa, I have these good tidings to share with my friends. Since we will leave in the morning it must be tonight. It is also your last chance to share a story with these people. Many have asked you to speak of a whale hunt but always Saunuch turns the words to the hunt of the great bear. Will you tell your story while you can?"

"Gladly, Mihikin." Kepa answered, grasping for the first time how greatly he would miss many of the men he'd met here. "Lead the way."

Word circulated quickly and soon thirty men were gathered together in the wigwam of a distant relative of Mihikin. Unable to hide the intensity of his happiness, Mihikin told them all about the future birth of his children. This created such an uproar of congratulations that it was several minutes before voices quieted and Mihikin could again be heard. "My heart is full tonight," he said. "It is good to sit with all of you and talk. This is the final night we have Kepa among us, and he has agreed to speak of his time as a whale hunter. Though our way of speaking is new to him he is a fine storyteller. I ask that we do not turn him from his tale once he begins."

All heads pivoted toward Kepa, the angles of their faces bronzed and sharpened by the glow of the fire. Voices hushed. Bodies shifted then stilled. Arms hung relaxed over the knees of crossed legs. The air smelled of leather and sweat and the smoke of burning spruce.

Kepa had considered with care what story he should tell. He'd almost decided to let his story recapture that last and nearly fatal hunt, but then he'd rejected it because he couldn't faithfully tell its ending. He'd been unconscious at the time. So he'd chosen another incident to recount, one he hoped would interest these men. He knew that his mind and mouth would occasionally stumble over a word, but his audience would forgive him for this. Their tradition and nature made correcting or belittling a guest at such a gathering unthinkable.

"My people have hunted the whale for generations beyond count," Kepa began with slow deliberation. "The men of my family have hunted these huge fish or built ships for ages. We sail the sea as your people roam the forest, for there we find food to nourish us and oil to light our homes." The faces around him looked back at him absorbedly, hanging on his words.

"I have whaled for only two summers, but in that short time I have seen many wonders upon the sea. Some were beautiful and some were terrible. Some were almost beyond what a man can believe.

"On my very first voyage we were sailing north of my land in search of whales. I had heard of a great whale that bears fifty teeth, not baleen such as the whales of this coast. Each tooth is rounded and curved, and at least this big." He unsheathed his knife and showed them the section extending seven inches from the tip. Grunts of amazement and appreciation for such a creature circled the group as Kepa went on, "I had handled one of these teeth when I was young and when I began to sail I wondered if I would see such a whale. I have only heard of a few ships that dared to hunt these beasts. My captain sought mostly the Viscaino whales, the Right whales. But then on a calm, clear day in early summer our captain allowed one of our boats to be towed behind the ship so that several of our men could fish from it."

Kepa's eyes now narrowed a bit, seeing again the scenes of that day. "I was watching the boat as the men were hauling in a net when suddenly I saw something huge and gray rising fast beneath the boat. I yelled out a warning but there was no time for them to act. The whale burst from the sea with its jaws open and leaped into the air with the boat clamped tightly in its mouth. It rose straight up, at least five times the height of a man, its tail whipping from side to side, clutching our boat. We watched from the ship in horror as the jaws tightened and snapped the boat in half. Our fishermen were crushed or flung into the sea."

A few sharp breaths were sucked in as wide brown eyes remained locked on Kepa.

"Our captain ordered another boat lowered to rescue our swimming men, and the second boat was soon in the water. I was one of the men rowing but I kept my harpoon close by. We all expected the whale to return at any moment, and we watched with every pull of our oars for his open jaws to come rising up beneath us. We rowed far from the ship and one by one pulled our men from the sea, but still the whale did not show himself. We managed to recover all but two of our men. Even after much searching, the bodies of these last two could not be found. We returned to the ship and still that whale did not spout for a breath, which is a rare thing after so close a meeting. Some men who had watched from the ship believed the whale took our friends down with him to the bottom of that ocean, to keep as his prize. Perhaps this is so.

"Since that day I have never again seen a toothed whale. I am glad. Once was enough. That is my story."

"Kepa, to see such a whale!"

"A fine story!"

"Another, Kepa, another!"

"Yes, another!"

"One more!"

Smiling at their insistent prodding, Kepa said, "I will tell a short tale but it is not really my story. It is only one I have heard."

"Fine, fine!"

"Tell us!"

With an acquiescing nod, he began, "There was an old whaler named Patxi who lived in my village, a man older even than Wapitikwa. Patxi once showed me a long stick that tapered to a point and was made entirely of bone. It was as long as this lodge is tall. It was pale and beautiful, and very strong. Though it was straight, it showed lines that twisted around it as they rose upward. I looked at it in wonder for a long time and then asked Patxi where it had come from. He winked at me and said, 'Some think it has magical powers, and I let them think this, but I have known your family for many years and I will tell you the truth.'

"This is what he told me. When Patxi was middle-aged his whaling ship sailed far to the north, so far that they began to see mountains of ice floating upon the water. As they drew closer to the ice flows a scout shouted to his captain that something strange lay in the water ahead. All hands ran to look and there, rising up from the sea, were several of these bone lances. They extended straight out from the heads of small whales! The whalers stared in disbelief as two of the whales began to fight each other with their tusks. Boats were lowered and they rushed toward the fighting bulls. Several of the whales were killed and brought aboard, where the crew studied them in astonishment. The captain kept the tusks, but he later gave one to the old whaler when he had married Patxi's daughter. It was his most prized possession.

"So, my friends," Kepa drew his tale to a close, "not only do some whales have a jaw full of huge teeth, some have one tooth as long as a lance. When hunting such creatures, a man should always be wary. He must be watchful of the many dangers and marvels of the sea."

Satisfied nods and chattering ensued and several requests were made for Kepa to tell more but he politely declined. For the rest of the evening he let himself enjoy the storytelling talents of his host and the other guests, reveling in the warmth of the fire and the congenial company. He tried not to dwell on the fact that, after he left tomorrow with Achaku's family, he'd never see many of these men again.

Several days after Kepa and Achaku had returned to their lakeside campsite the restless preoccupation that had possessed her the morning after her sweat bath returned. Again she was reluctant to explain her feelings, and Kepa began to wonder if she had become pregnant. When he asked her about this directly, she shook her head and said, "No, Kepa, there is no child."

Two nights later, Kepa was awakened by her sobbing. He reached out, calling her name as she wept, but Nimu's voice said hastily in the dark, "Do not wake her. We must let the dream come."

Still crying, Achaku rose to her knees and then stood, her hands outstretched and seeking. Kepa could barely make out her silhouette so he hurried to stir the banked fire and add a log. Slowly, agonizingly, as if it took every ounce of her strength, she pulled her hands back and clasped them to her chest. Her head came down and she started to teeter to the side. Kepa caught her as she fell. Her glazed eyes flew opened, startled and confused, and as her mind returned to the present a few more tears silently fell. Sitting back stiffly and reaching for her fur to wrap around her, she moved as if she'd been aged fifty years by the dreaming.

Now Kepa could see her stricken face more clearly. "Achaku, tell me, is it your dreams that have been troubling you all this time?"

Her head bent down, her tussled hair falling forward to hide her face.

He reached out and took her hand. "Share them with me. What do you see?"

174

Nimu edged closer to his mother and took her other hand, trying to hide his concern.

Loosening her hand from Kepa's, Achaku wiped her face and pushed her hair back behind her ears. She attempted to meet his gaze and failed. "I have had dreams since the night before the caribou hunt. In them...in them I see you leaving. I see you standing alone on the hill in the bay you call Aldapak. Alone, Kepa. Your men and their ships are below, waiting."

She took a breath, forced herself to look at him, and admitted, "I have been hoping you would stay with us. You told me not to hope but I have been holding tightly to it. Now, after tonight when the dream was so clear, I know I must accept your leaving."

With great effort she edged closer to the fire, her brow furrowing and her gaze becoming distant.

"I will sit with you," Kepa said.

"No, Kepa. Sleep. This is for me to deal with, for now."

Reluctantly, Kepa returned to his covers but he lay with his head on his bent elbow and watched her by the fire's glow, his stomach and his thoughts tumbling. What could he say to her that would not bring her more pain, other than that he would stay? And that he could not say.

He tried to comfort her in small and large ways over the next few days, and slowly she began to smile more often and even to laugh. The things that seemed to cheer her most were the antics of Nimu and his new puppy, which the boy had named Watcher. This name was apt, Kepa thought, since the young dog seemed to let nothing escape his notice, be it smoke or animal track. Considering how well Nimu's training of the pup progressed, Mihikin had proclaimed that Watcher might even rival Tracker as a hunter one day.

Achaku's tense expression began to ease as the dreams ceased. On the third night after her last dream Nimu asked to sleep in the lodge of one of his cousins and Achaku assented. The unusual degree of privacy this allowed inspired a freedom in their lovemaking that heightened the joy and fulfillment for them both. Afterward, they held each other for a long, long time, but they kept their deepest thoughts guarded and unspoken.

Farewells

18

Achaku's dreams of Kepa's departure had halted completely but it took nearly a week before she allowed herself to sleep soundly. Though she kept her feelings silent, every touch, glance, and whisper they shared seemed to grow more precious and poignant. They vigilantly avoided discussing his leaving. Only once, after they'd made love, did Achaku say, "I will miss you."

With the passage of each new day, Kepa studied the land, sky, mountains, trees, fish, animals, and people, especially the people, with the appreciation of one who will soon leave what he has come to greatly admire. And yet, the pull of desire to see his cousins, friends, and homeland again began to build.

Winter was showing its first willingness to relinquish its frigid hold by allowing fissures to open in the ice at the edges of rivers, creeks, and lakes. The warmth of the midday sun often melted the topmost layer of snow and caused the branches of trees to weep from above. These short hours of melting invited the breath of the night wind to freeze a thin crust over the surface of every drift, flat, and limb. Even so, within days the people would need to leave this country in order to return across the larger rivers in safety.

This morning the snow crunched and compressed beneath Kepa's wandering snowshoes. It was the kind of brilliantly sunny, deafeningly still day that a man was born to spend lingering in wild places. He had invited only Nimu and Watcher along and he hunted only half-heartedly. The clan and he had been fortunate to find food throughout even the coldest of months. He'd shot a doe only yesterday, thin though she was, so there was no shortage of meat.

He halted on a small rise above the embankment of a creek, the radiance of the sun reflecting off the snow forcing him to squint as he scanned the vicinity. The only sounds were those of their own breathing, an occasional *pfuff* of snow falling from a high limb, and the ice-muffled gurgling of the small stream. Looking down Kepa saw fresh deer tracks leading to the edge of the water. The melt-weakened snow bank had given way under its weight and lay cracked and tilted toward the creek. Reminded of the frigid baths he'd endured this winter, he smiled inwardly to think of the deer's surprise at its sudden splash into the sliver of water at the edge of the ice. He glanced downstream but the hilly terrain blocked his view of the bank where he guessed the deer had emerged. No compulsion to follow the animal tugged at him, no urge to hurry.

Kepa inhaled, set his hands on his hips, and gave the arresting scenery the full attention it was due as he slowly exhaled. His eyes feasted on the shimmering magnificence of the forest until he noticed with amusement that Nimu stood beside him in a pose that perfectly imitated his own. He grinned at the boy and said, "The forest is awakening."

"Yes, the melt is coming fast," said Nimu. "Are we going after the deer?"

"Soon."

The boy nodded, content to simply share Kepa's company. "While we wait, will you tell me about your family?"

"I have told you about my cousin Urdin. He is all that is left of my family."

"Then, will you tell me about when you were young?"

Hunger for a good story was clearly reflected in Nimu's voice and on his face. "We will let the deer leave us behind," said Kepa. "Come, sit with me and talk."

While drawing his knife he walked to a nearby tree. He trimmed off a number of its thinnest lower boughs and brushed them free of snow and ice with his mittened hands. The branches were loosely woven into a mat upon which they seated themselves and removed their snowshoes. Young Watcher scampered around their resting place in an ever-widening circle, his nose to the snowy ground, darting after any new scent, pausing occasionally to look back at them with an expression that asked if he was being missed.

When Nimu looked up at Kepa expectantly, he began with, "I was lucky to be born into a good family. My parents were kind, patient teachers to my brother and me, and we were happy. It seems to me now that everyone in my village was happy. Everyone worked hard. We all had enough to eat. Then, when I was a little older than you, a terrible sickness came to our town, and to a great number of towns. They called it the Black Death. It killed my father. It killed many, many people."

"Does your heart still remember him, your father?"

"Oh yes. He could tell wonderful stories, and he loved to work with his hands: big, rough, strong hands. He knew the secrets of building large ships. He built the one you saw at Aldapak. We called her *La Magdalena*. Every ship he finished he took out on her first voyage, but only her first. He missed my mother whenever he was away. He was a fine man. I remember him laughing often, especially when he and my mother were together."

"Did your mother teach you to be a healer?"

Kepa paused for a moment, seeing the image of his mother's face. She had died suddenly a month after his wedding, before he could be called to her side. In his memory, she was still vibrant and beautiful. He said warmly, "She taught me about life, about people, even about myself. She taught me many things, but it was other people and books who instructed me about healing. For that, I traveled to a large city called Toledo to learn things from other healers."

"To-le-do. Did the books show you how to heal my arm?"

"Books and much practice."

"Someday, will you come back and bring me such books to read?"

So, here it was, the question Kepa had been wrestling with for weeks, and here were Nimu's eyes upon him, pure and hopeful and shining with anticipation.

He forced his mouth to form the words and his tongue to utter them. "I have given this much thought, Nimu. It would be better if I do not come back." Saying it, facing his own loss of everyone and everything that he cherished in this pristine land, was even harder than he'd imagined. And the burden grew much worse when he looked at Nimu, his head so low it rested upon his drawn up knees. Kepa saw a tear fall down Nimu's cheek, then another.

Nimu's voice broke as he said, "It is because of me."

"You? Nimu, no, how could it be you?"

He looked up, his eyes welling with tears and pain. "That day long ago, when you were angry with me and wanted to heal my arm, when your heart still mourned for your wife. My mother said

178

we must heal those who cannot cure themselves. She was telling me to help ease your pain, Kepa, to help heal you. I have tried, but I have failed." His eyes fell to the spruce boughs. "If I had not, if I were a more powerful healer, you would not go back to your land. You would find happiness here. You would stay with us." His eyes squeezed shut and more tears fell. "I want you to stay."

"Nimu," Kepa said softly, his ribs clenching his lungs. "Nimu, look at me." When Nimu obeyed, Kepa said earnestly, "Son, it is not because of you. You have given me much joy, always. But I miss my home, as you would miss yours if you went to a far off land. And after I have gone your mother will marry another man, as she should, perhaps even your father. I do not want to bring them pain." He did not mention what pain it would bring to himself to see Achaku with someone else, but he sensed that Nimu knew this without such words. The boy started to say something but Kepa went on. "Also, the voyage is very far and very dangerous. Many things can take a man's life when he is on the sea. I may not be able to return."

He pulled off a mitten and gently wiped Nimu's wet cheeks with his hand. "Listen now, my brave boy. If my cousin returns to your land after I have sailed home, I will ask him to bring some of my books here. I will ask him to find you. With these books, I will also send letters that I have written to you." Watching Nimu's wet eyes and pinched mouth, Kepa could see that this wasn't enough, not nearly enough.

But Nimu managed to say, "Any of your letters that come to me, I will keep all of my life. And when I reach the end of my days, my people will bury the letters beside me so I can keep them close even when I travel to the stars." Then Nimu reached out, his eyes pleading, and Kepa embraced his small frame tightly and let him cry.

Kepa would always remember the trek back to the cache cave, and then on toward the summer camp as a trip during which the snow and ice diminished in direct proportion to the miles left to travel. Choosing the date of their departure from the lakeside camp with his uncanny ability to judge the changes of the season, Mihikin marched ahead of their group as they moved out. That he continued to hold this position day after day proved how well he was flourishing under the care of his lively young wives. The fondness between the three was evident, and the young women showed great respect for the remains of Liachita they helped to haul along.

The passion and affection between Achaku and Kepa also grew, but so did the quiet times when words trailed to a halt and couldn't be restarted. Nimu sensed the uneasiness of their silences and often tried to fill it up with conversation. The days passed with only the storminess of wind, sleet, and snow showing themselves.

After they camped and ate each night, Nimu's dedication to his reading became so intense that it threatened to infringe on his arrow making skills. Many nights, when slumber had overtaken the boy, Kepa would ease lettered hides from the small hands and tuck them away.

On the day they reached the cave the sky was raining lightly, the first true rain they'd seen since fall, and Achaku took it as an omen that their stay here would be a short one. Although temperatures dropped sharply the next day, Achaku proved to be right in this prediction. Mihikin was determined to reach their summer camp just as the ground thawed enough to allow for Liachita's burial, and he began visiting other campfires to encourage the clan leaders to depart soon. After just two days spent resting, hunting, and reuniting, the group loaded their travois and left the cave behind.

They made their way along trails covered with diminishing snow and ice, crossing melting rivers and streams with extreme care. Only once were they forced to pause and wait out a storm for two days before setting out again. Finally, Kepa began to recognize the terrain not far from where the fateful bear hunt had taken place the previous autumn, and by that afternoon they'd reached their former encampment. Here, with the weather still chilly, even Mihikin seemed content to remain for a short while. People plodded the final steps to the sites of their old cooking fires and eased the travois polls from their sore hands with a sigh of relief.

Once the wigwams had been constructed, Mihikin appeared at Achaku's door and said, "It is time for us to visit your old friend, Kepa. You too may come, Nimu."

Kepa was just about to ask the identity of the man they would be visiting when he began to suspect the answer. So he rose and stood beside Mihikin, content to wait for a while to find out if he was correct.

Nimu quickly tied Watcher to a stake in front of the wigwam.

The dog whined sharply but received no response as the humans set out and left him behind. Leisurely, the two men and the boy sauntered through camp, pausing to share a word here and there with another until they walked past the final wigwam and beyond. They halted at last before the stand of trees near a pole that rose straight from the ground. Upon it was perched the skull of Kepa's great bear. Though the brightness of its painted surface had faded greatly, it still sat high and proud as it overlooked the vastness of the valley.

Mihikin asked, "Do you wish to sing to him, Kepa?"

"Today, I ask Nimu to sing for me. He too has a special bond with this great animal."

Surprised and pleased, the boy's face quickly became grave as he began to chant words of praise to the bear's spirit. His small feet joined in to shuffle with the rhythm of his song.

Listening to the pious young voice, Kepa stared at the skull and slowly began to reflect on how his observations of the inner workings of these people's religion had led to a growth in the respect and love of his own. His had evolved into something more expansive, more accepting, and somehow now encompassed the need to celebrate the fundamental value of all living things. And while he would never believe that rocks and bones were alive, or that animals had spirits, he felt the practices of these people to honor them did no real harm. What they believed and practiced fit harmoniously with their world.

While studying in Toledo he'd occasionally taken time away from his medical lessons to read the teachings of Islam and Judaism, for Toledo was the home of many Moors and Jews. In these beliefs as in his own faith the message was clear; live an honorable life and you will be rewarded. That conviction was also practiced here, regardless of the unique rights and customs in which it was celebrated. Even when a child sang to a bear's skull.

When he returned home, would he dare to discuss such things with fellow Christians? *With Urdin, yes,* Kepa thought. *Urdin always understood.*

Dear Urdin, how was he faring now? For the hundredth time Kepa prayed that Urdin would come back to Aldapak this year. Perhaps his cousin had taken a wife, and even sired a child. Kepa began to wonder why Achaku had not become pregnant during the months they'd shared. Perhaps it was not meant to be so, because it was for the best. Until her future was more secure, the care of an infant would be a formidable burden.

Just how deeply he'd sunk into his reverie became clear when he suddenly realized that the singing had stopped and Mihikin and Nimu were gazing at him speculatively.

"Is your mind speaking to the bear's spirit, Kepa?" Mihikin asked.

"Ah, um, my mind is speaking of many things." He glanced one last time at the skull and noticed that the blue of the sky above it was fading to gray. "We should go back to camp before darkness comes."

They left the holy place behind and slowly retraced their steps, and Kepa was thankful to find Achaku and a hot meal awaiting their return.

By the time they reached the summer camping grounds the weather had warmed considerably, so even before the wigwams were raised a gravesite was chosen for Liachita.

Kepa cut down two young trees that stood between the grave and the running water so, according to Mihikin, "She can see all that passes by the river." While Kepa did most of the digging, both men seemed content to take in the sounds of the murmuring ripples and migrating birds rather than their own voices. Now and then Kepa would begin to hum as he shoveled and Mihikin would smile, enjoying the strange but lovely tune emanating from the ever-deepening grave. Hours later, when Kepa judged the hole to be adequate, he threw his shovel over the brim of the grave and climbed out caked with mud and sweat. Brushing some of the dirt from his hands, he said with an exhausted grin, "It is ready."

Mihikin raised an eyebrow. "You are not yet ready. There is still time for you to wash."

Sitting down near the pile of dirt and resting his forearms on his bent knees, Kepa said, "Even the cold water of the river will feel good today."

"Kepa, I am glad you are with me to see my first wife's bones join those of her people. It would please her to know you are here. She thought very well of you." His eye's warmed, fondly remembering. "Did you know? She had a special name for you, 'Bear

Man' and sometimes just 'Bear', because of the hair on your face and chest. When you killed Short Tail, she said to me, 'A stronger bear won the battle today. Our Bear.'"

Kepa shook his head, his eyes tender. "She showed me much kindness."

Mihikin's face saddened as he asked, "When will you leave us, Kepa?"

"The ships might arrive in ten days, perhaps fifteen. I will leave after the moon is full."

"And if they do not come?"

Kepa had asked himself this question many times, but always returned to the same conclusion. "If no storm is strong enough to turn them back, they will come, and our ships have sailed through many storms."

"We have spoken before of the many different kinds of people who live in the lands across the sea. How many of these will come here in ships?"

"I do not know this. I only know that my people are very good at keeping their fishing discoveries secret. It may be a long time before those from other lands come."

Mihikin said tentatively, "We have few enemies. The game and fish are plentiful and there is enough for all. Yet there have been times when men from the north have come, men who sometimes eat the flesh of human beings, and the battles have been fierce." He looked directly into Kepa's face. "Would your people war on us, Kepa?"

Giving his answer the gravity Mihikin deserved, Kepa said, "I pray they never would. Although they can be courageous warriors when defending our land, they do not generally seek to conquer the lands of others. They are mostly fishermen and traders."

"With the weapons you have told me about, the muskets and cannons, they could cause us great harm if they chose to."

"They could, yes, but my people cherish their own land and their families. If you share the fish of the sea with them, they will want peace here, and they will want to return home."

"And you share this same love for your land and family."

"That is why I must go."

Mihikin sighed heavily. "I will try not to think of your parting until that day comes. Now, my friend, we must prepare for the funeral."

When Liachita's village had gathered together at the gravesite several men respectfully lowered her body, positioning it so that her feet pointed toward the river. To give comfort and aid to her during the afterlife, Mihikin and Achaku deposited Liachita's dearest possessions and food to rest beside her remains. Other people then filed past the open grave and left small gifts, and Kepa bent down and offered a spoon he'd crafted from a caribou bone. On its handle he'd carved a single delicate feather.

Voices, led by Achaku, began to rise in a song of mourning as several shovels slowly filled the hole with dirt. Then the entire camp began to dance a slow circle around the grave. Kepa danced beside Achaku in a place of high honor.

Until late in the night the singing continued. In the minds of Liachita's loved ones, her many kindnesses were remembered, and these memories were stowed away as treasures.

Finding Kepa sitting outside his wigwam one evening, sharpening and oiling his knife while Achaku cleaned a beaver pelt, Mihikin greeted his niece and then said to Kepa, "It is a fine day. Walk with me before it grows dark." Achaku nodded encouragement and the two men left her side to follow one of their favorite paths.

Their steps led them little by little to the site of Kepa's stone kiln, which had weathered the winter with very little damage. Only one rock had shifted out of place from the lip of the ring. They stood over the circle looking down at it, both of them remembering Kepa's first clumsy forging efforts.

Mihikin glanced over at Kepa and said, "Achaku has told me you will set out for the whaling bay tomorrow."

"This is so, Mihikin." For a moment silence as heavy as a stone stepped between them, one nearly as painful as those that too frequently now separated Kepa and Achaku.

But Mihikin soon went on. "Achaku's dream, the one where she saw you going alone to your ships, it was very powerful. She told me it was one of the strongest dreams she has ever had, so it will happen just as she saw it. I have told several of our people that they must not follow you when you leave. They will let you to go

184

on this journey alone, though many wish to come; even Saunuch intended to walk with you."

They traded a poignant glance.

"I will miss them, even Saunuch. Many here have been good to me. Mihikin, I have something I wish to give you. It is a small thing to offer after all you have done." He unslung his crossbow and held it in his hands.

Mihikin protested, "Kepa, not your bow! It holds much of your power."

"Whatever power it holds I wish to come to you. But first I will take it with me on my short journey to the bay, in case there is need. I will leave it buried by the large mossy stone where you camped with your friends while Achaku and I visited the cove. You can find it there on your next fishing trip. Now, would you like to fire it?"

"My heart fills with joy at what you have said, Kepa, but I ask that you give your weapon to Nimu. He is too young to use it now, but it will be his greatest possession." He placed a hand on Kepa's shoulder and held his gaze. "You have been a father and a friend to Nimu. Leave your weapon at the bay for him to find. I will tell him it waits there."

Kepa nodded. "Then, will you accept the iron-tipped arrows that fit your own bow?"

A wide smile broke out on the dear old face. "Those, I will take. When will be a good time to bring Nimu to the bay?"

"I ask that you do not show yourselves until our ships leave. Your people are strangers to the whalers and, as you know, they have guns. If strangers come near them, especially in great numbers, they may use them out of fear. It would be wise for now to be cautious. Also, Mihikin, I do not want to lose the strength to sail back with them, as I could if I see you again."

"You need not worry. There are many places for us to fish and hunt along the coast. I will talk to our people."

"That is very kind of you."

Mihikin's voice grew reflective and melancholy as he asked, "This land of yours, is it more beautiful than ours, Kepa?"

"Its beauty is different in many ways, more tamed perhaps, but wonderful. You have heard me speak many times of my village and my house. It will be a lonely place now that my brother is gone, but it is where my parents are buried."

This, Mihikin understood well. He sighed and sat down with a short groan on the edge of the forge. "Tell me about the women across the sea. Are they as lovely as our women? Are they as helpful, as loving?"

It was clear that Mihikin intended for this discussion to take some time, so Kepa settled down beside him and began with a twinkle in his eye. "Our women are as fiery as our men."

"Ohhhh."

"Yet they are also gentle."

"Gentle, this is also good."

"They are very hard-working, but they can be playful too, sometimes as playful as young children. When they are most happy, they love to dance and sing. They are lovely when they dance, stepping and turning."

"Go on, Kepa, go on," Mihikin said, closing his eyes. "I am beginning to see them in my mind."

He delved into the details, embellishing just a bit, much to Mihikin's delight.

On their last evening together Mihikin and his new wives joined Achaku, Kepa, and Nimu for a late meal. Stories old and new were told, stories of things other than departures or ships or lands across the sea. When Achaku's guests departed, the three who remained talked until the fire had been built up and burned low again three times. Nimu's head began to droop toward his chest. At last he lay down and fell asleep, and Kepa pulled a sleeping fur over his small curled body.

Now it was just Achaku and he. They knelt face to face and Achaku said, "I will not let sadness steal what joy we may find in this last night. Love me, Kepa."

And he did, with every nerve, muscle, sense, and emotion he possessed. When at last they slept, very little of the night remained.

The next morning as he paused outside the wigwam he was still savoring the feel of her body. But now she stood in front of him, clothed and waiting quietly beside her son. Kepa crouched down and took a gentle hold of Nimu's upper arms. He stared into deep brown eyes that were fighting bravely to remain dry.

"You will stay with me, Nimu, in my heart and mind all of my days. I will remember the many times you helped to make me well, and how you fought so bravely on the bear hunt, and all the nights you wrote your letters by the fire's light." *And a thousand other times, oh, a thousand other times.* "I ask that you watch over your mother."

Nimu tried to speak but it came out as a choking gulp. He tried again but still could say nothing. So he turned and walked away from them, his steps quickening until he was trotting and then running toward the trees. Kepa took a step toward him but Achaku touched his arm. "Let him go, Kepa. The forest will give him comfort."

Her voice was so calm, as was her face. It was Kepa now who felt the stinging at the back of his eyes and the clenching of his throat. Achaku pulled the folded piece of hide from her belt and looked at it with tenderness. Sketched upon it was a simple likeness of Kepa's large, stone house in Mutriku. He'd given it to her only moments before. "I will show him this when he speaks of you, and when he looks at the one you drew of your ship. The stone lamp you also left for him will bring light to many of his evenings." Her voice stilled at this, asking nothing more from him.

Kepa looked into her eyes and said, "Achaku, when you—" just as Mihikin approached them. There was so much more to say to her, and yet what could he say that would matter? Mihikin was now standing at his shoulder wishing him a safe journey, and still Achaku's features were strong and serene. Kepa felt himself lingering and knew he must find the willpower to match hers.

"It is time," he said. He bent down and hugged her to his chest, kissed her hair, her cheek, then forced himself to turn to Mihikin.

"Take care of your family, dear friend. You are as fine a man as I have ever known." His eyes trailed to Achaku. "Take care of them."

"I will pray that the Great Manitou blesses you always, Kepa. Do not forget us."

Kepa grabbed Mihikin in a huge bear hug then spun around, snatched up his pouch, crossbow and quiver and strode away. Villagers called out warm wishes as he passed by, but he kept his face turned away. The only response he dared to offer was a wave and a nod.

Achaku and Mihikin followed his steps with their eyes until he'd disappeared beyond the screen of the trees.

Then Mihikin looked closely at his niece, studying her features. "You did not tell him about the child."

Achaku lowered her chin. "I could not."

"A man should know he is to have a child, Achaku."

"I could not," she repeated. When she lifted her face to him the tears were falling freely at last. "He might have chosen to take our child to his far land. I am not strong enough to lose them both, Mihikin. This part of him I must keep with me."

Return to the Bay

19

It seemed that every step Kepa took toward the bay awakened a new memory so fresh and sharp that it overpowered his attempts to think ahead. Here was where Achaku had laughed last fall at the antics of Nimu and his friends. Here, she'd pointed out a pair of hawks teaching their hatchlings to fly. Hear, his newly healed ankle had begun to tire and Achaku had stopped to bandage it.

With an effort he focused on estimating the day of the year. Early June? He might have to wait a week or two for the ships. Surely they would come. The beautiful Basque ships. Oh, what joy it would have given young Nimu to be shown around a ship. Why had he not brought the boy with him? Because it would have made his parting even harder? Or, because of Achaku's dream? Did he even believe in her dreams, completely? Yet he had come alone.

Stop this, he ordered himself. *It's done, it's been decided for a long time.* And yet, had it really been a decision? Hadn't he always simply planned to return? Hadn't he?

Stop this!

Soon he would see men of his own country, men who spoke like him, and drank, and ate, and lived like him. Perhaps even Urdin would come. Urdin, wouldn't he have been charmed to meet Achaku?

Kepa stopped in his tracks and cursed loudly. Then he cursed again with more feeling.

Telling himself he felt better now, he walked on for quite a while as he kept his thoughts directed firmly forward. How long would they be whaling in the bay before sailing home? He had no wish to resume his role as a harpooner. If Captain de Perea returned, Kepa would accept his request to resume his past officer's rank and take on the duties as the ship's physician.

He was ready for that now, ready to take on the lives and deaths of others. It was Achaku who had made him ready, she and Nimu, and Mihikin. His quick pace slowed gradually until he had almost halted again, but then he recognized the hill that separated him from his first view of the bay. Resolving that he would camp at the tree line on the other side of the rise to await his countrymen's arrival, he began to climb.

He crested the hill, lifted his gaze toward the bay, and there they were. Three ships, their anchors lowered and their sails snugly furled, lay at rest. Kepa's legs started to buckle but he quickly righted himself. His breath came in short gasps as he watched the two boats pursuing whales beyond the island. Another chalupa was towing a dead whale toward a new rendering station on the mainland beach inside the eastern curve of the bay. So, they've come ashore within easier reach of the forest. They know they need fear the natives less now that their numbers are stronger.

Quickly, he scanned the ships more closely. Yes! One of them was *La Magdalena*! As he hurried down to the edge of the trees, his eyes searched hungrily for a glimpse of Urdin. He stood still, squinting, concentrating, but could not find him. Suddenly he spotted Todor! Good, faithful Todor was barking at the rowers of the boat towing the whale in. Again Kepa skimmed the area with his gaze, intensely sweeping the cooperage, the tryworks, and the ship, but there was no sign of Urdin. It was unlikely that he would be below decks on a day like this. Did he not sail with them, then?

With crushing disappointment, Kepa realized that Urdin had every reason to stay behind. He'd known great hardship on the last voyage. He'd lost, or so he believed, both of his cousins, and because of this he'd inherited both of their families' properties. He was a wealthy man. Why would he risk the treachery of the Atlantic Ocean to revisit a land he barely knew? One he may even dread. He would not.

Kepa sat down heavily, his brain bombarded with so many conflicting thoughts that all clarity was soon lost. He kept his gaze on the activities below and let his mind race for several minutes. Very gradually, his confused speculation became meditation and, even more slowly, shaped itself into one undeniable fact. He was still here, sitting alone, hiding in the cover of the trees while his own countrymen worked below him within hailing distance.

If he stood up right now, walked into the open, and cried out loudly, they would come to him, laughing with joy and surprise at his return. They would embrace him warmly and probably celebrate his rebirth throughout the night. It would be a merry reunion. They would ask to hear every one of his stories again and again, and he would gladly share much of what had happened to him. And it would be wonderful to learn what life had handed to each of them and to the people of their village during the past year.

He would live among them again, his good, strong, brave, boisterous, loving people.

And then, and then he would never see Achaku again. Or Nimu, or Mihikin, or the others. No, if he showed himself to the whalers, he would not be allowed to leave their numbers to go his own way. Not here. Even if Captain de Perea would tolerate Kepa's desertion because of his extraordinary circumstances, which was unlikely, the other captains would definitely not. And they would be well justified. If they let him leave, how could they keep others from doing the same? They would be surrendering the strict discipline necessary for a crew's survival.

He'd wanted so desperately to return to his homeland yet had he, in his very soul, understood, even before he'd left Achaku, how badly he wanted to stay? Searching deeply within himself with his eyes closed he realized that he had. He had. Today this awareness had held him quietly sheltered among the trees, and here he still sat. Lifting his gaze, he stared longingly at the men and ships below. He shook his head, sighed deeply, shook his head again, and felt his mouth spread into a gentle smile.

The weight that he'd been carrying since saying his farewells at the encampment fell slowly away and a sense of tranquility came to him. It did not erase the powerful yearning to go down and speak to his men, to laugh with them, as they had never seen him laugh. He was not the same grief-stricken, bitter man they had known just before his disappearance. But now he would keep their friendships as memories, nurturing them to greater richness with time.

Perhaps, he mused, after his service and commitment to *La Magdalena* had long been forgotten, one of his children would meet his friends' children.

This he could hope, but he would not make his own presence known. Achaku was waiting.

For just a few minutes more he watched the whalers' movements and felt again the rhythms of their lives. Then he saw three men emerge from the trees near the mouth of a stream that ran not far to his left. Two of them were rolling a barrel dribbling water from the path beside the watercourse. Kepa would have to stay well out of sight as he headed back. He had no way of knowing how many others were hunting or exploring in the area.

It was time to go. Moving with greater stealth than when he'd come, Kepa got to his feet and trotted in a crouched position, careful to screen himself from the bay. He'd nearly reached the rise above the stream when a shout from below stilled him. He stopped and peered from behind a tree. Several men were filling two more water kegs seventy feet down the hill. Trying to get a better look around the trees to account for all of the men in the water-gathering crew, Kepa took a step forward and a dry branch beneath his foot snapped loudly. The voices below suddenly hushed as Kepa ducked back behind his tree. He could feel their eyes searching the forest around where he stood, feel their fear and excitement. Several muffled words reached him, then the talking resumed.

A voice said, "It was only a branch breaking off. These trees pop and groan more than my dear old grandfather."

This was greeted with light laughter and the sound of one barrel being rolled down the path. Kepa dared to peek out and saw that the last barrel was now being filled. He let out a long breath, looked once more at the men below, and crept from his tree to the next and then the next. When he judged that he had progressed safely beyond their hearing and vision, he increased his speed.

Listening for any unnatural sound from behind, he came over the top of the hill and eased his pace. Glancing at a slight movement to his side he found himself staring into the wide barrel of a raised musket. "Don't move," said a tight voice.

Kepa jerked to a halt and stared at the man clasping the musket. For an instant he couldn't breathe. He fought to pull in a gasp of air and croaked hoarsely, "Urdin." He stumbled toward him, his arms reaching out.

The barrel leaped an inch higher to aim straight at Kepa's heart, but he kept running toward his cousin, crying louder. "Urdin! Urdin!"

A sharp strangling noise came from Urdin's throat as he gaped at the savage racing at him and calling out his name in Kepa's voice.

He took a startled step backward and dropped his musket. His mouth moved but seemed unable to make another sound. Kepa was only ten paces away when Urdin accepted this miracle and remembered he had legs. He leaped toward his cousin with his arms flung wide, tears nearly blinding him as he sprinted.

They crashed together, both sobbing now, clutching tightly, thumping the other's shoulders, their legs fighting for balance. They each pulled back only long enough to stare into the face before him, gaining assurance of this reality, then embraced even tighter and hung on and on.

Kepa was the first to come to his senses. He stepped away, one hand still clasping his cousin's bicep while his other hand held a finger to his own mouth to signal Urdin to silence. Receiving a nod of understanding, Kepa motioned him farther from the water gatherers below. Urdin followed, too dumbfounded and elated to wonder at his cousin's desire for secrecy.

When they'd drawn behind another small hillock, Urdin wiped at his eyes and said, "By God, I thought you were a ghost!" He reached out and felt his way up and down his forearm. "It's you, though, in the flesh. And, Kepa, you look as hale as any man I have ever seen. But how? How did you survive the water? We searched for hours."

"You will never believe me."

"You are here before me. I will believe anything after this day."

"Very well, do you remember the orca with the white fin?"

"The one we call the devil fish? Of course. He is deviling us still."

"I was near death, had lost consciousness, and that orca lifted me from the water near shore."

Urdin searched Kepa's face for a sign of insincerity. "By all that is holy," he said in awe. "Saved by a fish. It sounds like a Jonah's tale. Then, we must not have seen you because of the fog."

"I surfaced around the eastern point of the bay in a small inlet, beyond your sight. My head and leg were injured."

"And we left you, Kepa. We left you for dead!"

"I know. I saw my grave."

"God have mercy on us, and you as well. You were injured and alone. And yet you survived." Before Kepa could respond, Urdin eyed Kepa's clothes from his neck to his feet. "I would wager a season's profits that you did not make those yourself. So you found the native people, or they found you. Tell me everything, everything!"

"First you had better hail your men or they'll send the whole crew to look for you. The captain would be sorely aggrieved to think he's lost his pilot."

"That may be true, but come with me," Urdin said, tugging on Kepa's sleeve. "The men will go mad when they see you. The moment you...Kepa, what is it?"

"I want a little time alone with you first, Urdin. Go now, and tell them you'll soon follow."

Urdin was already hurrying away. "Stay right where you stand. If you move, I will fear my seeing you was nothing but a vision!"

Although it seemed a long time to Kepa, Urdin soon returned carrying the musket he'd dropped. They found a place sheltered by the trees and sat on a fallen log, both smiling again, basking in the mere presence of the other.

"Now then," said Urdin, "tell me how you rejoined the living."

Kepa told him all of it, from the moment of his awakening in Achaku's wigwam to his return to Aldapak. When his story at last trailed to an end Urdin sighed in admiration. "You have done well, my cousin. It warms me greatly that you've come back to us."

Kepa's gaze shifted away. "I am with you for only a short time, cousin. I have decided to remain here."

"Well, we will not sail for several weeks. Do you wish me to say nothing for awhile?"

"I mean not to return to the crews at all. I will leave today for Achaku's village."

A silence followed, one Urdin needed in order to understand what he'd just been told. "You mean never to return to Mutriku?"

Kepa gave him a slow nod.

"Is it the woman, then?"

"Yes."

"And the boy."

"Yes, Urdin."

Urdin picked up a small branch that lay at his feet and rolled it between the fingers of both hands. "So, after thinking you dead, after mourning you for a year, you ask me to give you up again for them?"

194

"I ask even more than that, dear cousin. I ask that you tell no one you've seen me, ever. Let me remain dead in the minds of my countrymen, to everyone but you."

Kepa watched him now as pain, understanding, anger, and compassion struggled against each other in Urdin's heart. At last he said, "If the captains knew you were alive, they would never let you stay. They could not."

"No, they could not."

Urdin snapped the twig in his hands and stood suddenly.

"Damn all that's seduced you, all that's made you want to stay!" He shoved a hand roughly through his dark hair and stomped three steps away.

Kepa waited for him to turn back, knowing he would, loving him all the more because he knew that he would.

Urdin did turn, and stepped closer, his eyes filling again. "And yet, God bless them too." He sat down and cocked a blurry, affectionate glance at Kepa. "She's even got you practicing your medicine again."

A smile played at the side of Kepa's mouth. "She has indeed."

"I wish I could meet her, truly I do, but it would not be wise for her to come here."

Wrapping an arm around Urdin's shoulders, Kepa said, "I wish you could meet as well. You would love each other." He felt his cousin's shoulders slump in final surrender.

"You have always told me I am too soft-hearted. And you must be right. I have allowed you to talk me into letting you go." He looked at Kepa, still struggling. "I know this is not easy for you either."

"I have wanted nothing more than to see you, to work with you, to return home with you for all these months. Or so I thought. It wasn't until I left her that I began to see how I had found a new home, one that needs me more than my old one."

"What of your property, your birthright?"

"It is yours now, and it pleases me greatly that it is. You must marry that fine woman who has been waiting for you and start a family."

Urdin's eyes shone despite his turmoil. "Both of these things I have already done."

"Urdin, that is fine! But, why did you come back here when you have a wife, and a child on the way?"

Shaking his head, he answered, "It is not easy for me to explain. I simply had to come once more, to visit your graves, perhaps, yours and Gotzon's. Or maybe I sensed you were still alive. Whatever led me here, I am thankful that it gave me the chance to see you. Even for a little while."

They let the country around them do the talking for a few moments, the birds and trees and squirrels. Then Urdin asked, "What supplies should I leave for you?"

"Iron would be most useful. If you bury some in the small cave I used last summer, I will come back for it."

"Have you become a blacksmith too?"

Kepa slung his crossbow from his back and handed it to Urdin and then showed him his knife.

Urdin eyed them thoroughly. "They are far from beautiful, but they must serve you well." He handed them back. "I will leave what iron I can. What else?"

"Books, if you can spare them."

"I have two with me. They are yours. And…?"

"Whatever became of my txistu? I miss playing it very much."

Urdin let out a short laugh. "I have taught myself how to play it, to remember you. It is aboard the ship. I will leave it in the cave. Is that all?"

"That will be enough."

"Tell me what she is like, this woman of yours."

How did one describe Achaku? "When she dreams she sees things that will come to pass. She saw me coming here today, though she did not see beyond my arrival. She's a healer of much consequence among her people, Urdin, and her cures include the touch of her hands and the use of singing and dancing. Magic, some would call it."

Surrendering to a smile, Urdin said, "And she has worked her magic on you. She must be beautiful."

"As lovely as this land." He sighed deeply. "I remember she once described our ship as a brown swan, but it is she who possesses such gentle grace, such rare beauty. "

Urdin muttered thoughtfully, "Well then," and let Kepa's last answer disperse his unasked questions.

As if an unseen sandglass had been measuring out their allotted time, they both knew there was more to be said than could be uttered now that the turning was near. It loomed before them, unstoppable. So they stared at each other, praying for the strength they needed to part.

"I already buried you once," Urdin said. "Today I must leave you again. Yet, even knowing how I will miss you, I am so very glad to have seen you, Kepa. Now I can think of you here, with a family, and know you have found a life to replace what you lost years ago."

Slowly, they stood up together and Urdin said, "I must get back."

Kepa wanted to tell him a thousand things, about Nimu's writing, about the grizzly hunt, and the land of the caribou, but there was no more time.

Facing one another with their hands clasping the other's shoulders, their nearly identical brown eyes drank their fill. This final look must last a lifetime. They embraced with the rough force of their concussive emotions, then Urdin broke away.

Before he dropped from view on the other side of the hill, he paused and looked back.

Kepa had not moved. He stood amid the gently swaying trees, the fringe on his wild clothes and his long hair dancing with the breeze, his face touched with longing but also with a serenity Urdin had not seen there in a very long time. *Live well, cousin*, he thought. Urdin raised a hand high and waved it once, then pivoted and headed down toward the bay.

From below Kepa heard voices shouting, "There he is! Pilot! Pilot, the captain threatened to chain us all for leaving you!"

Other cries, excited and relieved, reached Kepa in snatches but his feet were already moving in the other direction. In moments the human sounds faded away completely.

He set a loping pace he could maintain for hours, and his meditations of the visit with his cousin now kept him company. Once, twice, a third time his mind relived their meeting, committing every impression to his memory as a pirate hoards his gold. Their talk, the encounter Kepa had nearly missed, had surely been a gift.

His mind gently shifted and he began to wonder why Achaku had not foreseen his encounter with Urdin or his return to her.

Perhaps, he concluded, it was a good thing that some things could still surprise her. Yes, it was preferable that certain revelations be left to their own time and place of discovery.

Such as his homecoming. He pictured her reaction when he found her this evening, and when he took her in his arms. He could see her smiling through her tears. What was she doing now? As his thoughts focused on every aspect of her pretty face his pace steadily increased. His legs lengthened their stride while his heart beat a smooth, accompanying rhythm. He felt his lungs expanding, felt his spirit lifting as the vast, feral country enfolded him into its enormity.

"Do you see me, Gotzon?" he whispered. "Run with me, brother. Run with me."

~~~~

The Author

Photo by Dr. E. Wilfred Richard

The photo above of Christine Bender was taken while she worked as a digger with the Smithsonian Institution team of archaeologists at the Basque whaling site in Hare Harbour, Quebec. Christine lives with her family in Boise, spending her free time in the mountains of Idaho. She can be contacted through her website at www.christinebender.com.

More Caxton Press titles from
Christine Echeverria Bender
WWW.CAXTONPRESS.COM

Sails of Fortune
Christine Echeverria Bender
ISBN 0-87004-449-4
Trade Paper - 5.75 x 8.75 - 416 pages - $16.95

Challenge the Wind
Christine Echeverria Bender
ISBN 0-87004-422-2
Trade Paper - 5.75 x 8.75 - 362 pages - $16.95

For a free catalog of Caxton titles write to:

CAXTON PRESS
312 Main Street
Caldwell, Idaho 83605-3299

or

Visit our Internet web site:

www.caxtonpress.com

*Caxton Pres*s is a division of THE CAXTON PRINTERS, Ltd.